"Perhaps I would want you to see me clearly,"

Cord said huskily.

"You told me that I was blind as a bat with or without my glasses," Sarah said, trying to keep her voice light. "So there's no point in taking them off, is there?"

Cord's mouth twisted. The lady was too innocent. "Don't trust me too much," he warned. "There's a good bed upstairs in Simon's apartment. At the moment, I'm tempted to drag you into it."

Sarah felt her heart beat a little faster. Small flames glinted in his smoky eyes, but the look he gave her was softer, gentler. "But you won't," she said quietly, very sure that he would keep his word and not cross the invisible line. Of course, that didn't mean that he wouldn't try to tempt *her* into making the first move....

And, dear God, she was so tempted.

Dear Reader,

Hot weather, hot books. What could be better?
This month, Intimate Moments starts off with an
American Hero to remember in Kathleen Korbel's
Simple Gifts. This award-winning author has—as
usual!—created a book that you won't be able to put
down. You also might have noticed that the cover of
this particular book looks a little bit different from our
usual. We'll be doing some different things with some
of our covers from time to time, and I hope you'll keep
your eye out for that. Whenever you see one of our out-
of-the-ordinary covers, you can bet the book will be out
of the ordinary, too.

The month keeps going in fine form, with *Flynn*,
the next installment of Linda Turner's tremendously
popular miniseries, "The Wild West." Then check out
Knight's Corner, by Sibylle Garrett, and *Jake's Touch*,
by Mary Anne Wilson, two authors whose appearances
in the line are always greeted with acclaim. Finally, look
for two authors new to the line. Suzanne Brockmann
offers *Hero Under Cover*, while Kate Stevenson gives
you *A Piece of Tomorrow*.

I'd also like to take this chance to thank those of you
who've written to me, sharing your opinions of the line.
Your letters are one of my best resources as I plan for
the future, so please feel free to keep letting me know
what you think about the line and what you'd like to
see more of in the months to come.

As always—enjoy!

Leslie Wainger
Senior Editor and Editorial Coordinator

Please address questions and book requests to:
Reader Service
U.S.: P.O. Box 1325, Buffalo, NY 14269
Canadian: P.O. Box 1050, Niagara Falls, Ont. L2E 7G7

KNIGHT'S CORNER

Sibylle Garrett

Silhouette® ™
INTIMATE MOMENTS®

Published by Silhouette Books

America's Publisher of Contemporary Romance

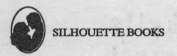

SILHOUETTE BOOKS

ISBN 0-373-07573-1

KNIGHT'S CORNER

Copyright © 1994 by Sibylle Garrett

Books by Sibylle Garrett

Silhouette Intimate Moments

SIBYLLE GARRETT

is a world traveler who finally settled down on Long Island with her husband of twenty-two years and their two children. Her love of books, vivid imagination and a desire to share her many personal adventures eventually propelled her toward a career in writing. Writing romances satisfies the dreamer as well as the realist in her.

Chapter 1

The Coyote Lounge wasn't a place where a family man would stop for a drink on his way home after a hard day's work.

The dingy, sprawling adobe structure, eight miles out of town, hadn't seen a coat of paint in years. With dark shutters covering its windows, no welcoming light spilled out into the rainy January night. A faded, poorly lighted billboard on top of the flat-roofed building announced auctions on Tuesdays and Thursdays, and "Ladies' Nite" on Fridays.

Cord Knight slowed his muddy pickup truck and glanced past the swiftly moving wipers to the building. There were many places like it along the Texas-Mexico border. They dealt in everything from alcohol to dope to counterfeit green cards. During his eight years as an antismuggling agent for the INS, the Immigration and Naturalization Service, he had seen the inside of a fair number of them, had even cleaned up a few. The Coyote Lounge outside of his hometown of Knight's Corner had been one of the latter. *Coy-*

otes, the smugglers of illegal aliens, had avoided the place ever since.

Or they had until a year ago. And things changed little around here.

The sign suggested that Rusty was still up to his old tricks, auctioning off stolen merchandise. Cord doubted that a "lady" had set foot inside the place in years. Cowhands would drop by for a drink and a game of pool, sometimes bringing along a woman for the evening, but men with steady girlfriends went to Josie's Café in town.

Turning into the parking lot, he groaned. It had rained hard for three days and the large, unpaved area was half under water. At the back, the light over the two gas pumps bounced off twin ribbons of water where truck tires had left deep ruts in the soggy ground.

Half the pastures in the county were flooded, as well, and, after dragging cows out of the mud near a flooded creek all day, he was tired and wet and chilled to the bone. He would have headed straight home—it was only another nine miles to the ranch house—but his gas gauge had been flashing empty for some time. He might make it on what was left in the tank, but his luck had been nothing to brag about lately. The only other station around was next to the Vista Motel, on the other side of the flooded bridge.

Only three muddy pickups were parked out front. Cord frowned as he drove past them. The last time he had been here on a Saturday night, business had been booming. Still, it was early yet, not quite six, and the floods may have kept some of the regulars away. His eyes narrowed on one of the trucks. Tan-and-white, it had bull horns decorating the front. Rod Snyder was here.

He grimaced. The Coyote Lounge was the favorite hangout for the rough bunch from the Devlin ranch. There had been bad blood for years between the Circle K and the neighboring Devlin spread. Since his return to the ranch six weeks ago, he had avoided any kind of confrontation, though lately, Devlin's bulls had been annoying the hell out of him. He sighed. Sooner or later he would have to do something about the latest of Devlin's get-rich-quick schemes. But not tonight. All he wanted tonight was a hot shower, a shot of smooth whiskey and a thick juicy steak.

Cord pulled up close to the rear exit, shifting into Park. For a moment he held his stiff cold hands in the streams of hot air blowing from the vents, flexing them. During the past year, he'd spent a lot of time in the jungles of Southern Mexico. He wasn't used to the damp cold anymore. Taking out a five-dollar bill, he pulled the hood of his slicker over his head and slid from the cab, leaving the engine running. His mouth twisted. Even six weeks after he'd walked away from his job, he was still jumpy. Not that he'd anything to fear. Everyone in the smuggling business knew that the former hotshot agent had lost it. A yellow-bellied coward was like a snake with its venom sacs removed. But old habits died hard.

The short narrow hallway was just as dingy as he remembered it. Only the stacks of beer cases were gone. In the past, Rusty had used the hall as a storage room, creating a fire hazard. The house was old, older than Simon's place had been, and that had caught fire so fast, the doc had been trapped inside. The firemen had managed to get him out alive, but he'd died in a San Antonio hospital two days later of smoke inhalation. Cord sighed again. He had been shocked to learn of Simon's death upon his return from Mexico. Dr. Simon Durand had been a close friend of his father, and he had liked the man.

Opening the door, he slid inside unnoticed. The music blaring from the jukebox was loud enough to swallow any noise. For a moment he paused to let his eyes adjust to the bright lights from the bar on his right. The place reeked of smoke, liquor and stale cooking odors. The walls above the dark, scarred paneling were a dingy gray and decorated with dusty, lurid, velvet paintings. The plastic furniture looked fairly new, but the chairs didn't match, as if they were being replaced one or two at a time after each brawl.

At the moment everything was calm. There were only four cowboys at the back, playing pool. Cord recognized two of them: Lefty, and Rod Snyder.

Lefty, a lean black-haired young cowboy, was shooting balls into pockets with swift accuracy. Cord knew that he was just as good with the knife he kept inside his left snake-skin boot.

Rod Snyder was a burly gray-haired man with a thin cruel mouth and mean blue eyes. He was Devlin's foreman. Cord's hard mouth tightened at the sight of him. He'd once watched Rod flog a young wetback—an illegal—nearly to death. Cord had been only fifteen at the time, but he had never forgotten the sadistic grin on Snyder's face as the whip repeatedly slashed across the boy's blood-streaked back.

Cord briefly studied Snyder's companions; they didn't look any friendlier. Both men were Hispanic, probably Mexican, judging by their taste for fancy clothes. Their boots were highly polished and they wore jackets with white snap-button shirts and string ties. They sure weren't from around here, Cord thought, watching one of them pick up a pool cue and take his turn. As the man bent over the table, Cord noticed a slight bulge at the lower part of his back.

Since when did a cowboy wear a gun in the small of his back?

Silently he took two steps into the room, keeping his back to the door. Turning to the big, red-haired man polishing glasses behind the bar, he drawled, "Evening, Rusty."

Rusty spun around. His mouth, framed by a dark red beard, dropped open and his small hazel eyes widened as if he was seeing a ghost. "Evening, Cord. Heard you were back," he finally said, keeping his voice low as if he didn't want to alert the men in the back. "Didn't expect to see you again. Had ourselves a big party when we heard the sharks had made a meal of you."

''Nice to be appreciated.'' Cord's mouth curled. He hadn't expected much else. For as long as he could remember, Rusty had been in trouble with the law. Since he had bought the lounge five years ago, he'd run rigged poker games, auctioned off stolen property and had done a little smuggling on the side, shipping stolen goods across the border and returning with truckloads of tequila, rum and Mexican beer.

Cord had known about Rusty's little side businesses, and could have put a stop to them at any time, except for one thing. Rusty'd had one thing in common with him. He had always been dead set against smuggling dope and illegals.

Rusty didn't like *coyotes* any more than Cord did. There had been an unspoken agreement between them that Rusty would let him know the moment an organized smuggling ring tried to move back into this neighborhood. And in return, Cord wouldn't run him in all the time for his ''moonlighting.'' ''You should've known that I was too tough for fish bait. So how's business?''

For a moment Rusty hesitated, then shrugged. Turning to the shelf behind him, he placed the dried glass on it. ''Pretty dull around here,'' he said reaching for another mug draining next to the sink. Wiping it dry, he glanced at the three-inch scar cutting across Cord's left cheek. '''Appears the sharks took a nibble out of you. Doesn't look bad enough for you to retire, though.''

Thoughtfully, Cord ran a finger over his left cheek, wondering what was going on. Rusty almost sounded as if he regretted Cord turning in his badge. Since his return, he hadn't paid much attention to what was happening in town. He felt certain that someone—either Maisy, his housekeeper, or Chuck, the foreman at the Circle K—would have told him if anything unusual was going on. He shot a sharp glance at the two strangers, wondering who they were, then turned back to Rusty. ''I see you took my advice about clearing the hallway. Or was it Doc Simon's death that finally scared you into it?''

The innocent comment rattled Rusty, and the still-wet glass slipped through his fingers, landing on the tile counter with a thud. Swearing, he picked it up, holding it up against the light. "Chipped," he muttered, glaring at Cord. Then he dropped the mug into the garbage can at his feet, wiping the counter with meticulous care. "Was a real shame, the doc dying like that," he said. "Shocked everyone in town."

Cord felt his gut tighten. The fire had happened three weeks before his return. That Simon's office had been vandalized shortly afterward had bothered him, but his father had assured him the thieves had only been after the drugs. The apartment above the office where Simon had lived before he'd bought the house had not been touched. As far as he knew there had been no suspicion of foul play. So why was Rusty so jumpy at the mention of Simon's death?

"Shocked everyone, did it?" he asked softly.

"Sure." Rusty turned his back to Cord. "Doc was well liked around these parts. Folks felt real cheated when the daughter buried him in New York and none of us could even pay our last respects." He turned around, anger in his eyes. "Wasn't right, if you ask me. Doc was born and raised here and he should have been buried here, too. Heard the daughter was adopted. One of them foreign orphans he took in while he was in I-ran years back. Damn foreigners. He should have left her there, if you ask me."

Cord felt unease prickle down his neck. Rusty might be a small-time crook, but he had a strong patriotic streak. Since his younger brother had been killed in Operation Desert Storm, his dislike of foreigners had turned into hate. The last time Cord had talked to him, Rusty had been furious because Simon had been treating illegals without reporting them to the authorities.

A movement from the back suddenly caught Cord's attention. Snyder had finally noticed him and was slowly coming toward him. Tensing, Cord slapped the five-dollar bill on the counter. "I need gas."

"Is that what you came in here for?" Rusty swiftly slipped the bill off the counter, as if he didn't want Rod to see that he was selling gas to Cord.

Cord's gray eyes sharpened as he turned to the short stocky man. The atmosphere around here had changed. Rusty had never been scared of Devlin or his men before.

"Rain finally flush you out?" Snyder asked, stopping a few feet away, his pale blue eyes as hard as diamonds. "Haven't seen hide nor hair of you since you got back. Never did believe you died in that explosion. Always figured sinking your boat was just a ruse to get the law off your back."

"Did you?" Cord shrugged, the insults sliding off him like rain off the slicker. He'd heard them all before. Besides, he noticed with grim amusement, for all his sneering, Snyder kept a careful distance of several feet.

Snyder glanced over his shoulder, as if hoping his friends would join him. But so far they were more interested in their game. "How'd it feel having cuffs clapped around your wrists, Knight? Too bad your daddy bought off them Mexican government officials. Me and the boss was really looking forward to visiting you in jail."

Cord's mouth stretched into a thin dangerous grin. "Mighty neighborly of you." For years, Hugh Devlin's father, Ed, had bought illegals from the *coyotes,* treating them worse than slaves, working them eighteen hours a day and housing them in subhuman conditions. A few years back, Cord had sent Ed to prison, where he had died a few months later. Unfortunately, he hadn't been able to make the charges against Hugh and Snyder stick, and they had been trying to get even with him since. The news of his own arrest must have given them immense satisfaction.

He wondered what Rod would say if he knew that one of Ed's former "slaves," the young wetback he had nearly killed sixteen years ago, was now a colonel with the Mexican Immigration Service and had helped him clear his name. "Since we're on such friendly terms these days, I wonder if you'll give Devlin a message from me." His voice remained soft, but it had an edge of steel to it when he continued, "The next time one of his rodeo bulls tears down my fences and strays onto Circle K land, I'm sending it to the slaughterhouse."

Without waiting for an answer, and with his ears tuned to the slightest hint of danger behind him, Cord walked out the door, closing it firmly behind him.

Driving around to the other side of the parking lot, he kept his eyes on the rearview mirror, just in case Snyder and his men decided to follow him. But the doors remained closed. None of them wanted to ruin their two-hundred-dollar boots in the mud. He smiled grimly. He had been counting on that.

Both Ed and Hugh had always been big spenders, buying flashy boots, Stetson hats, cars and planes, and their ranch hands were of the same ilk. Come to think of it... Cord frowned. The fines after Ed's conviction had nearly bankrupted the ranch, and until a year ago he knew for a fact that Hugh had barely been able to scrape enough together to meet the interest payments on the loans. If Devlin could afford to hire new help, raising rodeo bulls had to be more profitable than he'd thought.

Unless the bulls were just a blind and Devlin was involved in some shady business, Cord thought grimly, as he drew up at the pump. But then, that was difficult to tell right about now. Since his return, he hadn't paid much attention to what was going on in town. His name might have been officially cleared, but Snyder wasn't the only one who believed that "Big" John—as everyone called his father—had purchased his freedom by bribing Mexican government officials.

Cord pulled the hood of the slicker up closer against his neck and slid from the cab, grimacing as his rubber boots sank deep into the mud. On the few occasions he had gone into Knight's Corner, men he had known all his life had looked straight through him and women had crossed the street to avoid him. Twisting the cap off the pickup's gas tank, he reached for the nozzle on the pump.

He had known that coming home wouldn't be easy. Guilty or not, a bad reputation stuck to a man like mud.

His eyes were narrowed with suspicion as he climbed back into the truck a few minutes later. Maybe it was time to take an interest in town affairs again and start asking a few questions about Devlin's new enterprise, as well as Simon's death. Something about that fire stank to high heaven. With his father away on business, Cord had been keeping an eye on Simon's office. Maybe if it stopped raining tomorrow he would take a closer look at the place.

Cord's mouth twisted as he considered Rusty's comment about Simon's daughter. His personal opinion of the woman was only a notch above Rusty's. Simon had been dead for two months and she hadn't found the time to visit Knight's Corner and pack up her father's few remaining possessions. He'd bet she'd found time to cash the insurance check, though.

Slowly he shifted into gear and eased the truck through the mud. Since Simon had moved back to Texas after his wife's death two years ago, Sarah Durand hadn't visited him once. Oh, Simon had made all kinds of excuses for her. She was a surgical resident and rarely had time off. She also had a daughter, and traveling with a small child wasn't easy, he had explained, and it gave him a good excuse to fly to New York frequently to keep an eye on her. Cord smiled thinly. Right. Dr. Sarah Durand sounded like a damned cold fish. He wasn't too fond of doctors in general and knife-happy surgeons ranked at the bottom of his list. He only hoped that his father would be back at the ranch when the woman finally found the time to settle Simon's affairs.

As he headed toward the road, a white Toyota turned into the parking lot. Cord slowed down to allow it to pass him, but it hit the slick muddy surface and skidded, its small tires sinking into the deep ruts. The driver suddenly accelerated and the car shot forward, splashing muddy water high over Cord's pickup and coating his headlights and windshield.

"Damn city slickers!" Cord muttered. With the roads flooded everywhere, no one else would be stupid enough to drive around in such a car. Waiting for his wipers to clear the windshield, he watched the car draw up close to Rusty's front entrance. Long seconds passed but the door didn't open, as if, after taking a closer look at the run-down place, the driver had second thoughts about entering it.

Finally the door opened and a woman climbed out. Frowning, Cord watched her pull the hood of a dark trench coat tightly around her face. She was small, her head barely topping the roof of the car. A year ago, he would have driven over and offered his help, but he was more cautious these days. Strangers around here were often illegals. With rain coming down in buckets and visibility no more than a hundred feet, this was a good time to slip across the border undetected. She was probably one of them.

Cord gripped the steering wheel tightly, his mind flying back to another rainy night a year ago, when he had rescued another female illegal. Mariela Noquez had been on the run from her lover, "Lobo" Rodriguez, a powerful *coyote* who Cord had been trying to convict for years. She had asked for asylum in return for information that would put Rodriguez behind bars for the rest of his life. Sensing a trap, Cord had taken her directly to the station and handed the bedraggled woman over to a female officer, then had returned to his apartment for a shower and a change of dry clothes. Upon his return to the station several hours later to question her, however, he found that she had accused him of battering and raping her.

He had spent the next ten months trying to clear his name, and he wasn't about to become involved again.

Some of Cord's tension eased when he saw the woman bend, as if talking to another occupant in the car. At least she wasn't alone, he thought, watching her close the door carefully and lock it, as if all her worldly possessions were inside. Then she dashed to the entrance and leapt up the steps. He watched as she opened the screen and, leaning against the door, glanced at his truck for long searching seconds. Then she balanced on one leg, took off her shoe and poured water out of it. Putting it back on, she repeated the action with the other one. Next she brushed off the bottom of her coat with long smooth strokes that reminded him of a cat licking her fur. Damn. Cord swore at her fastidiousness. She might not be aware of it, but she would be much safer entering the lounge covered with mud. She straightened and again looked at his truck, hesitating, as if reluctant to walk inside, making him wonder. What was she hiding inside the car that was so valuable she didn't dare leave it unprotected?

Drugs?

He thought of the two Mexicans he'd seen inside the lounge. Maybe she wasn't lost after all and was dropping off dope. It would certainly explain why she'd groomed herself.

And it would explain Rusty's uneasiness and why he'd sounded almost sorry that Cord had turned in his badge.

Cord didn't regret it for one moment. He'd had enough. The cocky, idealistic fool who had constantly put his life on the line to make this part of the world a safer place didn't exist anymore. Shaking his head, he prepared to leave. Whatever went on at the Coyote Lounge was no longer his business. With a last glance at the woman still watching him, he sped out of the parking lot. He was a civilian now. He'd do his civic duty and call the sheriff's office the moment he got home.

But what if the woman was just a stranded traveler? his nagging conscience argued as he sped down the road. *You're the one who got Snyder all riled up. Mean as he is, he'll be looking for someone to vent his frustration on.*

Cord slowed down as the track running between the Circle K and the Devlin ranch came into view. Thoughts of his mother or his sister, Vicky, being stranded ran through his mind and he hit the brake. No way could he leave an innocent woman in the hands of a man who would have flogged a young boy to death if he hadn't interfered. Cursing inwardly at his noble streak, Cord checked his mirror and swung the truck around. Damn. He was not looking forward to this.

Dr. Sarah Durand watched the truck leave, wondering if she had made the right choice. While cleaning her shoes, she had been debating whether to ask the driver of the pickup for directions, then had decided against it. A drunken cowboy was not a very reliable source of information. Also, she had wanted to conceal the fact that she was traveling alone with a small child, fearing that he might follow her.

Besides, as a New Yorker she instinctively felt safer surrounded by crowds. A bar—even a sleazy one—seemed the safer of her two options. On the other hand, as an emergency room physician, she knew safety in numbers was an illusion. People got attacked and killed in all places, in subways, buses and bars alike. In New York she wouldn't have thought of entering a place like this any more than she'd walk into a stripper's joint on Forty-Second Street.

Still, Simon had always talked about how safe and friendly his hometown was. "People leave their back doors open and their keys in their cars," he'd often said. Then again, Sarah thought wryly, she didn't have much of a choice now that the truck had left.

With her hand on the handle, she put her ear to the door to listen, but the loud blare of country music drowned out all other sounds. She hated to leave Angel alone, even for a few seconds, but her daughter was safer inside the car. Taking a deep breath, she opened the door, waving at her daughter before walking inside.

The moment she closed it behind her, she realized she'd made the wrong choice. Though the entrance was somewhat hidden by a freestanding coatrack and bulky rain slickers and coats partially shielded her from the casual eye, she had walked right into the middle of an argument. At the moment, the four men in the front of the bar were too busy shouting at the burly red-haired bartender to notice her, but she was certain that wouldn't last long.

She took the opportunity to study the men. They looked like many of the patients the police brought into the emergency room of the large city hospital where she worked the midnight shift. The bartender seemed to be the most trustworthy of the lot. He was a big man, with the beefy arms and ham-size fists of a bouncer, and he carried enough weight to wrestle every one of the more slender men to the ground. His hazel eyes, almost hidden by fat jowls, were more crafty than cruel.

Her eyes slid over the mismatched chairs grouped around chipped tables. They reminded her of the abused furniture in the waiting room at St. Anne's. At midnight, the trauma ward frequently resembled a combat zone.

She waited a moment longer, hoping that the argument would die down. She didn't have much of a choice, she thought practically, unless she wanted to spend the night on the road with a five-year-old child and a cat. She had made reservations at the Vista Motel, but she hadn't been able to find another road on the map that would take her into town.

Lifting her glasses off her nose briefly, Sarah ran a weary hand over her wet face and rubbed her burning eyes. Since leaving San Antonio four hours ago, she had met one obstacle after another. No one had warned her just how bad the flooding was down here. The local weather report had warned of pastures being underwater and cattle getting stuck in mud, but the roads were supposed to have been clear.

Her mouth twisted, wondering if she would ever see Simon's small friendly haven of a town. Every time she'd made plans to visit him since he'd moved down here, something had gone wrong. Besides, Simon hadn't wanted her to come to Texas until he'd had the house fully furnished.

Now Simon was gone and the house had burned to the ground. All that was left was a vandalized office. Regret and sorrow rushed over her in an unexpected wave, but Sarah fought it. This was not the time or place.

She stiffened as the gray-haired cowboy suddenly threw a punch at the bartender across the counter and yelled, "Why'd you sell him gas? You two looked real cozy there for a minute. What'd you tell him, Rusty?"

"Nothing," Rusty growled, evading the punch with surprising ease.

It was time to leave, Sarah decided, regardless of her need for directions. Cautiously she twisted the doorknob behind her, trying to sneak out without calling attention to herself.

With a roar the gray-haired man leapt on top of a barstool. "I thought I heard ya talking about the fire—" He lunged again.

Glasses scattered and a big water-filled pitcher toppled off the counter, soaking the assailant's jeans before shattering on the floor. This was the moment Sarah should have escaped, but the word *fire* sent a sudden shock through her and she hesitated.

"Stop it, Snyder." Two Mexican men, dressed in jackets, reached for the gray-haired cowboy and dragged him back down. "Devlin'll be angry if you wreck this place again."

A slender black-haired man rescued his mug of beer and took a step back. "Don't worry. That yellow-belly damn near ruined Rusty's business. Rusty wouldn't say nothing to make that coward suspicious.''

Snyder struggled against the hands holding him, swearing viciously. The curses provided Sarah with the few seconds she needed to open the door. Backing out, she heard him growl, '' 'That coward' used to be the toughest, meanest agent the INS had, and I don't think he's changed.''

"Lost his nerve and guts in the explosion. Everyone knows that," one of the Mexicans argued. "Hell, even his own partner refused to work with him afterward. That's why he quit."

Sarah cautiously started to close the door, feeling sympathy stir for the burned-out agent they were bad-mouthing. Then she heard Rusty yell, "We was talking about fire hazards, if you have to know. When he used to snoop around, he always threatened to notify the sheriff if I didn't get the hall cleared. He just wanted to know if the doc dying in the fire finally made me do it. Told him that it did. I liked the doc. He was a good man. Can't understand why he would adopt one of them damned foreigners that's always stealing our jobs."

Suddenly he looked up, his eyes narrowing when he spotted Sarah. Then he growled, "Boys, we've got company. Come in little lady. We won't bite."

Heads jerked around and ten eyes pinned her like a fly to the door. Sarah hesitated. She was a plain woman and chances were the men would take one look at her and leave her alone. Still, she hovered in the doorway, calculating her chances of getting away, but dismissed the idea almost instantly. Leaving now would make the men suspicious. All she could do was brazen it out and hope that Rusty's regard for her father had not been faked.

Briskly she walked into the bar, her fingers closing around the keys in her pocket like they would a talisman. "I'm Dr. Durand, Doc Simon's daughter. The foreigner," she introduced herself crisply as she walked farther into the lounge, stopping halfway between the door and the bar.

At her announcement a sheepish look crossed Rusty's face and the men chuckled. Sarah felt her apprehension ease. "I couldn't help but overhear your words," she explained, forcing a slight smile on her lips. "Actually, I'm only half a foreigner. My mother was born on a farm near Tucumcari, New Mexico."

She rarely thought of her mother's relatives. She had been only twelve the last time she'd seen them. They had disapproved of her mother marrying an Iranian physician and moving to Iran. And after her family had been killed by Khomeini fanatics, they had been afraid to take a "little heathen" into their care. The only reason she mentioned the connection now was to ease Rusty's resentment toward foreigners.

"Well, now, that makes you nearly one of us." Rusty placed both forearms on the counter as if preparing for a long chat. The men drifted toward a nearby table and sat down. The black-haired cowboy raised his beer mug and said, "Glad to meet you, Doc. I guess you're here to pack up the doc's things."

Sarah nodded, trying to mask her impatience, hoping that Angel wouldn't be too frightened. Her daughter had been as apprehensive as Sarah about stopping at the "spooky" place. "I came in here to ask if there's another way into Knight's Corner. The bridge up ahead is closed."

Rusty shrugged. "Happens every time it rains hard. We don't mind 'cause it keeps strangers out. Where'd you plan to stay?"

"At the Vista Motel. I made reservations. They're expecting me."

Rusty shook his head. "Not tonight. If the bridge is flooded, the road on the other side is underwater, too."

Dismayed, Sarah considered her other options. She only knew two people in town. Unfortunately Simon's former nurse, Pilar Torres, was on vacation. That left only Big John Knight. She had met the big rancher and his family in San Antonio at the time of Simon's death. Since his son, Cord, had died a year ago, her father's friend had spent most of his time with his daughter, Vicky, and his divorced wife, Renee, so she wasn't certain if he was in Knight's Corner at the moment. That left the apartment above Simon's vandalized office.

But before she could make a decision, Rusty said, "Your best bet's the Circle K. It's the closest and they'll be glad to have you, seeing as how your father and Big John were close. The land on the other side of the road all belongs to the Knight family. You just follow the fence line for about five miles until it stops, then take the track for four miles."

"Are you sure this is the right way?" Angel asked fifteen minutes later, craning her neck to look above the dashboard.

"We're on the right track," Sarah said soothingly. And that was exactly what it was, a narrow cow path with crumbling pavement running between two deep, water-filled ditches. If she hadn't seen the faded sign, Knight's Corner, 13 Miles, as she had turned into the lane, she would have suspected Rusty of pointing her in the wrong direction. Even now, with less than a mile to go to the crossroads, she was apprehensive. Rusty had seemed too friendly, too helpful, and she hadn't quite trusted him.

Besides, since leaving the Coyote Lounge, a truck had been following her. Sarah glanced in the rearview mirror and looked at the lights. The pickup was keeping its distance.

"Well, I don't like it," Angel said. "It's spooky. Sheba doesn't like it, either," she said, when the cat meowed plaintively.

"Sheba doesn't like the carrier," Sarah pointed out calmly, wishing for the hundredth time that she had left the cat with her neighbor and baby-sitter, Terry. But Angel was an impressionable, sensitive child. Her grandfather's death two months ago had shaken her secure little world and she had refused to be parted from her pet.

"Mommy, watch out," Angel cried, pointing at a big bulk that had suddenly appeared in the beam of their head-lights.

"I see it," Sarah said. She peered past the swiftly moving wipers, sucking in her breath sharply as the bulk took shape. A big bull was blocking her way. He stood with his head held high in challenge, blowing hot breath from his nostrils. His curved horns gleamed wickedly. Blood was running down his massive chest and mud-splattered hide.

"It's a monster!" Angel said in a hushed voice. More awed than frightened, she scrambled to her knees. "A big ugly monster. And it's bleeding."

"Get back down into your seat belt," Sarah said sharply. "It's a bull, not a monster." This was all she needed, she thought grimly, easing off the gas and gently stepping on the brakes. The car slowed down, but refused to stop, sliding over the slick muddy surface... and toward the bull. For a moment the bull stood trapped in the beam of light, his mud-splattered hide rippling nervously, his small eyes reflecting the light, gleaming menacingly as the car moved closer. Then it pawed the ground, lowered its head and charged.

In a desperate last-ditch effort to stop the car, Sarah floored the brake, but the rear wheels skidded and the car fishtailed out of control. Which was when the bull buried his horns in the front fender, sending the car into the ditch.

Angel screamed and Sheba let out a frightened howl.

The sound caught the bull's attention, riveting his attention on them. For a moment he stood frozen. Then, with a snort, he suddenly turned and charged down the lane toward the oncoming lights behind her.

Chapter 2

City slickers.

Cord couldn't believe that anyone would be stupid enough to attempt this track with anything less than a four-wheel drive. The white Toyota slid sideways and its rear wheels became deeply buried in the water-filled ditch up ahead. In the beam of the headlights he could see the woman from the parking lot in the driver's seat. Cord's mouth curled.

Seeing the bull, he cautiously eased his truck close to the Toyota's bumper, driving the animal ahead of him. The truck was equipped with a cattle guard and, after taking one swipe, the Brahma bull lost interest. Sighing, he blocked the lane to keep the bull confined to the other side of the car and rolled down his window. He turned on the inside light so that the woman could see him. "Are you hurt?"

Sarah pushed the button to crack the window open, still slightly shaken from her ordeal. Recognizing the truck with its distinctive grid in front from the lounge's parking lot, she expelled a swift sigh of relief. She wondered if the driver was the burned-out agent, the one who had caused the brawl in the lounge.

From the distance of about ten feet between their vehicles she could see him quite clearly. His shaggy blond hair was sun-streaked and shone like old gold in the overhead light of his cab. His shoulders were broad and a steel gray rain slicker added to their width. He was deeply tanned, with the rugged, just-short-of-handsome looks women generally found irresistible, she observed clinically. A scar slashed his left cheek, adding to, rather than distracting from, his daredevil looks. She couldn't see his eyes, but the set of his wide, hard mouth was grim.

If he hadn't turned on the overhead light so that she could see him, she would have been worried. Now some of Sarah's tension eased. A man bent on crime didn't show his face, she reasoned. He looked grumpy and disgusted. Well, she felt the same way. "We're fine," she called out, watching the bull's restless pacing at the edge of the light. "In better shape than the bull. He needs a vet."

Cord shook his head in disbelief. That bull had just taken a swipe at her car, had caused her to slide into the ditch and all she could think of was calling the vet? With her black, wire-rimmed glasses and her hair pulled into a tight bun she looked prim, like a teacher or a crusader. Her accent was from the Northeast, probably New York. It figured. New Yorkers had their priorities all screwed up. With people getting murdered right and left, New Yorkers would stop traffic on a six-lane parkway to allow a poodle safely across! At the thought of having the ASPCA breathe down Devlin's neck, however, his mood brightened considerably. "Do you want me to call the vet before or after I get you out of there?"

There was just enough condescension in his drawl to set Sarah's teeth on edge. She didn't think it would be very sensible to anger him, though, so she kept her voice calm and firm. "Since mud and water are oozing into the car and my daughter is a little anxious, I believe the vet can wait."

Hell, she'd taken him literally. He couldn't stand females without a sense of humor. He could use a good laugh right about now, too, because, unless they were visiting someone else around here, he would damn well bet he was going to be stuck with them for the night. "Who were you planning to visit? I can try and raise them on the CB."

Sarah hesitated. "Why were you following me?"

"Following you? I was *behind* you, not *following* you. I'm on my way home. I stuck around the lounge to make certain you didn't run into trouble, that's all."

Angel scrambled to her knees and peered around her mother, looking at the stranger through the crack. "He looks just like He-Man," she whispered, "I think he's a good guy, Mommy."

Sarah gnawed her bottom lip in indecision. He probably was a good guy, but she didn't want to take any chances. "If you could get the sheriff's office, I would be grateful," she said. Once they were safe, she could decide what to do. "Would you contact him for me?"

Cord grimaced. She obviously didn't have a place to stay, but was too cautious to admit it. Glancing at the little girl next to her, whom he hadn't noticed before, he didn't blame her for that. A woman traveling alone with a child couldn't be too careful. "I can try. But we're ten miles out of town and the rain doesn't improve the signal. Unless there's a car nearby, I doubt I'll get through."

Cord reached for the CB and switched to the emergency channel. The town had recently elected a new sheriff. Cord hadn't met him yet, but from what he'd heard, Holt was a good man. As expected, however, he couldn't raise him. Switching to a different channel, he tried Pete's Garage next, hoping it hadn't shut down for the night. But again there was no response. Reluctantly he opened the door. "No one's picking up on it. I guess I'll have to take you into town."

Hearing the reluctance in his voice, Sarah would have loved to have thrown his offer into his face, but she couldn't. She was a practical, sensible person. Gritting her teeth, she said, "That would be nice."

"I don't think he wants to rescue us," Angel said a little anxiously, snuggling up to Sarah.

Sarah's arm tightened around her daughter reassuringly. She could handle disgruntled males. Actually, she found the cowboy's reluctance more reassuring than annoying. A smile and a glib tongue would have alarmed her much more. "He's probably tired and hungry," she said, watching him climb out of the truck. He was taller than she'd expected, and lean. His boots and jeans were streaked with mud, as if he'd spent the day outside chasing cattle.

Cord shivered as the rain hit him. Pulling his hood up and closer against his face, he slogged through the mud, stopping a foot away from the window so she could see him and wouldn't feel intimidated. He didn't want to spend the next hour coaxing her from the car. Bending down, he saw more clearly the small girl nestled right next to her mother. The child was staring at him with big brown eyes. She wore a fuzzy white knit cap and a bright red coat.

"Hi," he said awkwardly. He couldn't remember when he had last talked to a child, but she looked sort of cute. "How old are you?"

"Five." Angel slowly scrambled back to her knees. For a moment she stared at him searchingly. Then she smiled slowly, sweetly. "Thank you for chasing the monster away."

Her smile lit up her whole face. Cord felt one corner of his mouth kick up in response. "You're welcome, pumpkin."

At that moment a deep-throated howl came from the back of the car. Startled, Cord took a step back, running a hand across his wet face. An unaccompanied woman, a young child and what sounded like a very big cat. He hoped to hell they had a place to stay.

"That's Sheba." Angel raised her voice above the howl, looking up at him a little anxiously, as if afraid he would walk away. "She's a Persian princess. She's really very good. Only, she doesn't like the box much—that's why she cries. But my mommy said she would run away if we let her out."

Personally, Cord thought, it would be a blessing. He liked cats, the barnyard variety, but he didn't much care for the highbred neurotic type. But, faced with those big brown eyes, he found himself saying gruffly, "Don't worry. We won't leave her behind."

Then he looked at the woman, still studying him with faint apprehension, as if uncertain whether she should trust him or not. He could understand her anxiety, and tried to make allowances for it, but rain was running into his slicker and down his neck. "Look, lady, you're perfectly safe with me. So why don't you open the car door and I can carry you and your daughter to my truck. You can tell me where you want to go after that."

Sarah bit her lip. Something made her give the man another look, made her search his tanned wet face and finally meet his sharp gray eyes. She saw nothing there to reassure her. She felt an odd uneasiness, as if all her senses and instincts had suddenly gone on full alert. Drawing back a little, she asked, "Is there no way you can pull my car out of the ditch?"

Cord glanced at her car. Towing her to the road and sending her on her way would have been the ideal solution, but the ditch was steep and the road was slick. "I wouldn't get enough traction without putting chains on my tires. And I don't have chains with me."

His patient, patronizing tone was beginning to grate on her nerves. She didn't want to go with him, if she could avoid it. "Could you call a tow truck?" she asked.

"I already tried." Cord wiped a hand over his wet face again, praying for patience. He couldn't remember ever

having to work so hard trying to rescue anyone. There had
been a time when he would have simply opened the door,
picked her up and carried her to the truck. He had been
cocky then, believing that his honor and his badge would
protect him. But he no longer carried a badge, and his honor
had been dragged through the mud. These days, he was very
cautious in his dealings with women, if he couldn't avoid
them altogether. "Look, this is not the big city. We're miles
out of a small town," he drawled, "and Pete's Garage is
closed on weekends except for emergencies. And this hardly
qualifies as one."

Sarah shook her head in exasperation. *She* certainly considered being attacked by a bull and getting stuck in a wa-
tery ditch on a cold January night with a small child an
emergency. "Exactly what *does* it qualify as?" she asked
dryly.

One of Cord's brows shot up. "Stupidity?"

Sarah bit her lip to bite back an unexpected grin. She'd set
herself up for that one, she admitted.

Angel suddenly sat up straight and glared at Cord. "My
mommy is not stupid," she said fiercely. "And I don't think
you are a very nice man."

"Hush, Angel!" Sarah said firmly, startled by her
daughter's sudden attack. Angel wasn't an aggressive child.
She was sweet-tempered and often too trusting. But the trip
had tired her. And, Sarah admitted ruefully, her own uneasiness was rubbing off on her daughter, frightening her.
Hugging Angel reassuringly, she looked at their rescuer
apologetically. She wasn't prepared for the bitterness twisting his mouth, as if Angel's words had touched a sore spot.
"We're both a little tired," she said gently, opening the car
door.

"Sure." Before she could change her mind again, he
stepped past the door. The light inside her car had come on
and for the first time Cord could see her quite clearly. She
was younger than he'd thought. Late twenties, he guessed.

Bracing himself on the frame he bent down to look at the girl. Her delicate face was framed by brown curls peeking from beneath her cap. After her angry outburst she was a little anxious, but her chin was stubborn. Her mother's chin. Apologies didn't come easy to him, but he suddenly found himself saying, "I'm a little grumpy myself. I've been yelling at cows all day." She didn't shrink and the corners of her mouth lifted hesitantly.

"I don't know any cows. Are they very stupid?"

"Positively dumb," Cord drawled. "They were stuck in the mud and didn't want to be rescued." Then he heard a choking sound close to his ear and turned his head. The woman's face was mere inches away from his. She was sinking perfect white teeth into her quivering bottom lip. Hell, he'd really put his foot in his mouth this time, he thought, still staring at her soft lips. There was nothing prim or prudish about her mouth. It was unpainted, soft and full.

A jolt of awareness shot through him and his eyes narrowed in instinctive response. He glanced up. This close, her wire-rimmed glasses afforded her no protection. Her eyes were as big as her daughter's, tilted up slightly at the corners and as dark and sensual as night. At the moment they were sparkling with mirth, warm and unguarded. Another jolt went through him as their gazes locked. Desire, hot and completely unexpected, shot through him, stunning him. Her eyes widened and her laughter faded, a surprised look replacing the amusement on her face. For the space of three heartbeats their glances held; then she blinked, breaking the spell. When she opened her eyes again they were dark and mysterious once more. The lady had definitely slipped behind a veil.

"I don't think Angel will give you any problems," Sarah said quietly, still floored by the sudden sexual awareness that had flared between them. She hadn't been this conscious of a man in five years! This day had been filled with shocks, she thought, and the sooner she found a place for them to

stay, the better. With a few practiced strokes she pushed
Angel's curls into her knit cap. "You're the first one to go.
Don't wiggle," she admonished, pulling the hood of her red
winter coat over the cap. "I'll bring Sheba."

Cord glanced into the back, measured the size of the cat
carrier and frowned. "I don't think the box will fit into the
cab with us. Do you have a leash for the cat?"

Sarah tied the bow beneath Angel's chin. "I do. But I
think I should warn you that she still has all her claws."

Her voice never changed. It was still calm, reasonable,
cool. But this time Cord caught the gleam in her eyes. The
lady had a very wry sense of humor and she was gently
mocking him. Cord felt his interest quicken once again. He
looked at her hands. They were long-fingered with short
nails, and she wore no ring.

"I'm ready," Angel said, holding her arms out to him.

Cord lifted her. She was light, weighing next to nothing,
and he cradled her carefully. Bending over her to shield her
from the rain, he crossed the space to his truck.

She knew nothing about this man, Sarah thought as she
watched him carry Angel. Not his name. Or his address. She
had asked for none of the identification civilization demanded she should check before trusting him. But watching him place her daughter onto the bench of the pickup, she
suddenly realized that she knew him in a much more ele-
mental, instinctive, way. He was patient. He had a conscience. He was a little awkward, as if he hadn't been
around children much, yet he had a sense of humor and was
sensitive to a child's fears.

As he leapt down from the running board and moved
back toward her, she suddenly noticed that he walked with
the sure agility of a big cat. She became conscious of the tall,
lean streamlined silhouette of his body, the taut economi-
cal way he moved. Other things leapt into clear awareness—the rain, the mud, the earthy smell—facts she had

registered before but had ignored within the safe cocoon of her car.

With a mutter of impatience, she turned her mind to practical matters. Kneeling in her seat, she reached for her brown medical bag and her purse. She added them to the contents of her plastic overnight bag, then took Sheba out of her carrier. The bag, Sheba's carrier and their food chest were transferred swiftly to the back of the pickup.

"Is it safe to leave the rest in the trunk tonight?" Sarah asked, clutching Sheba in her arms.

Cord eyed the big orange fur ball warily. The cat glared back at him balefully from bright green eyes. "Safe enough. The water isn't likely to get any higher," he said, wondering how he was going to carry the animal without getting scratched. Coming to a sudden decision, he snagged one arm around the woman's waist, placed the other beneath her knees and lifted her, cat and all. "People often leave their keys in their cars around here."

Sarah stiffened, startled as much by his sudden move as by his words. "That's what Simon used to say."

Cord took one step, then froze at her words. The only man he knew named Simon had been *Doc* Simon. Suddenly he knew who this woman and child were, and startled, he lost his footing. Sarah tightened her arms around the cat, squeezing her. Sheba let out a yowl, and clawed at Cord. As the sharp claws went for his neck, Cord jerked back and they all landed solidly in the mud.

For a moment Sarah sat stunned, the breath knocked out of her. The leash slipped through her muddy hands and Sheba leapt to freedom. A few feet away, she paused, trying to shake the mud from her paws. Untangling himself from her, Cord lunged for the cat and missed, landing flat on his stomach in the mud. Sarah's attempt failed, as well. Angel, drawn by the noise, opened the truck door. With two bounding leaps, Sheba disappeared into the cab.

"Close the door!" Sarah and Cord shouted simultaneously.

With great presence of mind, Angel did.

For a moment Sarah just sat in the mud, too stunned to move. What a perfectly awful ending to an already awful day, she thought, looking at her reluctant knight. His face was streaked with mud, and a mixture of emotions crossed it. Disgust. Wariness. Amusement. Raising her hands, she found them to be covered with mud. A giggle welled up in her. "I'm sorry," she gasped. "Are you okay?

Cord nodded. He couldn't talk. Laughter was welling up in him, shaking him. It had been a long time since he had laughed, really laughed, and he now didn't seem to be able to control himself. "Welcome—to—Knight's—Corner, Doc Durand," he finally managed to say. Then laughter ripped free.

Startled, Sarah looked at him, giggles still shaking her. "How do you know my name?"

"I—knew—your—father—quite well," he explained between gasps. "He talked about—you all the time. In fact—I've been—expecting you. I'm—Cord Knight."

Sarah's laughter broke off abruptly, strangled by a sudden, ice-cold fear. Whoever this man was, he wasn't Big John's son. He couldn't be. Cord Knight had died in a boating accident a year ago.

Cord watched the laughter freeze and her eyes widen with shock from one instant to the next. Abruptly silent, she inched away from him. Her wide, apprehensive gaze darted between the truck, her car, then back to him as if gauging her chances of escape. His mouth hardened into a firm line. He had seen it all before. The shock. The fear. Then the retreat into a store or to the other side of the street as if he were a man on a rampage.

"*You're* Cord Knight?" she asked, her voice a shocked whisper.

He shrugged. Usually he didn't give a damn. But her re-action had caught him off guard. Maybe because she was Simon's daughter and her father had been almost family. Big John and Simon's friendship went back to first grade and, despite Simon's wanderlust, they had kept in contact over the years. Cord could remember Simon sending him Iranian stamps for his collection when he was ten. He could also recall the tense days of worrying at the beginning of the Iranian revolution, hoping that Simon and his wife had managed to escape. He'd known about Sarah since she had been smuggled out of the country on a fishing trawler after her family had been killed by fanatics. At sixteen, rescuing young damsels in distress had appealed to him. And there had been a time when he had fantasized about rescuing her.

Swearing, he leapt to his feet. Now that he had rescued her, he was tempted to leave her sitting in the mud. But he couldn't abandon Simon's daughter and granddaughter. He had some conscience left. If she didn't realize by now that she was perfectly safe with him, she wasn't as smart as Simon had always said she was. He had met some pretty dumb physicians during his career and she kept looking at him with her wide dark eyes as if she expected him to pounce on her any second now. Irritated, he walked to the back of the truck, opening the storage box to get a clean rag. "Relax, Doc. I don't rape muddy waifs."

At his scathing words, Sarah's head snapped back. There was no doubt in her mind now that he was Big John's son. The resemblance was startling. If she hadn't believed him dead she would have realized it before. "I know," she flung at his back, scrambling to her knees. "Ghosts are impo-tent."

Ghost? Startled, Cord jerked his head up and glanced over his shoulder, suddenly realizing the reason for her shock.

She didn't know of his return.

As far as she was concerned, he was still listed as missing at sea and presumed dead. She probably didn't know about his reputation, either. Simon had been no gossip and he doubted that it had spread all the way to New York. Some of his anger eased. "Hey, Doc, I'm no ghost," he drawled. Tossing her one of the rags, he began to wipe down the front of his slicker.

Because her glasses were splattered with mud, Sarah didn't see the rag coming and it hit her straight in the face. For a moment she was speechless. Then fury flared up. "Even ghosts are not that nasty. You are the rudest, grumpiest cowboy I've ever had the misfortune to meet." Snatching the rag from her face, she ground it into the mud with one hand while pocketing her glasses with the other.

"Grumpy?" Startled, Cord turned. The lady couldn't swear worth a darn. "Is that the best you can do?" he taunted.

"Not quite," Sarah muttered, flinging the muddy ball at him with all her strength. She aimed straight for his chest, the way her brothers had taught her long ago.

He saw the missile coming, but wasn't fast enough to avoid it. It hit him in the shoulder with enough force to make him wince. Surprise flared through him. He couldn't believe that the woman he had dismissed as frumpy and humorless had just flung mud at him! And with startling accuracy, too. A slow, reluctant grin kicked up. "Does that convince you that I'm no ghost?" he asked with dangerous softness as he slowly stalked her. "Just how many cowboys do you know, city slicker?"

Sarah felt a warning ripple down her back. Everything about Big John's son was just a shade darker, colder, harder than she'd have expected. This was no gentleman. But he had prodded and goaded her once too often. She was too furious to back down now. "One," she taunted. "And that's more than enough." She scooped up another handful of mud and got to her feet. "Don't come any closer," she warned.

Cord's glance moved speculatively from her hand to her face. "Since your experience with cowboys is somewhat limited, let me explain something to you," he said almost gently. "A cowboy doesn't back down from a dare." Her hair was mussed from her fall, thick, mud-coated strands stuck to her face and tumbled down her shoulders. There was nothing sedate about her now. Her dark eyes were narrowed and slightly tilted like a spitting cat's. Small white teeth were biting into her bottom lip as if she couldn't quite make up her mind whether to laugh or to swear. A jolt of desire shot through him. He advanced another cautious step. The mud came sailing through the air. This time she'd made the mistake of aiming at his face. He ducked easily and the stuff went right past him. She didn't retreat, but glared at him defiantly.

"Mommy, can I play, too?"

At the sound of Angel's eager voice, Sarah spun around. Excitement vanished abruptly and reality hit her with stunning force. She must be losing her mind, she thought, dazed and suddenly shivering with cold. Stark raving mad. She couldn't remember the last time she had thrown mud at anyone. "No," she called out. Her voice sounded strangled and she cleared it before she tried again. "No. It's freezing out here. And we weren't playing."

"Just what were you doing, Doc?" Cord asked softly for her ears alone.

"Getting even," Sarah said succinctly. She watched Angel's mouth droop with disappointment and sighed guiltily. She hadn't found much time to play with her daughter during the past few weeks. The last time she had seen Angel really romp around had been at the kindergarten's Christmas party three weeks ago, she suddenly realized. "Stay inside, Angel. We'll be right there. And hold on to Sheba's leash. We don't want her to escape again."

She waited until Angel's head had disappeared, then turned to the man watching her. The laughter had faded from his face and his eyes were once again guarded, watchful. She felt a brief stab of regret. He didn't look as though he had laughed much since his boat had sunk in the Gulf of Mexico.

She recalled Simon mentioning that he had been an anti-smuggling agent for the Immigration and Naturalization Service. Hunting *coyotes,* was the way he had put it. Sarah wondered if the hunter had become the hunted and if he had disappeared because of it. Whatever had happened to him, though, it hadn't been easy, she thought, looking at his hard closed face.

"I'm glad you're not a ghost," she said with simple sincerity, holding out her hand. With a grimace at the grubby sight of it, she added, "Welcome back to life, Cord Knight."

Apart from his family and a few close friends, this was the first genuine welcome he'd received. Slowly Cord took her small firm hand, surprised and touched at the same time. Gently he said, "I wish we could have met under different circumstances. I was very fond of Simon." His tragic death must have come as a shock to her, Cord thought soberly. Despite her two-month delay in getting to Simon's hometown, he knew they had been very close.

"Thank you." Abruptly Sarah withdrew her hand and brushed mud off her coat. She hadn't expected his gentleness. To her dismay, her eyes suddenly filled with weak tears. Dear God, breaking down and crying like a baby was all she needed, she thought, blinking furiously. Taking a shaky breath, she reassured herself. She was overworked, stressed-out, tired and relieved that they had found a safe place to stay. Tears were natural, if not welcome.

She hadn't realized until now just how much she had feared being stranded, of having nowhere to go.

It was an old fear, an irrational one, this dread of being unwanted. She'd thought she had dealt with her fears long ago, but since Simon's death, the old nightmares were coming back. Slowly she walked to her car and looked at the dented front fender. Another thing she would have to deal with, she thought. "Do you know the owner of the bull?"

"Yeah." She was a tough lady, he thought, a survivor like himself. He found the way she fought her emotion by brushing down her coat, then facing another problem, much more appealing than tears or broken sighs. He would have liked to go to her, to give her some comfort or reassurance, but something told him that she wouldn't welcome sympathy. "Let's go, Doc," he said briskly. "Don't worry about your car. I'll deal with Devlin."

"Devlin?" Sarah's brows drew together in a frown. "The name sounds familiar but—"

"Never mind," Cord said swiftly, before she could ask more questions. She was shivering and so was he. "I'll take care of it." Taking her arm he drew her away from the car and to the truck.

He was someone to keep at a distance, Sarah decided on their way to the ranch. Since George, Angel's father, had died two weeks before their wedding, she hadn't felt a spark of interest in another man. Shivering, she shifted closer to the stream of hot air pouring from the vents, content to listen to her daughter's never-ending questions. Angel was fascinated at the thought of spending the night at a ranch. Did Cord have horses? Pigs? Goats?

His patience surprised Sarah as much as the way he treated her daughter. Unlike most adults, he didn't talk down to her. Sarah watched him grin at Angel's description of how a goat had knocked her over at the Bronx Zoo, and she had the absurd wish to snatch Angel away from him. She didn't want him to become an important part of their lives during their stay in town.

But he wasn't a man to be dismissed easily. Questions kept flashing through her mind and she was too curious a person not to dwell on them. How had he survived the explosion? Where had he been? Why had he allowed everyone to believe that he had drowned in the accident? His parents had been devastated.

Maybe he had suffered from amnesia? She wasn't too comfortable with that idea. Total amnesia was rare. Besides, he had been some hotshot agent for the INS. She assumed that the search for him must have been more thorough and extensive than for an ordinary citizen.

"When did you come back?" she asked as he turned into a narrow drive beneath an arch with a Circle K.

"Six weeks ago." Cord slowed down to a crawl, his glance sweeping over the white-painted iron arch and the long drive lined with small evergreens and white fences along either side. On top of the small rise, he could barely see the red-tiled old Spanish-style ranch house and the cluster of buildings surrounding it. He never tired of the view. There had been times during the past year when he thought he'd never see it again.

"Did you go on a trip? Where did you go?" Angel asked.

Sarah saw his hands curl tightly. It was the only sign of emotion she saw. He loved this place. She felt as if she'd just been allowed a glimpse into his soul. "Angel, why don't you talk about our trip today,' she suggested, drawing her daughter's attention away from him.

While listening to Angel's chatter, Cord studied Sarah. She was very perceptive and sensitive, not at all what he'd expected. Frankly, he couldn't see her as a surgeon. The ones he'd met were all cold fish. "What took you so long to come down here?" he asked, when Angel had finished her story. "We've been expecting you for weeks."

Sarah hesitated briefly, reluctant to reveal too much of herself. "I had only two months left of my surgical residency. I decided to finish it first." Work had helped her get through the past two months.

"So what do you do now?" Cord asked.

"I work the midnight shift in the emergency room at St. Anne's, a city hospital."

Cord sent her a startled look. He'd spent more time than he cared to remember in places like that. And they all looked alike. They were madhouses. Combat zones. What was she trying to prove to herself? "Do you plan to stay there?"

"For a while. Until Angel goes to middle school, I guess. Simon—Simon had wanted me to look for a job in San Antonio. But now I—I have all my friends in New York."

She glanced around as the truck went up the rise. She couldn't live here. It was too isolated, too quiet. But she could see why Cord loved the place. In the shine of powerful floodlights, the sprawling adobe structure with its wrought-iron grilles looked solid, safe and enduring. There were barns, sheds and corrals. In the distance she saw lights burning in a small row of buildings, which she guessed were bunkhouses.

The main house was dark. Only the entrance was lit.

Startled, Sarah sat up straighter, suddenly uneasy. It looked as if no one else were home.

"The housekeeper is off for the weekend." Cord looked past Angel at Sarah leaning with her head against the back and the cat curled up in her lap. "My father's away on business. If you'd let us know of your arrival, both my parents would have been here."

"I guess I should have. I was looking forward to seeing them again. They were both very kind to me. But I wasn't quite certain when I would be free."

"Just where were you planning to stay?" Cord asked, pulling up at the side entrance. His father had expected her to live at the ranch. There was plenty of room.

"At the motel for a night or two. Then I planned to move into the apartment."

Cord nodded. Perhaps, with Big John away, it was better this way. Cord's reputation wasn't the best, and once she heard the gossip around town, she would probably want to move anyway.

The house was as quiet as a tomb. It was the first thing that came to her mind when she entered. There was no laughter, no bustle, no noise. It should have been shouting with joy, now that the only son and heir was back.

An hour later, after a long hot shower, and dressed in clean jeans and a sweatshirt, she felt more like her former self. But the emptiness and the silence still nagged at her as she crossed the long narrow foyer with its brown terra-cotta tiles and thick whitewashed adobe walls. Angel skipped at her side, her sneakers squeaking softly on the highly polished floor. Excitedly, she ran to a bunch of bright Mexican paper flowers arranged in a pottery vase next to a big oak chest. "I made you one like this for your birthday," she said, reaching for a bright orange one.

"Yes, you did and I love it." Sarah grabbed her hand just in time to stop her from pulling the flower out. "Don't touch anything," she warned. She watched Angel's eyes dart curiously around for another interesting object to admire, to feel and touch. Like Sarah, Angel was a tactile person, and often created the most amazing creatures out of putty and clay.

A smoothly carved alabaster mask on the wall caught her daughter's attention next. Her sensitive face turned thoughtful as she studied it. Sarah groaned. She had visions of masks appearing all around their apartment. But Angel surprised her with her perception, as she so often did. "The mask is crying," she said, pointing at a small brown imperfection in the almost translucent marble. "It makes me feel sad." She stepped back, her small hand stealing into Sarah's as she often did when something made her uncomfortable. "The house feels sad, too."

Sarah agreed with her. It had been only six weeks since Cord's return. After believing their son dead for over ten months she had expected at least some members of his family to be here, especially on a Saturday night. But perhaps the rains had kept everyone away.

Angel glanced at the oak staircase leading to the family bedrooms. Reading her daughter's intention, Sarah's hold tightened. "Don't you dare," she said sternly, drawing her swiftly down the hall. They passed a dining room with a banquet-size table of dark Spanish oak and heavy ladder-back chairs. It was a house built for a large family—strong, sturdy and enduring—yet Sarah's impression of echoing emptiness continued.

There were a great many silences around Cord, Sarah thought as she opened the kitchen door. Perhaps that was due to his arrogant take-it-or-leave-it-type attitude. The attitude of a man who was very sure of himself and saw no need for explanations. He expected people to take him at face value.

Sarah's lips compressed with exasperation. She dealt with men like him every day. Most of her professors and the older physicians she worked with had that same kind of annoy-ing—often deliberately intimidating—superiority. Person-ally, Sarah felt that a patient had a right to know what to expect. And frankly, she was curious about the reappear-ance of a man who had been thought dead for ten long months.

The big, tiled kitchen was empty, too, but at least there was noise. She could hear the faint sound of a dryer run-ning in the mudroom next door, reminding her that she had to wash their own muddy clothes. The big oak-and-tile table near the window had been set for three. A big pillow had been placed on one of the chairs; a glass of milk sat next to the plate. And a candy bar. Cord's unexpected thoughtful-ness stunned her. She felt a sense of welcome steal over her.

"Oh, goody," Angel cried, racing toward the table. "I'm starving."

Before Sarah could stop her, a voice from behind her said, "That's for dessert."

Startled, Sarah spun around, looking at the man framed in the doorway to the mudroom, carrying a platter with an enormous steak on it. He looked different. Clean, for one. And definitely more male. Soft faded denim clung to his long legs and rode low on his narrow hips. The blue chambray shirt molded his wide shoulders and broad chest. His freshly washed hair fell onto his forehead, giving him a rakish look. Soft, scuffed brown leather boots added another inch to his height, making him look even leaner and tougher. His eyes had changed to a deep smokey gray but were as distant as before. The expression, "Where there's smoke, there's fire," flashed through her mind, and she took a step back.

She had always felt more comfortable with sedate, quiet men, men like Angel's father, George. "I didn't mean to cause you all this trouble," she said, making a sweeping gesture that encompassed the steak and the table. "A sandwich would have done fine." She glanced at the steak and felt her stomach churn.

He shrugged. "It's simple enough. I wasn't expecting company." Her freshly washed hair was braided, the thick single rope falling all the way to her waist. The hairstyle softened her angular features. She wasn't vibrantly beautiful like his mother and sister—rather the opposite in fact. She had a subtle yet haunting allure that attracted him more than stunning beauty would have. The intelligence in her dark eyes was unmistakable and so was her honesty. Cord had never bothered to look for those qualities in a woman before. But since a woman's lies had cost him his job, his honor and almost his life, he now appreciated those traits. "I figured I at least owed you a hot meal for dropping you in the mud."

Sarah wryly shook her head. "I think we already settled that score." She didn't want to like him, but with every passing moment it became more difficult not to. "What can I do to help?"

"Potatoes are in the microwave. Baked beans and rolls are in the oven," he said, carrying the platter to the table.

Angel's eyes darted from her mother to Cord, then apparently decided that the man would be more easily charmed. "That looks good. I like steak," she said, smiling at Cord angelically while her hand sneaked past the glass of milk toward the candy bar. "Can I have one bite? I only want to taste it."

Cord's lips twitched. In another ten years the doc was going to have her hands full. "After dinner," he said firmly, reaching out to ruffle her dusky curls. "I don't want to get into trouble with your mother."

Angel looked over her shoulder at Sarah, then turned back to Cord. "Mommy never gets angry," she confided in a whisper. "She gets real quiet. Grandpa said it's because she's more hurt than angry. She's been very quiet since Grandpa went to heaven." Her smile suddenly became wobbly. "Everyone goes to heaven. My father and Lisa, too." With a last look at the candy bar, she sat down on the pillow. "Did you know my grandpa?"

"Yes," Cord said quietly, something inside him twisting. Since his return, he had kept everyone at a distance, but the sadness in Angel's eyes made him want to hug her, reach out to her. "He visited here a lot. In fact he used to sit in the chair you're sitting in now."

"He did?" Angel's face brightened at the words. "Did he talk about me and Mom?"

"All the time," Cord said gently. It wasn't a lie. Simon had talked about moving his family to Texas once his daughter had finished her training. "He was very proud of you. He showed me pictures of you, too." He suddenly recalled several of them in the zoo. Angel had been riding a camel, he recalled, laughing at a young woman in jeans and a blouse knotted at her waist, a baseball cap with Texas emblazoned on it shadowing her face. He'd nearly whistled at the way she'd filled out her clothes.

Involuntarily, his eyes swerved to the woman bending down to get the baked beans out of the oven, watching the way the soft denim stretched and molded itself to her subtle curves. Beneath that voluminous sweatshirt, the doc was hiding a figure that could give a man insomnia! And those long, long legs. For a moment he imagined her lean thighs wrapped around him and felt his body tighten in response, reminding him that he hadn't touched a woman in over a year. A long time for a man who had once enjoyed an active sex life.

"If you saw pictures of me before, why didn't you know me today?" Angel suddenly asked.

Cord's glance swerved back to her, sharply bringing his erotic thoughts under control. She didn't miss much, he thought ruefully, and he sure as hell didn't want her to start asking why he was staring at her mother. "I was away for a while. In the last picture I saw of you, you were a lot smaller. You've grown into a big girl since."

Sarah placed a pot holder on the oak table, then put the steaming casserole of baked beans on top of it. Keeping herself busy, though she was a guest in his home, was her only way of ignoring the fact that they were alone except for Angel. She had been aware of his glances, more than she cared to admit, and had studiously avoided looking at him or joining the conversation. But at his words, her curiosity finally got the better of her.

Straightening, she looked at him, then wished she hadn't, as their gazes locked in a flare of mutual awareness. For a moment the echo of shared laughter and the mud fight hummed between them. And the small flame grew. In the bright light of the stained-glass lamp, she could see shadows and weariness in his eyes, and deep lines of control and bitterness bracketed his mouth. Whatever hell he had been through, it was still haunting him.

"I'm in kindergarten now," Angel said, drawing Cord's attention back to her.

With a silent sigh of relief, Sarah turned away and opened the oven to take out the rolls. She doubted that he slept much at night. She knew all about nightmares, she thought, running a knife around the edge of the pan and loosening the rolls. The best way to fight nightmares was to bring them out in the open and confront them. She grimaced. The strong silent types always were the most difficult patients. They licked their wounds in private, as if, by forcing their mistakes to the deepest recesses of their mind, they would cease to exist. But they couldn't control their subconscious and would wake up screaming and bathed in cold sweat. Then they tried to exhaust themselves physically. When that didn't work, they either drowned their troubles with the help of drugs or alcohol . . . or isolated themselves. Like Cord.

With cops she often ordered a psychiatric evaluation.

Her eyes strayed to Cord, studying his strong profile, and she suddenly chuckled. She could just imagine his reaction if she suggested it to him. He would probably tell her very succinctly to go to hell and that he wasn't a basket case.

At the sound of her soft laughter, Cord glanced at her. His eyes darkened at the sight of her flushed face and the mischievous sparkle in her eyes. "Care to share the joke?"

"I—" Sarah felt her heart skip a beat, then begin to race. She licked her suddenly dry lips. There was little wrong with him, she decided wryly, nothing that a good rest wouldn't cure. And a woman. His reaction was that of a healthy male who had lately lacked the time and opportunity to play sexual games. He'd had something of a reputation, she recalled. "I was looking for the bread basket," she said once she was certain her voice would be calm and reasonable.

"On top of the refrigerator." Pouring coffee, Cord watched her stretch like a cat, standing up on her toes. As she reached for the basket, her shirt rode up, revealing the gentle swell of her hips and a stretch of creamy satiny skin. At the sight of it, the lingering ache in his body became a dull throbbing. This time, however, he did not look away, but watched speculatively as she placed the rolls into the basket.

Beneath that calm, practical facade the doc had a wicked sense of humor. He wondered what she had found amusing about him. A year ago, he would have pursued the subject. Now he was content to enjoy the novel experience of a woman not looking at him with fear or anger in her eyes.

He watched her sniff in the smell of freshly baked bread. There was something unconsciously sensuous about the small innocent pleasure. He suddenly realized that he had never taken the time before to notice such small things about a woman. His assignments had often lasted weeks, and what relationships he'd had had been brief and uncomplicated.

"Can I see your horses tomorrow morning?" Angel asked.

"Sure. If it's all right with your mother, you can even help me feed the foals. Does she ever run out of questions?" he asked as Sarah put the rolls on the table.

"When she sleeps." Sarah watched Angel's eyes droop a little and a big yawn split her face. The excitement was wearing off, she thought. "She'll hold you to your promises," she warned, slipping into the chair next to her daughter. "So don't make them lightly."

"I'll remember that," Cord said, but he wasn't worried in the slightest. There was something about a five-year-old's eagerness that brought life back into focus, like painting a drab gray barn a bright red. Angel accepted him at face value because he had driven her monster away. She trusted him. A man didn't have to guard against her. Smiling, Cord sat down in the chair at the head of the table and stretched his long legs beneath the table, determined to enjoy the brief pleasant interlude. "How much steak do you want?" he asked.

Sarah's stomach churned again. "I'm not hungry. I'll just have some bread and beans."

"Mommy doesn't eat red meat. It makes her sick," Angel said. "She says that she sees too much blood at the hospital."

"My mother doesn't eat red meat, either." Cord sent Sarah another sharp look, again wondering what she was trying to prove to herself. Then another thought occurred to him. Renee was also very perceptive and sensitive. And she, too, preferred city life.

There were a great many similarities between his mother and Dr. Sarah Durand.

Chapter 3

"I hope it doesn't rain tomorrow," Angel said an hour later as she climbed into the queen-size bed. A yawn escaped her and she rubbed her eyes with her pudgy hands. "I want to see everything. The horses, and the foals, and the kittens in the barn."

"That's a tall order. This is a very big place to explore all in one day," Sarah teased, tucking the bed covers around her daughter. Gently she brushed the soft curls away from the flushed soft face. The last time she had seen Angel so excited had been at the hospital Christmas party, she suddenly realized with a pang. Their lives had been very quiet during the past two months and the holidays had been a solemn, quiet affair. She had made an effort for Angel's sake, had even bought a Christmas tree, but every ornament, every song, had reminded her of some incident in the past. Now, for the first time in weeks, Angel was looking forward to tomorrow, in her eagerness forgetting the reason for the awful trip. Even the bull's attack had been turned into an adventure. And she owed Cord for that.

"Why can't we stay here?" Angel asked drowsily. "Grandpa did when he first moved here."

"Only until he had found a place of his own to live," Sarah pointed out gently, sitting down on the side of the bed, her glance moving around the big, comfortable room with its white painted walls, dark wood furniture and turquoise accents. "We have a place of our own. And the moment I have my car back, we'll move into town. The apartment may not be as big or as exciting as the ranch, but you can do things like buy the newspaper every morning."

Sarah grimaced. Ever since she had enrolled Angel in kindergarten, her daughter had wanted to buy the *Sunday Times* at Jim's Deli, a small corner store a block and a half away. But how could a small slice of freedom compete with kittens and foals?

Horses. If there had been one thing she had avoided over the years, it had been horses. At Angel's age they had played a very large role in her life. Her whole family had been horse-crazy. She had ridden from the moment she had been able to stay in the saddle. Her father had been a member of the Bakhtiars, a seminomadic tribe once famous for their horses. Her family had often spent weekends and long lazy summers at their camp.

For a moment her thoughts flew back to another time, a time before the world had gone crazy. She could almost feel the hot dry desert wind in her face, and her small black mare, Amshida, beneath her, trying valiantly to catch up with her three brothers riding ahead. Akim, the youngest and gentlest of the three—the only one with her mother's fair complexion—would eventually fall back and give her a chance to catch up with them.

Angel burrowed deeper beneath the comforter. "Why do we have to? Cord won't mind if we stay here."

Startled, Sarah looked at Angel. Apparently her daughter had missed the tension, but then Cord had gone out of his way to make her feel comfortable. She sighed. He hadn't been unkind to her, either, she admitted. Another woman would have felt flattered by his interest, would have enjoyed a little sexual banter. But she didn't want to play games. It wasn't that she was a prude. There had been times, during the first two years in med school, when she had enjoyed the easy, flirtatious banter that often went on between men and women. And then she had met George and had fallen in love.

Games too often turned serious and she never wanted to risk falling in love again.

Sooner or later everyone she loved died. Holding herself apart was the only way not to get hurt again. Since Simon's death, there were only a handful of people who even called her by her given name. At work she was Doc Durand and at home she was Mommy—and until tonight it had been enough. Now she felt a strange yearning that made her restless, and it would have to stop.

"The ranch is too far out of town," she said, getting to her feet. "It will be more convenient for us if we live at Grandpa's apartment. And we also have to think of Sheba," she added as the cat leapt onto the bed. "Here we would have to keep her locked up in this room and it isn't fair to her."

"Oh, all right." Angel smiled sleepily as her pet curled up close to her. "Good night, Mom. Good night Sheba."

"Sweet dreams." Sarah watched Angel's mouth curve briefly in response, then relax into sleep. For a moment she lingered, watching her breathing deepen, and a small sigh escaped. She didn't want to spoil Angel's fun and excitement, but staying here would create too many problems. Knight's Corner was a small conservative town and if Rusty's dislike of foreigners was an example, she would run into some prejudice because of her Iranian heritage. The fact that she wasn't married and had an illegitimate child would also raise some eyebrows. If she remained at the ranch with a dangerously attractive, single man, tongues would really start to wag, especially when she had a place of her own. For herself she didn't care, but she didn't want Angel exposed to unpleasantness. Everything about her daughter was soft and trusting and she wanted to keep it that way for a little while longer.

Sarah dimmed the bedside lamp. She knew all about small-town gossip and the power it wielded. Involuntarily, her thoughts flew back to a day sixteen years ago, shortly after her arrival in the States, when Simon had taken her to the farmhouse outside Tucumcari to meet her grandparents. Her grandmother had taken one look at her and had walked back into the house, declaring in a voice loud enough to carry to the outside, "She looks just like one of them terrorists on TV. I won't take that little heathen into my house. We'll never be able to hold our heads up again."

With an exclamation of impatience, Sarah bent to straighten out Angel's sneakers, then gathered her clothes scattered on the turquoise comforter. She hadn't thought of the scene in years. She hadn't wanted to leave Simon and Lisa and live with her grandparents anyway. After her grandparents' rejection, Simon had filed for adoption, making it all legal.

And now George, Lisa and Simon, too, were gone.

All she had left was Angel.

For a moment ice-cold fear gripped her heart. She couldn't deal with another loss.

Expelling a breath she forced the terror back. Moving quietly, she straightened out the room, brushing cat hair off the green overstuffed chair near the window, trying to slip back into the numb cocoon she lived in daily, but was suddenly finding so hard to return to.

She went into the white-and-turquoise-tiled bathroom and picked up the plastic bag of muddy clothes. With a last glance at her small family, Sarah quietly left the room.

Walking down the silent hall she wondered where Cord was. At the thought of running into him, she felt tension curl in her stomach. Annoyed, she gripped the bag tightly, wishing herself back at St. Anne's and dealing only with the easy companionship of the ER. Surgery was still a largely male-dominated field and she worked alongside men every day. She ate with them, joked with them and occasionally shared the same room trying to snatch an hour's sleep during a double shift. She had never felt the least interest in any one of them.

But then again, none of them were weary, bitter knights living alone in a castle on top of a hill.

It was the silence and the emptiness that disturbed her more than anything else, she decided. There was too much room in Cord's home for thought. Finding the kitchen deserted, she breathed a sigh of relief. The mudroom was also empty and Cord had emptied the dryer while she'd put Angel to bed. She looked at his clothes, neatly folded and stacked in a basket with his underwear on top, then swiftly turned her back and set the dial on the washer, tossing Angel's garments into the drum. She couldn't remember the last time the sight of a man's underwear had unnerved her. It was as if, removed from St. Anne's sterile environment, she was suddenly turning into a woman again. It was nothing more than a lingering rush of adrenaline, she told herself, rinsing her muddy pants in the adjoining sink. What she needed was a good night's sleep. Tomorrow she would feel perfectly in control again.

With a sigh, she tossed her pants into the washer, drained the water, then reached for her coat, grimacing at the muddy sight of it. Simon had hated it, she recalled. It made her look like a scarecrow, he had told her bluntly the first time he had seen it. Maybe it wasn't stylish, but she didn't buy her clothes with fashion in mind. At work she rarely got out of her blue surgical togs and at home she dressed for comfort and with an eye on the practical. And the coat was that. It kept her warm, dry and didn't show every speck of dirt, she thought, squeezing and rubbing, putting all her energy into cleaning it. When the muddy stains refused to come out, she filled the sink with warm sudsy water and decided to let it soak for a while.

A few minutes later, leaving the kitchen, she suddenly heard Cord's voice coming from somewhere nearby. Involuntarily, she stiffened, the deep sound of his voice making her tingle with awareness once again. Briskly she started down the hall, trying not to listen, but at hearing "... repair the fence before the Brahman can attack another car," she abruptly stopped and frowned.

Apparently he was talking to Devlin, the owner of the bull, and from the sound of his voice, it wasn't a neighborly chat. Suddenly anxious, she followed his smooth, deceptively soft drawl down the hall.

The door opposite the dining room was partially open and she peeked inside. Bookshelves lined the walls from floor to ceiling. To her left she spotted a computer system with the screen turned on. Cord was sitting behind a large desk, a beer in one hand, boots propped beside the blotter, holding the receiver away from his ear as if the party on the other end of the line were yelling into the phone.

Sarah hesitated, reluctant to intrude. He was perfectly capable of dealing with an angry neighbor and there was no reason to become involved. Besides, men tended to be touchy about the privacy of their study, guarding that space more jealously than their bedrooms, and she'd never knock on Cord's bedroom door!

Then she heard him say succinctly, "No one is cutting your fences, Devlin. They're rotting away. And I definitely expect you to pay for the damage of the car and apologize to Dr. Durand."

Sarah shook her head in exasperation. If Devlin was anything like his men, demanding an apology would be like waving a red flag in front of a bull.

She didn't need more trouble and certainly not over a two-hundred-dollar dent.

Exasperated, she pushed the door open and walked up to the desk. "I'd like a word with Mr. Devlin, please."

Startled, Cord looked up. His eyes narrowed when he noted the angry flush in her normally pale face and the angry sparkle in her black eyes. He wondered if she knew how sexy she looked, all flushed and with her damp sweatshirt clinging to her breasts, her ridiculous glasses perched on the tip of her slim nose and the long braid bouncing with each step. Probably not. From all he'd learned, she was still mourning for Angel's father and was dedicating her life to her daughter and good works instead. *She* might not think of herself as a woman, but having her around definitely reminded him that he was a man, and he didn't need the frustration.

"Hold on a moment, Devlin. I'll get right back to you." He pressed the hold button on the cordless phone, then turned to Sarah. "I don't think talking to Devlin is a good idea," he drawled, wondering how much of the conversation she had overheard. He might be down on his luck, but he didn't need her to fight his battles for him. Pity wasn't what he wanted from her. He raised his eyebrows and his gaze dropped down to her prim mouth. "Lighten up, Doc. If he insulted you, I'd feel compelled to teach him some manners. And I'm sure you don't want to provoke a fight."

His drawl was low and seductive, feathering down her neck like a tangible caress. Sarah stiffened against the urge to shiver. For a moment she was caught in the beam of his dark intense gaze, held captive by it, mesmerized. She gazed right back, refusing to be seduced, intimidated or side-tracked. Drawing in a slow, deep breath to steady herself, she tilted her chin and said firmly, "I don't provoke fights. A city emergency room at midnight is no genteel drawing room. I'm perfectly capable of dealing with men like Mr. Devlin in a calm and rational manner."

Cord grinned slowly, reminiscently. "I've seen you in action, Doc."

Sarah clenched her hands, determined not to let him goad her into losing her temper a second time. "From what I overheard, you weren't exactly avoiding a confrontation, either." She glared at him accusingly. "I don't particularly care for the fact that you are using me to goad Devlin."

Cord's jaw hardened at the accusation, tightening the scar on his left cheek. "Why, Doc, I didn't think you were the type to listen at keyholes," he taunted. "Actually, I was trying to make things easy for you. All I did was let Devlin know that if he gave you a hard time he'd have me to deal with."

He looked tough and dangerous suddenly and the transformation from the teasing devil he'd been only seconds ago sent a shiver of apprehension down her back. Sarah suddenly understood why Snyder didn't believe that Cord had "lost his nerve." He might be wounded, but he wasn't beaten yet. Not by a long shot.

Whatever the differences between him and Devlin, it was more than a dispute over broken fences or renegade bulls.

Wrapping her arms around herself against the sudden chill, she backed up and said fiercely, "I don't want you to involve yourself in my affairs. I'm going to let my insurance company deal with Mr. Devlin."

"Around here we handle conflicts more personally, city slicker," Cord teased her. Then his eyes suddenly narrowed with suspicion, wondering if anyone had talked about him at the *Coyote Lounge*. Until now he could have sworn that she knew nothing about his reputation, but she might have overheard Rusty and the others talk about "the coward." She was a practical, sensible creature and had probably decided to dismiss the gossip as malicious.

Until he had started flirting with her.

Damn. Would he never learn? It was his rumored luck with the ladies that had added to his troubles in the first place. The shrink at the arraignment had spouted all kinds of nonsense about inferiority complexes and a deep-rooted hate for women. Hell, yes, he had enjoyed women's company between assignments and no, he'd never hung around long enough to argue with them. There was nothing wrong with that. Any woman he'd become involved with knew the score. But perhaps the doc had listened to the same lectures as the shrink and the moment he'd turned on the heat a little, she'd gotten upset. "Anything you say, Doc. I was just trying to be helpful," he drawled, his eyes hard and remote. "Now, if you don't mind, I would like to finish my conversation with Devlin."

Sarah hesitated, instinctively aware that she'd touched an unhealed wound by flinging his protection back into his face. Cord didn't lack courage, but no matter how much he tried not to let other peoples' opinions affect him, it was obvious that, because of something in his recent past, others called him a coward, creating some self-doubts. She didn't want to add to them. "Look, it's not because those men called you—" she started to explain, then bit her lip, reluctant to bring up the subject. She was a stranger after all.

"—a coward?" Cord filled in for her coldly. He saw her shake her head in distress, as if she didn't want to believe in and repeat the gossip. But people had tiptoed around him too much during the past six weeks and suddenly he wanted to bring it out into the open. "Or are you wondering if it *is* true that I was charged with raping an illegal immigrant? That I jumped bail and blew up my boat to fake my death because I didn't want to go to jail? Except for the part about sinking my boat, it's all true, Doc," he taunted. He watched her face turn white and her eyes widen with shock. Hell, she hadn't known about it after all, he realized and felt a stirring of remorse. Wearily, he raked his hair back and growled, "Why don't you get the hell out of this room. And close the door on your way out."

Cord watched her spin around and make for the door, the long braid bouncing angrily with each step. The heavy shiny coil made her look vulnerable suddenly, like a little girl, and for a moment he was tempted to call her back and apologize. He was good at hurting people. He was an expert at it. His mother's eyes still filled with tears every time she saw him. And his independent, successful businesswoman of a sister, who'd never felt any restraint before at telling him off, only glared at him when he snapped at her and her mother.

Cord's jaw tightened with frustration. Every time he saw them, he felt guilty as hell. He had caused them a lot of heartbreak and suffering, but there had been no recriminations, no anger, and he wished they would just yell at him and be honest about their feelings.

Like his father. Big John couldn't even stand to be in the same room with him. He had gone on more business trips during the past six weeks than he used to during an entire year. His father was a man of few words. With him, actions spoke louder than words.

Raising his beer, he took a deep swallow and watched her grip the door handle. He'd apologized more during the past six weeks than he had in his entire life, and he was through with it.

Sarah gripped the handle as if it were a lifeline. She was shaking all over and she was cold. So cold. "You really like shocking people, don't you?" she snapped, turning back to him. "You're angry and bitter, probably with good reason, but you're not the only one hurting."

She stopped, swallowing the sudden lump in her throat. His bitterness was shredding the numbness she had wrapped around herself like a thick winter coat since Simon's death. Pain. Anger. Fear. She gripped the handle tightly, trying to hold back the emotions suddenly raging through her, blinking at the tears that pooled and burned in her eyes. "Simon used to say, 'Buck up, kiddo. Life ain't so bad.' We often disagreed on that philosophy. Life stinks sometimes."

Abruptly Cord got to his feet and walked around the desk. He didn't credit himself with having much of a conscience, but what he had was drawing him toward her. "Look, Doc—"

Sarah took a step back, mortified that he was witnessing her weakness. She was afraid that once she started crying, she wouldn't be able to stop, and she wanted to have at least some pride left. "I don't think you'd ever touch a woman in anger—you're the type to rescue them. And from what I overheard at the Coyote Lounge, you're hardly a coward. Those men hated your guts."

She took a steadying breath and bit her trembling lip, trying to hold back the tears. "I think men place too much importance on courage and honor anyway," she added with hoarse fierceness. "I'm the only survivor of a family of dead heroes and I prefer a live coward any day."

Closing the door in his face, she walked down the hall, back into the mudroom. She drained the muddy water from the sink, then filled it up again, soaking the coat and rubbing at the stains, as if by salvaging the coat, she could recover some of the numbness she had wrapped around herself since Simon's death. She knew that she couldn't hide forever or pretend that his death had been just another bad dream. Sooner or later she would have to deal with his loss and plan what she and Angel would do now that they were alone. Lifting the coat, she glared at a particularly stubborn stain, then dropped it back into the water and rubbed again. Later suited her just fine.

She had never pretended to be anything but a coward.

But at least she was alive.

Cord stood facing the door, listening to the soft pad of her receding footsteps, frowning at the look of panic he had caught in her eyes. Panic and despair, both of which she had tried to hide from him. She was such a bundle of contradictions, he thought. Practical and sensible on the surface and so fragile beneath. She hid her vulnerability behind a fierce, stubborn pride.

For a moment he was tempted again to go after her and apologize, but he sensed that she would not welcome his presence right now. Besides, he had some unfinished business with Devlin to take care of. He might not give a damn what went on in town—and from what he'd heard, the new sheriff was perfectly capable of dealing with Devlin—but the Doc was almost family, and whether Sarah liked it or not, he felt responsible for her and her daughter.

With a wry twist of his mouth, he opened the door again before returning to his chair. While he did keep people at a distance, he didn't want to necessarily be alone. He had spent a year in near solitude, afraid of contacting his family because their only protection had lain in their belief that he was dead. He hadn't dared linger in the small Mayan Highland villages near the Guatemalan border for fear of being recognized. The only human being he'd had contact with had been Luis, but his friend was working at the government offices in Mexico City and their meetings had been few. Now, having people around made him feel he was still alive, reminding him that the nightmare was finally over.

As always, the thought made him edgy. There was still a lot of unfinished business, and sometimes he wondered if he truly hadn't taken the coward's way out by walking away from it all.

Restless, he reached for the phone. Pressing the button, he listened to the dial tone. Devlin had gotten tired of waiting, he thought, punching the numbers again. But he answered almost instantly, as if he had been waiting near the phone. In fact, he'd been fairly reasonable so far and Cord was beginning to wonder why. It was time to start pushing a little harder, he decided. "About those bulls, Devlin. Did Rod give you my message?"

"Yeah. Your family doesn't own the whole damn county," Hugh Devlin growled.

Cord's mouth curled. "Maybe not. But the track belongs to us. We gave up a strip of good land to build a buf-

fer between your spread and ours. If you force me to, I'll
have one of my hands ride shotgun to keep it open and
safe.''

"Don't threaten me," Devlin snarled. "You have one hell
of a nerve barging into my lounge, throwing threats around
and getting my men all riled up. You want me to pay for the
dent, I'll send you a bill for the damage you caused.''

Cord felt a brief stab of satisfaction that Hugh's men had
wrecked the place. Then his eyes narrowed suspiciously.
"Since when do you own the Coyote Lounge?" Devlin
seemed to be very flush in the pockets these days and Cord
doubted that the bulls were that profitable. And Devlin
wasn't selling any of them, not as far as he could tell. Devlin's voice also sounded a little wary, as if he was regretting
the slip, when he said, "Bought it from Rusty about a year
ago. His brother's death got to him. He lost all interest and
didn't want the responsibility anymore.''

Cord frowned, wondering why Rusty hadn't mentioned
it. Had Devlin forced him to sell out? And where had Devlin scraped up the cash to pay for it? A year ago he had been
all but broke. "Did you inherit money? Or did you rob a
bank?'' he asked with deceptive softness.

"I won it. I'm not giving you a chance to send me to
prison on some trumped-up charges like you did my daddy.
It's all legal," Devlin snarled. "I won big in . . .''

I'll bet you did, Cord thought grimly, listening to Hugh
expand on his luck at the tables. But he doubted that the
money had come from gaming halls. It seemed like too
much of a coincidence that Hugh had come into funds
shortly after Cord's boat had been sabotaged. It was far
more likely that Harper had paid him to keep an eye on the
Circle K, just in case he hadn't become shark food.

Harper.

For a moment hate flared at the thought of the man who
had sold him out to the *coyotes*. Then he clamped down on
it. He had seen what revenge could do to a man. It ate at his

soul until there was nothing left but the need to destroy. Luis was going that way, he thought grimly, and it was a damn waste. A few years back, the critics had called his artist friend the new Diego Riviera. Now the half-finished sculptures and paintings in his studio were gathering dust. Luis didn't have much of a choice but to keep on fighting. For Luis it was a matter of survival, he thought soberly. But he himself had been given a chance to walk away from it all and he was determined not to blow it.

" . . . and I kept the receipts—"

"I'm sure you did," Cord cut through Devlin's words, suddenly weary of the game. He wasn't going to learn anything more tonight anyway. Devlin had become cautious after the one slip and wouldn't be riled into losing his temper again. "Since you're doing so well, you won't mind settling with Doc Durand. And keep those damned bulls penned up," he said coldly, hanging up the phone.

Frowning, he stared at the beamed ceiling, wondering if Devlin was still working for his former boss. Harper had quite a deal going with "Lobo" Rodriguez, the *coyote* who controlled a sizable percentage of the goods being smuggled into the U.S. When Luis had first warned Cord about Harper, he'd had a hard time believing it. Harper was a wimp. He turned green at the sight of blood. He was pedantic and cautious, always double- and triple-checking information before acting on it. He didn't have the stomach to deal with ruthless men like Rodriguez. And he disliked foreigners almost as much as Rusty did.

If the tip had come from anyone but Luis, Cord would have dismissed it as a joke.

Even so, it had taken him weeks of checking computer files to find evidence that Harper had been providing green cards, Social Security numbers and false passports to Rodriguez's wealthier clients. Unfortunately, when he'd tried to copy the file, it had crashed. He had no proof.

And who in their right mind would believe the word of a man with his blackened reputation over Harper's word?

Slowly he ran his finger along the scar while his other hand balled into a fist. Harper had set him up, sold him out to the *coyotes* and something in him still craved revenge. He could feel it pulling at him now. Slowly the beamed ceiling slid out of focus and he was once again lying on his back in the jungle staring at the canopy of leaves, the green hell closing in on him in a world of silence and cloying heat and Rodriguez's men beating the bushes around him.

Abruptly he pushed back his chair and walked from the room, crossing the foyer in long strides. After his presumed death, Mariela had been sent back to Mexico. It had taken him months to find her, but he had eventually. He had snatched her right from Rodriguez's well-guarded *finca* in Southern Mexico. With a little persuasion, she had signed a statement and the charges against him had been dropped.

He was a free man.

Then why are you holed up here on the ranch? his inner voice asked snidely. The INS had even offered him another job. A desk job in Texarkana—hundreds of miles away from Brownsville and from Harper—with the warning that they would not tolerate any more accusations against his former boss. That was when he'd finally accepted that some crooks got away, that it was time to quit and cash in his chips while he still could. A cynical smile curled his lip. The doc had pegged him all wrong. He was no hero. He was just another cowboy, down on his luck and smart enough to accept defeat.

But hell would freeze over before he allowed Devlin, Harper or anyone else to encroach on his territory. He wasn't beaten yet.

He opened the front door, crossed the covered porch and ran down the steps. The rain had stopped and the sky had lightened, a cool breeze chasing the clouds away. The temperature must have gone up, because he didn't feel the cold nearly as much. Slowly he raised his face and breathed in the clean cool fresh air. The day's depression slid away and suddenly he felt something inside him quicken, a fresh eagerness he hadn't felt in months.

Welcome back to life, that inner voice piped in again.

Rounding the house on his way to the barn, he saw the light burning in the mudroom. He stopped abruptly, frowning, then walked to the door. He owed the doc an apology and he may as well get it over with. And maybe he should call his sister, as well; one word of encouragement was all the excuse she would need to drive down here. He didn't want his family around—not yet. Not until he knew what Devlin was up to.

And not until he'd taken a closer look at Simon's house.

Opening the door, he found the doc bent over the sink, looking like a waif, trying to scrub that awful coat as if it were the only garment she owned. The impact of the impression slammed into him like the kick of a mule and he sucked in his breath. "Why don't you let it soak overnight," he suggested quietly. "You won't need it tomorrow. The rain has stopped and it's warming up."

Sarah stiffened at the sound of his voice. She had kept an eye on the kitchen door, but she hadn't expected him to come in from the outside. He sounded gentler, his soft drawl soothing, and warmth stole into her. She hoped he wasn't going to mention the embarrassing scene in the study because she couldn't deal with it right now. Turning the water off, she straightened, reaching for the towel lying on the washer before looking at him. His tawny hair was ruffled from the breeze and a fresh sharp outdoor scent clung to him. He seemed different, less tense, more alive. His crooked half smile slid beneath her defenses. "I think the coat is beyond help," she said with a grimace, reaching for the glasses she'd placed on the shelf above the sink and pushing the frame onto her nose. "But I'm too tired to care one way or another. It's been a long day. I'm going to turn in now."

Cord watched the shield slide back into place. Turning to the coatrack, he lifted his tan leather jacket from a hook. "I have to check on one of the horses. Simon's are stabled in the same barn. Want to take a look at them?" he asked casually.

Puzzled, Sarah glanced at him. "Simon didn't own any horses. He talked about looking around for a pony for Angel so he could teach her to ride, but he never said anything about having bought a horse."

Cord shrugged. "Guess he wanted to surprise you. Maybe they were supposed to be a Christmas present." And one hell of a Christmas present they would have made, too. He'd give his eye teeth to own even one of the beauties. Simon had always had an eye for horses. "Did you ever look at the list of assets my father sent to the lawyer?" he asked slowly.

Sarah shook her head, still stunned by the news that Simon had owned horses. "No. No, I—I didn't have the time," she said, unwilling to reveal that she hadn't been able to make herself look at the list because it had seemed so final. Horses! She felt a sudden spark of eagerness. "How many?"

"Three." With satisfaction he noticed the sudden spark of eagerness. "Do you ride?"

"I used to," Sarah said slowly. "A long, long time ago." She ran a shaky hand over her face. "What am I going to do with three horses?"

Cord took in her stunned expression, his glance thoughtfully lingering on her trembling hand. He suddenly realized why she hadn't shown any interest in her inheritance, why she had waited nine weeks to come to Knight's Corner. A part of her wanted to deny that Simon was gone and as long as she didn't have to deal with reality, she could pretend that it was all a nightmare.

He couldn't shield her from the pain, he thought soberly, surprised at how much he wanted to do just that. His thought flew to the vandalized office. His father had boarded it up and straightened out the place, but she was in for a shock nonetheless. Perhaps those three beauties out in the barn would soften the blow for her. He settled his jacket firmly across her shoulders and steered her toward the door. "Take a look at them first. You can decide what to do with them later," he said gently, ushering her out the door before she could recover from the shock.

But even as Cord herded her outside, the cool breeze blew straight into her face and reality set in. She stumbled backward and dug in her heels, clutching the open flaps of the jacket against the chill. She didn't want to see the horses. Not tonight, anyway. And certainly not with Cord watching her. "It's too cold and too late," she muttered, huddling in the coat. It was one thing to be a coward, but another to announce it to the rest of the world. "We took the seven o'clock flight out of La Guardia and I'm beat."

Cord glanced down at her bent head. She was such a little thing, her head barely reaching to his shoulder, and the wind was getting stronger. His arm slipped down to her waist and he drew her against his side protectively as he guided her down the pebble-strewn path. "We're halfway to the barn. The breeze will blow the cobwebs away."

Sarah dug in her heels, resisting being dragged along, resisting the temptation to lean into him. She glared at him indignantly, avoiding those sharp eyes that had already managed to see past her carefully erected defenses too many times for comfort. "Maybe you have antifreeze in your veins, but I'm freezing solid."

They had stopped at the edge of the floodlights and Cord could see her face clearly. He grinned at the flash of temper in her dark eyes. It was one hell of an improvement over the despair he had glimpsed only moments ago. "You may be a city slicker, but you're no hothouse flower, Doc." Then he

noticed the apprehension behind the anger and he withdrew his arm slowly. "And if it weren't for the fact that you
still have some doubts about me, despite your protesta-
tions, I'd prove to you that I have real blood in my veins."

Denial rose instantly to her lips. "That's not true. If I had
any doubts, I wouldn't be standing here arguing with you."
She scowled at him fiercely, her eyes sliding over the jagged
scar. For a moment she wanted to reach out and run her
finger over it, try to soften the hard tissue. But she was more
woman than physician at the moment. She fixed her gaze on
his mouth, watching the corners quirk with amusement as
if he knew just how aware of him she was. "And that's not
an invitation," she warned in exasperation, trying to ignore the inherent sex appeal in her statement. But something warm and forbidden curled in her stomach and a blush
stole into her face. She pushed up her glasses, trying to hide
the blush.

Cord felt hunger rip through him. He wanted to lift those
ridiculous frames off her nose and show her ways to deal
with their demons together. In the old days, he wouldn't
have hesitated to kiss her and deepen her awareness of him.
But he was a man with a reputation and a shady past and he
had no business touching her.

Besides, something warned him that if he did, he might
not be able to walk away from her.

"I read you loud and clear, Doc. I'll keep my distance,"
he promised wryly. "But the next time you throw mud at
me, the deal's off."

Uncertainly, Sarah stared at the wry smile that told her
not to take the flirtation seriously, that it was only a game,
a way of distracting her and himself and of easing the tension between them. But since she didn't feel like playing, he
was backing off, waiting for her to make the next move.
"I'm not in the habit of throwing mud balls." She tried to
give him a stern look and failed, a helpless giggle escaping
her instead. "I still don't know what came over me. There

won't be a next time, I can promise you that. In another day or so the ground will be too dry. Even if you riled me enough to feel tempted, it wouldn't be impossible.''

"A lot can happen in two days," Cord teased, hooking his thumbs into his pockets.

"God, the size of your ego is something else." Sarah sniffed, pushed the glasses up her nose again and raised her face into the breeze, suddenly feeling better and stronger than she had in months. The trip had knocked her badly off-balance. Each disaster she had run into today had sliced away at the comforting numbness, shaking loose the many feelings she wasn't ready yet to deal with. But Cord had distracted her from the emotional whirlpool that was threatening to suck her under. She shot him a sideways glance, wondering if he knew that she hadn't felt much of anything during the past two months, not anger or the need to laugh. "Let's have a look at the horses."

Chapter 4

The inside of the barn was warm and dim. For a moment Sarah hovered near the door, sniffing the familiar scents of horse and hay, listening to the rustle as animals moved, and she watched wisps of dust dance in the beam of lights.

"Like hospitals, barns smell the same all over the world," she said lightly. Slipping out of the coat, she hung it up on the rack beside the door. Her glasses were fogging up so she took them off and slipped them into her pocket. "It's been a long time since I've seen the inside of one." She had forgotten how good a barn could smell and how soothing the sounds were. Smiling slightly, she looked up at Cord and found him close to her. Too close. And he was looking at her as if they had known each other all their lives.

She wished they had. She wished he was someone she could talk to, lean on and share things with. Longing needs she had thought put aside long ago, sprang out fresh and terribly strong. She wanted to give in to them and feel, just feel.

Cord watched her nostrils flare as if sensing a threat. He had practically twisted her arm and dragged her in here, hoping to chase away some ghosts. Now he wondered if he hadn't raised a few instead. He decided to give her a few minutes by herself to sort through the memories. Maybe there were some good ones mingling with the bad. "While I check on some things, why don't you go ahead and look over your horses by yourself. They're in the last three stalls on the right. But watch out for the bay—she spooks easily."

Sarah's eyes widened. How had he known that she wanted to be alone? Apparently he didn't miss much.

Cord shrugged, giving her a crooked smile as if to say that he understood. "I know a thing or two about ghosts myself. If you need help with your demons, call me. I'll be around."

A soft gasp escaped her. "Careful, cowboy, your shield is slipping," she scoffed.

Cord grimaced and shook his head. "You've got your metaphors all mixed-up, city slicker. Shields are for real knights. There's only one knight left in this corner of the world and his name is Big John. I'm just a mean cowboy with a hide so thick and tough, even the sharks were afraid of losing their teeth."

Something wrenched inside Sarah. Before she could stop herself she reached out to him, her hand lifting to his face, tracing the scar. She felt him draw a sharp breath, go rigid, motionless. "Sharks have pea brains, thank God," she said gently, tracing the taut tissue with the tip of her finger. She could feel a tingle, as if she had touched electricity. The current pulsed through her, warmth spreading with every beat of her heart. "I have a medical degree and you don't fool me. If you want my expert opinion, the toughest part about you is this scar."

"But then you're blind as a bat with your glasses off," Cord said wryly, catching her wrist.

They were so close that she could see the flames in his smoky eyes, the desire, the need. For a moment their eyes locked and held. Without thinking, without being able to think, he tightened his hand around her wrist. The need to feel her hands slide all over him was stronger than anything he had known in a long time. It was crazy to want like this. The way his father still wanted his mother, even five years after their divorce.

Crazy.

He had sworn to himself never to allow a woman to slip beneath his skin, to seep into his soul. Especially not a city person like his mother. His father had lost a part of his heart when his mother had left to pursue her artist's career. Cord had vowed that he wasn't going to end up like Big John. He was lonely, yes, but his loneliness was only a temporary thing. Sooner or later the scars would soften, the last year would slip into oblivion and he would be a whole man again.

Slowly, aching all the way, he drew her hand down, released it and walked toward the tack room and the small kitchenette stacked with veterinary supplies, tossing over his shoulder, "Go look at your horses, Doc. It's a lot safer to pet one of them."

As if burned, Sarah stuffed her hands into her pockets. What had gotten into her? For a moment she had forgotten all the lessons life and medical school had taught her.

One of the first lessons taught in medical school was not to become too involved with those in need, to remain aloof, or she would lose her objectivity. She knew herself to be a person without half measures, with very strong feelings and a tendency to put herself too easily in the place of others. Too often, she was unable to draw the line between sympathy and empathy. The only thing that had saved her sanity thus far was the nature of ER work: involvement was temporary. In her ER work she could reach out fully without having to guard against overinvolvement. For once a patient was stabilized, he was moved to another part of the hospital and into someone else's care.

But there was something about Cord that made her want to reach out to him. He didn't seem like a stranger. Perhaps because she had known about him for years. Both Simon and Lisa had been only children and had lost their parents early. The Knights had always seemed like distant relatives. She could still remember when Cord had graduated from high school; for some time she had studied the photo that had arrived with the invitation to his commencement exercises. He'd looked devilishly handsome, cocky, a lonely young girl's fantasy. But, because schools closed earlier in Texas than in New York, only Lisa and Simon had flown to Texas to attend.

Her thoughts flew to George, the gentle fellow med student who had wooed her with such persistence. It had taken him months to break through her resistance, until she had finally agreed to a date. George had been so solid, so real, a big cuddly teddy bear, a forever-kind-of-guy.

Two weeks before their wedding, an enraged psychiatric patient had killed him, bashing him from behind with a chair.

Shivering, she hugged herself and walked down between the stalls. There was no forever. It didn't exist. And whatever Cord stirred in her was best ignored. They were two lonely, vulnerable, shell-shocked people turning to each other in need of warmth. She couldn't let anything happen between them, she told herself sternly as she stopped in front of the first of the stalls housing Simon's horses. The sooner she got away from this place, the better.

She wanted no more ties.

"Oh," A soft gasp escaped her as a black mare with a white star poked her head through the bars, looking at her with dark liquid, wide-spaced eyes. She was a dainty princess—sleek, gentle, inquisitive, with muscles rippling beneath a satiny coat.

Sarah stood as if frozen. Closing her eyes, she willed the vision to go away. "Oh, Simon," she whispered, digging her teeth into her trembling bottom lip and curling her fingers into fists. "I should have known. You always had a passion for our fleet desert creatures."

At the sound of her voice the mare's ears picked up and she whinnied softly, tossing her beautiful triangular head impatiently. Sarah hesitated, afraid to step closer, afraid to run her hand over the silky neck. Once she did, she would lose her heart—and what was she going to do with horses in New York? Three of them! They would cost a fortune to stable and it just wasn't practical.

Keeping her distance, she walked to the next stall.

The dapple gray stallion with the silver mane stood two hands taller than the little princess and was more powerfully built. Simon's horse, she was certain, the one he had planned to ride. A lump formed in her throat at the thought and tears pricked her eyes when she thought of what might have been. God, how she missed him, this man with a heart as big as Texas.

But it was the bay mare with the white blaze, watching her through the bars, too shy to poke her nose out and ask for attention, that tugged at her heartstrings the most. Blinking back tears, her hands stuffed into the pockets of her jeans, she inched closer, talking softly.

That was how Cord spotted her when he rounded the corner. He paused, the bucket of oats in his hands forgotten as he watched the struggle on her face. He could see her hands slide out of her pockets, still balled, wanting desperately to touch, but very much afraid. Her struggle went on for minutes as she coaxed and cajoled and moved forward again and again. The bay, just as cautious, moved closer from the other side until they almost stood nose to nose, taking in each other's scent, both of them so wary and cautious. "I'm not afraid of horses," Cord heard her say. "I just don't want to become attached to you. There have been so many losses in my life. Every one I loved is gone. Except Angel. And sometimes I'm so afraid that I'll lose her, too.''

Then the mare stretched and pushed her head through the bars right into Sarah's face. Cord watched her sway back, and held his breath. Sarah's arms came up as if to hug the strong silky neck. For a moment her arms hovered and her fists opened.

Then she spun around and ran past him, dashing blindly out into the night.

Sarah heard the door creak open. Abruptly she came awake, sitting up in bed. It took her only an instant to realize that she wasn't in the small physician's lounge, snatching an hour of sleep, or in her own bed in their rent-controlled apartment on Eighty-Seventh Street. She was in the guest bedroom on the Circle K ranch.

And Angel was sneaking out of the room.

''Hold it right there,'' she said, blinking at the sight that met her scratchy eyes. Angel had dressed herself. Sort of, anyway. The buttons of her red-and-white-striped sweater were open at the back. The suspenders of her denim overalls trailed down her back and the flap hung down the front. Her shoelaces were untied. But she had run a brush through her curls, her face was shiny and her eyes were bright.

Groaning, Sarah shook her head. Usually she was a light sleeper. She couldn't believe she hadn't heard Angel moving around. But she had lain awake for hours in the dark before exhaustion had finally claimed her. ''Where do you think you're going?''

Angel looked at her warily. ''To the kitchen. I'm hungry. I heard Cord talking to someone.''

Cord. At the mention of his name, last night leapt sharply into focus. She couldn't believe what she had done last night. Looking back, it seemed like a surrealistic dream. She couldn't possibly have done all those things. Feeling her face flush with embarrassment just remembering, she wanted, for a moment, to slide back beneath the covers. If she stayed here long enough, Cord might be gone by the time she went into the kitchen.

"Maybe you want to sleep some more," Angel said, taking two sneaking steps into the hall.

"No. Don't you dare take another step," Sarah said. Brushing her hair out of her face, she glanced at her watch. It was barely 7:20, but their internal clocks were still on New York time, which added an hour. They were both early risers and Angel had been very patient. "I'm sorry, sweetheart," she said contritely. "I overslept. Come back while I take a shower and get dressed. I'll show you the barn before breakfast."

Angel's eyes darted longingly down the hall. "Why can't Cord show me? He's already up."

Fear welled up, like it did every time she left her daughter at the kindergarten, every time her baby was out of her sight. Cord wasn't used to small children and had no idea that they could vanish in the blink of an eye. "Let me close those buttons and get you dressed properly."

At the sound of their voices, Sheba came out of the bathroom and paused at the bottom of the bed. Spotting the open door, she suddenly made a dash. "Watch out, Angel," Sarah warned, but her words came too late. Tired of being cooped up in the room, Sheba gained her freedom. Angel shouted, "Sheba, come back—" then chased after her.

Muttering a curse, Sarah leapt out of bed, snatched her jeans from the chair and jumped into them, her blue cotton nightshirt flapping around her thighs as she raced after Angel and Sheba, hoping to catch the cat before she ran into Cord.

In the middle of the foyer, Sheba stopped, the tip of her bushy tail flicking with excitement as she viewed her choices of adventure. Sarah groaned at the thought of having to chase after her up the stairs. "Don't you dare," she threatened. "I'll lock you into the crate until we leave."

Not overly concerned, Sheba glanced back, waiting until Angel had almost caught up with her. Then, flicking her tail in disdain, she lightly ran into the foyer and leapt on top of the armoir.

Cord was discussing towing Sarah's car with his friend and foreman, Chuck Mendoza, over a cup of coffee when he heard the commotion through the open kitchen door. Turning his head, he listened to Angel's shrieks and giggles, one corner of his mouth kicking up. It felt good to have the house come alive again. "The cat must have gotten out."

Chuck glanced at Cord curiously. He was a few inches shorter, with a wiry build. A shock of black shaggy hair fell onto his broad-lined forehead in front and brushed the collar of his black-and-white-checked Western shirt in back. His leathery face was lean and his sharp hazel eyes missed little, not the limp of a horse or a rotting fence post. Or the slight grin on Cord's face.

"Ain't you going to help catch it?" he asked, searching his friend's face. Big John had given him and his mother, Maisy, jobs when his father had run off with a younger woman eighteen years ago. Since Big John had all but moved to San Antonio, shortly after Cord's disappearance, to be near his wife and daughter, Chuck had been responsible for the day-to-day running of the big operation. He blamed his few gray hairs on the heavy responsibility and had been glad to hand it over to Cord upon his return.

"Not me. I'd as soon chase a tiger cub." Cord ran a finger down his neck. "You want to help, go right ahead."

Chuck tilted his head, listening to the little girl's giggles and a woman's chuckles. "Must have been quite an evening," he said. "Was boring as hell at Aunt Billie's house. Even Ma couldn't take all that gossiping after a while. The floods gave us a good excuse to leave early."

Cord grimaced. "I'm glad you did. I was thinking of asking Maisy to come back this morning anyway. By now, Hugh's mother has probably spread it all over town that the Doc spent the night in my bed."

Chuck's eyes sharpened speculatively. Cord might have played the field and behaved like a young healthy tomcat at times but his moral fiber was as strong as his daddy's. No matter what the temptation, he wouldn't have taken advantage of a stranded guest in his home. Still, there was something. Raising his mug, he asked casually, just to get a rise out of him, "Did she?"

Angry denial flared up at the question, a desire to protect and to shield. Cord caught himself just in time before he could make a fool of himself. "You haven't met the doc yet. She's all prim and proper." After the way she'd run from the barn last night, it was a safe bet that she'd appear in the kitchen with her hair twisted into a bun and her glasses firmly in place. "She's some kind of trauma specialist in a big-city emergency room. A saint, more interested in good works than men."

At that moment the saint threatened, "I'll wring your neck if you don't come down from there this minute."

"Some saint," Chuck remarked dryly, his eyes widening when a big fluffy orange striped cat charged into the kitchen. Spotting the two men, the animal stopped abruptly in the middle of the floor. Recognizing Cord, she flattened her ears and hissed.

Chuck raked a hand through his straight black hair, raising his bushy brows as he looked from the spitting cat to Cord. "Must have lost your touch with females. I don't think she's too fond of you."

Cord chuckled, his eyes fixed expectantly on the half-open door, wondering what would happen next. "I dropped her in the mud last night," he explained just as the door burst open and Sarah charged through it. Barefoot, black mane flying wildly around her shoulders, she was wearing nothing but jeans and a collarless cotton knit shirt. All four buttons at the neck were open, revealing her slender long throat and just enough smooth creamy skin to make every muscle in his big body tense with arousal. Sarah lunged for Sheba, skillfully evading the half-sheathed claws, grabbing her by the scruff of her neck before she could leap on top of the refrigerator. Holding her in the crook of one arm, she ran her hand over the ruffled fur, soothing her with smooth strokes and the gentle sound of her voice.

Suddenly she became aware of the stares of the two men at the table. And her state of undress.

Embarrassment sent a flush up her neck. Pride, however, made her raise her eyes and say with commendable calm, "Good morning." Avoiding Cord's charismatic glance, she looked at the dark-haired man with a rueful shrug. "Hi, I'm Sarah Durand. This pest here is Sheba."

Glancing over her shoulder, she watched her daughter storm into the room, laces and suspenders flapping, her face flushed and her eyes sparkling from the chase. "And this imp is Angel."

At Chuck's chuckle, Cord glanced at his friend, his eyes narrowing at the appreciative gleam with which he was eyeing Sarah. Chuck couldn't seem to get his eyes unglued from her long enough to say hello, and Sarah didn't seem to mind him staring at her. Slowly he placed the mug on the table and got to his feet, deliberately placing his big body between them as he reached for Angel.

"Hi, imp," he said, lifting her high in his arms until she wiggled, kicked and squealed. Lowering her, he glanced at Sarah, raking her with hard, cold eyes. He knew he was behaving like a possessive Neanderthal. Caveman tactics weren't his style, but he seemed unable to stop from drawling, "We'll take Angel with us to the barn while you take care of the cat and get changed."

Sarah scowled at him, anger mingling with sudden anxiety. "Angel isn't dressed properly yet," she said. Ignoring her daughter's protests, she willed Cord to put Angel back on her feet.

Cord studied her expression for long seconds, reading something like fear. Fear of him? he wondered, startled. That was ridiculous. He had given his word that he was going to keep his distance. Or was it something much more fundamental, like the fear that had made her run from the barn last night, run from temptation as if the devil had been chasing her? As if she were afraid to let herself care too much?

Because all the people she'd loved had died.

And she was terrified that the only person she still had, would be taken from her, too.

His eyes softened, and his voice was a little rough when he said, "Don't worry about Angel. Nothing will happen to her while I'm around."

Sarah looked at her daughter, securely wrapped in his strong arms, her eyes shining with eagerness. "Oh, please, Mommy, I won't run off. I promise."

Then she looked back at Cord, the knight who had placed his life on the line for years to make this a safer world, the bitter lonely man who thought he didn't deserve to be called a knight because he thought he had failed somehow. It was her own fear, not lack of trust in him, that made her hesitate, but she doubted he would believe her and she didn't want to add to his wounds. "Don't even blink," she warned with a slight catch in her voice. "Angel is like a *djinn*—a sprite," she added, when she saw Cord's puzzled look. "With her it's definitely a matter of now you see her, now you don't."

Before she could change her mind, she left, frowning over the fact that for the first time in sixteen years she had lapsed into Persian.

At the age of twelve she had wanted nothing to do with the people who had murdered her family and had angrily rejected her father's heritage. For years she had feared that she would be sent back to Iran. With Simon and Lisa's help, she had eventually come to terms with her loss, and the irrational fear of being sent back had vanished in time. These days she no longer denied her roots, but she didn't draw attention to them, either.

Then why had she slipped into Persian after all these years, especially in a place where foreigners were regarded with suspicion? she wondered uneasily.

Closing the door to her room, she released Sheba and stood in the pool of sunlight coming through the window. She could feel herself changing. Emotions she had long suppressed were tearing at the wall she had built around her heart. She was shedding the cocoon. Things were rapidly sliding out of her control. She was becoming involved once again.

Suddenly she could almost hear the Fates laughing.

A shiver ran through her at the thought.

Fate. She had grown up surrounded by the mysticism of the East and a part of her, the part she tried to deny and hide from, *did* believe in karma and kismet. The American in her and the logical rational physician wanted to believe that she could control her life, that people's actions determined their futures. But actions were triggered by emotions, and emotions were not so easily controlled. And how did one explain why one person could be blessed with repeated good fortune while another was continually haunted by accidents?

With a sigh she went into the bathroom and turned on the cold shower.

When Sarah returned to the kitchen half an hour later, dressed in jeans and a gray sweatshirt, her hair pinned loosely at the back with a barrette, she had herself back under control. Cleaning the bathroom and packing their few belongings had calmed her. She had also informed her insurance agent of the accident and he had promised to take care of the problem.

She found a slender elderly woman with steel gray hair flipping pancakes on a griddle. Spotting Sarah, the woman wiped her hand on the white apron covering her blue flowered dress, then held it out to her. "You must be Doc Simon's daughter. I'm Maisy, the housekeeper. You met my son Chuck earlier."

With a rueful grimace, Sarah shook the work-roughened hand warmly. "Briefly. I was too busy trying to catch our cat before she could disappear outside. I'm Sarah." She glanced at the mudroom door, wondering where Angel was. "Did you see my daughter?"

Maisy nodded. "The men took her with them to the barns. Don't you worry about her none. With Chuck and Cord both watching her, she won't get into no trouble."

"I don't know about that. Three months ago she and another five-year-old climbed over the eight-foot chain-link fence at their school during playtime to buy candy at the corner store."

Maisy's parchment white skin creased into myriad fine lines when she grinned. "She's a real charmer. I couldn't believe my eyes when I came in here and found Cord trying to fix her suspenders as if he'd dressed little ones all his life. Did my heart good to see him smile and joke around like he used to." Blinking, she opened the oven door and took out a big platter already heaped with pancakes, stacking the fresh ones on top. "It's been a bad year."

Sarah nodded, turning toward the mudroom. "I just need to rinse out my coat. I'll give you a hand in a minute."

Maisy returned the platter to the oven. "I already hung your coat outside. There's orange juice in the fridge and I made a fresh pot of coffee. Just sit and relax. You look like you haven't been sleeping too well."

Sarah glanced at the table set for five. "I'm not good at watching people work," she said quietly. She took butter and orange juice from the refrigerator, then poured a glass of milk for Angel.

Placing thick slices of ham on the griddle, Maisy slanted her an understanding look. "Cord says you're a vegetarian like Miz Renee. She can't sit idle, neither. Always doing something. Since she left, this place has been like a tomb, like the soul just went out of it. The whole family, old Mrs. Knight and Cord's aunt and uncle and their families, used to come down most every weekend. Now they all meet at her house in San Antonio."

Sarah knew she should not encourage Maisy to gossip, but she was curious about Cord's parents. They were so much in love with each other that it was painful to watch them hide it. Renee had said that they were too different to live together, that she was too bohemian in her tastes and that the conventional small town had stifled her creativity, but Sarah suspected that there was more to it. "I stayed at Renee's house last November. She's a lovely person."

"That she is. It was a real shame, her leaving," Maisy grumbled, taking out a big frying pan and slapping it down on the burner. "Big John could have stopped her from leaving, but he's too damn proud, too stubborn to bend. And Cord's just the same, burying himself on the ranch, just like his daddy did after Miz Renee left. Neither one is much for wearing their hearts on their sleeves. Last time Miz Renee and Vicky came down here, Cord sent them packing. Said he wanted some time to himself. Well, maybe now that you and your daughter are here, he'll get out more."

Sarah sent Maisy a troubled look, watching her break eggs into the pan. "I won't be staying here. The moment I have my car back I'll move into Simon's old apartment."

"You will? Whatever for?" Maisy frowned at Sarah. "Cord didn't say nothing about you leaving. And I know Big John wouldn't like it if you did. I don't think it's a good idea, you living downtown, not with that office being boarded up and Devlin causing all this trouble."

Sarah's eyes narrowed with apprehension. "Just what kind of trouble? My father never mentioned any Devlin, but ever since my arrival, his name seems to keep cropping up at every turn."

"Doc Simon had a few run-ins with Devlin. But I guess he didn't want to worry you." Jamming her hands on her hips, Maisy turned around, her eyes flashing with anger. "The Devlins are a bad lot, all of them. Old Ed used to buy cheap labor from the *coyotes*. Bankrupted quite a few of the smaller ranchers and farmers. They just couldn't compete. Then Cord put a stop to it and sent Ed to prison about five years back. He died a few weeks later. In a knife fight, they said. Hugh's been trying to get even ever since."

Maisy picked up the spatula, waving it like a weapon before turning back to the stove. "With Big John spending so much time with Miz Renee and Vicky in San Antonio this last year, Chuck's had his hands full. Those bulls broke down fences faster'n he could put them back up. Since Cord's return, Devlin's been more careful, but he's been spreading all kinds of stories about town, like how Big John bought off Mexican officials to get the charges against Cord dismissed. It ain't true, of course, but there's plenty of folks that believe it. That boy can't go into town now without someone sneering at him. And after everything he's done for them, too. It makes me so mad—"

She broke off abruptly as the outside door into the mudroom opened and Angel called out excitedly, "Mommy, where are you? I held the kittens. And Cord let me sit on one of Grandpa's horses." Seconds later Chuck strolled into the kitchen, followed by a windblown, bright-eyed Angel with her soft small hand clasped securely in Cord's big callused one. Spotting Sarah, she ran toward her, in her excitement almost tripping over the words as she continued, "The kittens are so small and they all have blue eyes. Cord said I could have one, but I have to ask you first."

Sarah hugged Angel, smiling down at her, trying to hide the niggling resentment flaring up within her. She didn't want another cat and she didn't like him planting the idea in Angel's head. She guessed she should be grateful that Angel wasn't pleading about taking the horses with them to New York. Yet. "We'll talk about it later," she said gently. "Breakfast is almost ready. Go wash your hands and run a brush through your hair."

Noticing the agitation in both women, Cord's watchful glance slid from Maisy to the Doc, then back to his housekeeper. The trouble with longtime employees was that after a while they became family. These days, Maisy was behaving like a surrogate mother, and from the way she was waving that spatula, he could tell that she had been pouring all her grievances over the trouble Devlin was causing into the Doc's sympathetic ears. "Are you attacking the doc? What did she do?" he asked humorously.

"Doc? What doc?" Maisy flipped the eggs, a confused look crossing her face. Then she glanced at Sarah and smiled. "Oh, he means you. You don't look like no doctor I've ever met." Turning her attention back to Cord, she looked at him with wise old eyes. "I think she's too pretty and too young to be called only Doc. When you call her that, I think of her father. Anyway, I was just warning *Sarah* about Devlin. You didn't tell me that she was planning to move into town."

Cord didn't move, his mouth twisting into a humorless smile. He should have expected it, should have been prepared for it. She had told him last night that she didn't want any trouble while she was here. An association with him would stir up trouble. The old biddies in town would make her life miserable if she stayed here.

Hell, he should be glad that she was leaving. Both she and her daughter had slipped beneath his defenses. He'd even looked forward to spending the day with them. So it was just as well that they were leaving.

But, damn it, it still felt like a betrayal, as if she were moving into the enemy camp. He shrugged. "I guess I forgot."

Sarah said nothing, just stood there for a long moment. She wanted to explain that it had always been her intention to move into town, that Maisy's words had nothing to do with it.

Distressed, she looked at Cord and found him watching her with cold distant eyes, his face expressionless. "We'll tow your car out right after breakfast." Opening a narrow kitchen drawer, he withdrew a bunch of keys and handed them to her. "My father had the locks and the broken windows replaced and boarded up. Last time I checked, everything seemed in order. You have electricity and water, and there's enough oil in the tank to last you a few weeks."

"Thank you, I appreciate it," she said quietly, her fingers closing around the keys. She pushed her glasses up her nose, trying to hide the guilt washing through her. She felt as if she *were* deserting him.

Damn him for making her feel like a coward.

Maisy had been listening to the words, but had been too busy putting eggs on a platter to see the silent messages passing between them. Handing the platter to her son, she turned to Sarah, a troubled look in her eyes. "Well, I don't like it none that you're going to live on Main Street with the little one. It's deserted after the stores close down."

Sarah smiled slightly. "You're talking to a New Yorker, remember? Simon always used to describe this town as a place where people can leave their back doors open and the keys in the cars."

But Maisy was still uneasy. "Things ain't what they used to be. There's lots of strangers in town these days. And Lorna Devlin, Hugh's mother, is a vicious woman, so you watch out for her. A few months ago, she caused your father some grief."

Cord tensed and asked sharply. "What kind of grief?"

Maisy shrugged. "Doc Simon treated a few illegals without notifying the sheriff. Lorna had the biddies in town protesting in his waiting room. The doc finally called the sheriff, who dragged her off to the station." She looked back at Sarah. "If she causes you any trouble, you come right back to the ranch."

Chapter 5

"Why didn't you tell me about this business with Lorna before?" Cord asked Chuck half an hour later, as he turned into the track. It sometimes shook him just how much he had missed during his absence.

He had lost a whole year of his life and the worst part was that he had so damn little to show for it. There was no sense of accomplishment, no sense of pride for a job well done and, no matter how much he didn't want to dwell on it, it ate at him.

"Didn't think you were interested." Chuck rolled down the window, checking the fence line as they drove past.

With a shrug Cord acknowledged the jab. "Lorna Devlin never was one of my favorite people and I couldn't care less what she's been up to. Simon, however, was."

Chuck slouched deeper into his seat. "Is that why you all but tossed his daughter and granddaughter out?"

Cord's hands tightened on the wheel. He already felt like a heel and he didn't need Chuck's censure. Sarah had hardly eaten anything at breakfast and the smiles Maisy and Chuck had coaxed from her hadn't reached her eyes. Even Angel had sensed something was wrong and had looked slightly subdued. Slanting Chuck a warning look, he growled, "It wasn't my decision. She couldn't get out fast enough after Maisy told her about the gossip."

"Is that what you think? I thought you knew women better than that." Chuck had his own ideas about the scene in the kitchen. He didn't think Sarah had been frightened away by anything his ma had said. But whatever her reasons for leaving, Cord didn't like it and it was forcing him to take interest in town affairs, something he himself had tried and failed to get his friend and employer to do. Tipping his hat lower against the fresh breeze, he decided to rub it in a little more. "You were kind of hard on her, weren't you? Seems like we're always hardest on the people we like best."

Cord slanted his friend a warning look. The tension Chuck had noticed between them was purely physical. "Keep out of it!"

Chuck grinned. "Whatever you say, boss. D'you think Sarah could be tempted to move down here and take over her daddy's practice? We need a new doctor. Big John hasn't had much luck finding one."

Cord's mouth compressed in exasperation. "She's a specialist. Not much work around here for a trauma surgeon," he growled, easing the truck over the ruts. The ground was still muddy, but the water level in the ditches was going down. Then he noticed a fresh set of tire tracks. Eyes narrowed against the glare of the morning sun, his glance swept past the cacti growing along Devlin's fences, but he spotted nothing unusual.

Chuck sent Cord a sly knowing glance. "Oh, I don't know. We have our share of accidents around here. Besides, little Angel sure enjoys running around free, and Sarah would do anything to make that little one happy. She agreed to take the kitten, didn't she? I'll bet if Angel didn't want to leave here, she'd consider staying."

Cord shrugged. For a while maybe. His mother had stuck it out, too, until Vicky had finished college. In fact, the similarities between his mother and Sarah were startling at times. "I doubt it. One run-in with Lorna will change Sarah's mind real fast," he said cynically. "Now, are you going to tell me about the incident or not?"

Chuck frowned. "There isn't much to tell. Doc Simon told Lorna bluntly that he was a physician, not a politician, and that he didn't care if a patient didn't have an *amica,* a green card. Lorna's in charge of the fund-raising for the new church and she lords it over the other women in the group. She made them all gather in Doc's office to protest." His mouth curled. "So much for Christian charity! But the woman always was a hypocrite. Anyway, soon the whole town was gathered outside, arguing." A grin appeared. "Little Mary Lou Coombs threatened to frizz Lorna's hair but good the next time she came to her beauty shop if she didn't leave the doc alone."

Funny though Chuck's description of Mary Lou's reaction was, Cord wasn't amused. He wished he hadn't been so hasty handing over the keys. If he had known about this business with Lorna, he would have hung on to them until he had made certain that it was safe for Sarah and Angel to move into town. The mere thought of anyone threatening both of them made him furious. "Where the hell was that new sheriff of ours while all this was going on?"

"Oh, he was there, and the deputies, too. Holt was a little miffed because Doc Simon refused to press charges. Dan Holt's been trying to get someone to file a complaint against Devlin for months, but people are too scared of Devlin's boys. Not the doc, though. He wasn't much scared of anything. He just didn't want Lorna to spend a night in jail. Said she'd be sure to throw a fit and he didn't want to be called out at midnight to attend to her."

"How long before the fire did this happen?" Cord asked grimly.

"About two months." Chuck pushed his hat back and slanted Cord a narrow-eyed glance. "I don't believe Devlin set the fire, if that's what you're thinking. He's a bully, but he's no killer."

Cord's thoughts flew back to Harper and how he'd underestimated the man. "Devlin has some tough boys working for him these days, the type that don't like to draw attention to themselves." He briefly described his stop at the Coyote Lounge. "Did you know that Rusty sold the place to him?"

Chuck shook his head, suddenly becoming apprehensive, too. "Still, we couldn't find anything that suggested arson. Big John, the sheriff and I were all there when the fire inspector and the insurance man went over the site. And we made damn sure that nothing was overlooked. The only thing out of place was that the lid to the fuse box was missing, but then, the house was old and that lid could have come off some time ago." He paused. "Why don't you talk to the sheriff?"

"I think I will. Simon wasn't a careless man," Cord said tautly, slowing down as the Toyota came into view. In fact, he seemed to recall Simon talking about having the whole place rewired before he moved in— His thought broke off abruptly when he noticed the truck with flashers on the roof parked behind the Toyota and the khaki-clad figure leaning against it. He swore softly. "I guess that's Dan Holt."

"In person." Frowning, Chuck sat up, eyes narrowed on the officer. "I wonder what he's doing here?"

"Maybe making sure I didn't molest another woman." Cord's mouth compressed into a grim, bitter line. Pulling up close to Sarah's fender, he gave the man a closer look. The sheriff was about his own height, around forty, with a lean, tough build. He was an ex-marine drill sergeant who had come back to town after twenty years of service. Gos-

sip had it that he ran his department like a boot camp. Cord
took in the short haircut, the hard, lined, but honest face,
the military bearing, the sharply creased pants and the
brightly polished badge and brass buckle.

A little rigid, but nobody's fool, and his own man, he
thought. With a grimace he opened the door. He was prepared to like the man, but judging by the sheriff's hard,
narrow-eyed stare, he doubted Holt would be as open-
minded. With a mental shrug he walked up to him, but
didn't extend his hand. "Hi, Sheriff, I'm Cord Knight."

Sharp brown eyes clashed with remote smoky ones as they
took each other's measure. "Heard you were back. The
town's been buzzing for weeks," Dan Holt said. His glance
slid off Cord as if reserving judgment, his face easing into a
grin as Chuck walked up. "Haven't seen you in a while,
Chuck. Missed you at the Tuesday night poker game."

Chuck stopped next to Cord and gave the sheriff a level
stare. "I don't much like the company these days. We stick
together on the Circle K. If one of us isn't welcome, we all
tend to take it personal. Being a marine, you ought to understand that."

The sheriff's eyes narrowed at the veiled warning. His
glance swerved to the Toyota, then back to Cord, his mouth
curling. "Rescuing women seems to be your specialty,
Knight. I heard that this time it was Doc Simon's daughter.
I'd like to talk to her, if you don't mind."

Chuck took an angry step forward, growling, "Just what
were you trying to imply with that crack?"

Cord's hand clamped down on Chuck's arm. "I'll handle this. The sheriff's only doing his job. You get the chain
from the truck." He waited until Chuck had walked to the
back of the pickup before facing Dan Holt, his eyes hard
and his jaw set. "You're welcome to follow us back to the
ranch," he said smoothly. "Doc Durand needs an accident
report to file a claim with her insurance company."

A gleam came into the brown eyes. "D'you think she'd file charges against Devlin?"

Cord pushed back the open flaps of his leather jacket, sliding his hands into his pockets. "Not a chance," he drawled. "Doc Durand is a sensible woman. She doesn't want trouble any more than I do."

Dan Holt's glance strayed to the two shotguns mounted on a rack against the rear window of Cord's cab and his lip curled. "Is that why you're armed?"

Cord shot him a bland look. "A precaution. I'm not into bull wrestling."

Dan Holt wasn't deceived. "Don't mess with me," he warned softly. "I know all about you, Knight. I've read your file. You like to stir up trouble, but run like hell when the going gets rough."

Cord's hands slowly curled into fists, but his expression remained bland, refusing to give the Sheriff the explanation he was pressing for. Partly it was pride that kept him silent. He was through defending his actions and having his explanations tossed back into his face, but there was also that lingering sense of self-doubt. "The trouble with you military boys is that you're not encouraged to think for yourselves," he taunted.

There was a slight softening in Dan Holt's hard voice. "The court dropped all charges against you and that's good enough for me. But I have a problem with you blowing up your boat and jumping bail. In the military we call that desertion."

Cord felt some of his tension ease. Unlike most folks around here, the sheriff was keeping an open mind and was giving him a chance to present his side of the events. The novel experience made Cord unbend slightly. "Personally, I don't see any honor in going to jail for a crime I didn't commit and having my throat slashed in my cell." A mocking grin suddenly twisted his mouth. "Hell, even being a live coward beats being fish fodder any day. At least I lived to

tell the tale." Even if no one was willing to listen to him, he
added silently, bitterness surging through him.

Grudging respect flickered in Dan Holt's eyes. "Maybe
some time, when you feel like talking, I'd like to hear about
it." His glance went back to the shotguns. "I don't like those
damn bulls any more than you do. Unfortunately, I can't do
anything unless someone is willing to press charges. But no
one is going to shoot cattle and start a range war in my
town."

"*Your* town, Sheriff? Hell, we Knights founded it and we
still own a good part of it."

Dan Holt folded his arms across his broad chest. "Maybe
so, but your daddy offered me the job six months ago when
old Skaggs retired because he didn't like what was going on
in town. So, whether you like it or not, I'm the law around
here. And if you take it into your own hands, I'll have you
thrown in jail so fast, you won't have a chance to skip the
country. And this time there won't be any bail."

"Then I suggest you do something about those bulls before someone gets hurt," Cord growled.

"Hey, squirt, wanna take a ride on the little princess
here," Jimmy T. shouted across the yard as he led the black
Arabian out of the barn.

Angel was sitting on the top rail of the fence encircling the
pasture, watching the activity in the yard. Leaning against
the rail next to her, Sarah was keeping a wary eye on her
daughter and the road at the same time. It had been months
since she'd had an idle moment to spare and she was enjoy-
ing the sun and the mild breeze. At the ranch hand's words
she looked up sharply, apprehensive as she recognized the
mare. She had been freshly groomed, Sarah noticed with a
tug of guilt. In the bright morning sun, her coat gleamed like
blue-black satin. Whether she wanted the horses or not, they
were her responsibility and she should have taken care of

them this morning. "Angel doesn't know how to ride," she explained.

Jimmy T. was a short squat man with a weather-beaten face, graying brown hair and the bowlegged rolling gait of a man who had spent a lifetime in the saddle. At Sarah's words he pushed back his straw Stetson and grinned, revealing two gaps between his front teeth. "Then it's past time she learned," he said laconically.

"I want to learn." Eagerly, Angel climbed down from the fence, hopping up and down in front of Sarah. "Oh, please, Mommy, pretty please," she begged.

"The boss usually rides them other two. Won't let anyone else near 'em. But this filly here is too little to carry his weight and I've been takin' care of her. She's a real sweetheart and more gentle than one of them ponies most people buy for their kids. I figure your daddy bought her with the little lady in mind."

As if realizing that they were talking about her, the mare tossed her head and sidestepped daintily.

"See, she wants me to pet her," Angel cried, grabbing Sarah's hand and drawing her across the muddy yard.

"It won't take but a minute to saddle her up," Jimmy T. said, a crafty look in his eyes.

Sarah stopped a few feet away from him, keeping a firm hold on Angel's hand. But her emotions were not so easily controlled. Sarah itched to run her hand over the mare's neck. "Did the boss put you up to this?" she asked suspiciously. She had agreed to take one of the kittens the moment they were weaned if Sheba would accept it, but the horses were a different matter.

Jimmy T's brown eyes widened with childlike innocence. "Boss said nothing about the little lady. All he told me was that if you wanted to ride, not to let you take out the bay. She's too skittish, that one."

Resentment flared up in Sarah. These were *her* horses and if she wanted to ride the bay, she would, no matter what the "boss" said. Then she suddenly became very still. Until now she had thought of them as Simon's horses, but they *were* hers, a legacy from Simon.

"Mommy, please," Angel pleaded again, straining against her hold.

Sarah could feel herself weaken. With a sigh she stepped closer and held out a flat hand, instructing Angel to do the same. Angel giggled as the mare daintily absorbed her scent and blew warm air into her palm. With another sigh Sarah gave in to temptation. "If you show me where the tack is, I'll saddle her."

With a beatific grin Jimmy T. led the mare to the corral, securing the reins around the top bar. "I'll do it or the boss'll have my hide. Our Western saddles are too heavy for you to carry."

Sarah's mouth compressed in exasperation. "What else did the boss say," she asked dryly.

"Well, nothing much. Just that you knew your way around horses, but that it's been awhile since you sat one." He scratched the back of his neck, pushing his hat deeper into his face. "It'll be a lot safer for the little one if you take her up in front of you the first few times."

Sarah bit her lip, temptation and dread warring within. "You know what I think, Jimmy T?" she asked softly. "I think you're a con artist."

"Me, Doc?" he asked, his wide mouth twitching. Walking away, he tossed over his shoulder, "You're accusing the wrong man. Blame the boss. I reckon his shoulders are broader than mine."

The moment she swung into the saddle a few minutes later, and took the reins from Jimmy T.'s hands, Sarah knew she should have resisted temptation. Just walking the mare around the corral stirred a longing inside her to ride over open fields, to loosen the reins and feel the wind tug at her hair. She wondered where she could stable the horses in New York. There were several places within easy reach on Long

Island and in Westchester County. Stabling them would be no problem, but finding the time to ride them would be. She was mad, stark raving mad, she thought, nudging the mare into a trot. But, oh, it was a glorious madness.

"Mommy, stop, I want to ride with you."

Reluctantly, Sarah pulled in the reins and rode over to Angel, who was sitting on the top rail with Jimmy T. holding on to her. "You'll do," he said approvingly, lifting Angel in front of her. "I'll just stick around, in case the angel gets scared."

Sarah settled Angel securely before her. "Nothing much frightens Angel," she said, gathering the reins. "I'm the one who's scared." She was beginning to care about too many things, and she feared that one day she would wake up and everything would be snatched from her again.

With wise old eyes, Jimmy T. watched her ride the mare along the fence. "You're scarred, Doc, not scared, and there's a difference," he muttered to himself. "But there's nothing like riding to take your mind off things."

When Cord drove the mud-splattered Toyota into the yard five minutes later he couldn't believe his eyes. He had talked to Jimmy T. this morning. But after the scene in the kitchen, he hadn't dared hope that the doc would go anywhere near the horses. Yet here she was, walking the mare around the corral with Angel securely held in front of her. Shaking his head, he climbed out of the car. He didn't think he'd ever understand her.

Sarah watched Cord get out of the car, frowning when she spotted the police truck parking behind him. Chuck followed next. When she reached Jimmy T. again, she handed him the reins, lifting a protesting Angel down.

With a thank you, she slipped between the rails, drawing Angel with her, her glance uneasily moving from Cord's expressionless face to the sheriff's craggy one. "Is something wrong?"

Cord shook his head. "The sheriff wants a word with you." He smiled at Angel, listening to her excited chatter, commenting on her riding skills. Ruffling her curls, he said, "Why don't you and Chuck see if you can't persuade Maisy to give you some ice cream. You must be hungry after that long ride."

"Goody," Angel cried, and made a dash for the door. Chuck followed her at a slower pace.

Sarah wondered what it was Cord didn't want Angel to hear. Introducing herself, she said, "Since the car seems all right, I assume something happened at my father's office again."

Dan Holt's dark brows drew into a puzzled straight line. "Last time I checked the locks, everything was fine. I dropped by to make sure you and your daughter are all right."

Understanding dawned. Sarah felt a fierce stab of anger rush through her and she took an instinctive step toward Cord. "Maisy warned me about the gossip circulating in town," she said, looking at the sheriff accusingly. "But I didn't expect you to believe it. If you want to know if my daughter and I were harmed in any way, the answer is no," she stated bluntly.

Her bluntness startled the sheriff and the fierce direct look in her eyes took him aback. "I'm just doing my job, Dr. Durand."

"Spreading gossip is your job?" Sarah asked with raised brows. "If you had been doing your *job,* Sheriff, I wouldn't have gotten stuck in the first place. You should have posted one of your men at the flooded bridge. Or put up detour signs. Do you realize that I had to stop at the Coyote Lounge to ask for directions? That's another place that requires your attention."

Dan Holt shot Cord a suspicious glance. "Did you put her up to this?"

"Nope." Cord leaned against the sheriff's truck, stunned by Sarah's unexpected and fierce defense. Damned if he could figure her out, he thought, a small crooked grin lifting the corner of his mouth. "Maybe I should have warned you that the doc is a trauma surgeon at a Manhattan hospital. Patching up casualties is her specialty."

"Is that right?" A speculative look flashed across Dan Holt's face. "Takes guts to work in a place like that."

Sarah glared from one man to the other. "I'm glad you find this amusing. Let me tell you, Sheriff, I didn't find it very funny last night."

The sheriff's smile faded abruptly. "I can believe it," he apologized slowly. "Especially having a bull take a swipe at your car. I'll post a deputy at the bridge tonight, but I need your help to do something about the bulls."

The sheriff's words wiped the grin off Cord's face. "You're not using her to get at Devlin," he said flatly.

"I imagine Dr. Durand is perfectly capable of making up her own mind."

Sarah glanced from one man to the other. "There's no point pressing charges against Devlin, when I'm only here for a few days. I've already called my insurance company and they're handling everything. All I require is an accident report."

A slow grin spread over the sheriff's face. "If I can't get you to file charges, siccing an insurance company on Devlin is the next best thing." He opened his truck, reached for his pad and started to take down information.

Watching them, Cord swore softly beneath his breath. Last night, he hadn't worried too much about Sarah's decision, but last night he'd merely been speculating about Simon's death. After everything he had learned today, however, he didn't dare dismiss the suspicion that the fire had been set deliberately and that, somewhere, Devlin was involved. He wondered if Holt would still be so damned pleased with himself when he found out that Sarah didn't plan to remain at the ranch where Devlin couldn't get to her. He'd started to mention her move into town, when the door to the mudroom opened and Chuck called, "Cord, your mother is on the phone."

Impatiently, Cord glanced over his shoulder. "Tell her I'll call her back later."

"Chuck, wait a moment." Sarah looked at Cord pleadingly, wondering how many times he had used that same excuse and not called his mother back. She was a mother herself and knew how painful it must be for Renee. "The sheriff and I can deal with the report."

Her eyes were as dark as midnight, as uncertain as a child's and he couldn't resist her any more than he could resist her daughter, not after the way she had defended him a few minutes before. With a sigh of resignation, he turned to leave. He could always drop by the sheriff's office later.

When Cord walked out on the front porch to call Sarah to the phone fifteen minutes later, the yard was deserted. Uneasy, he strode around the back, where he found Maisy rinsing off two brown suitcases with a garden hose. A few feet away Angel was tossing pebbles into the puddles. "Where's the doc?" he asked, glancing at the garage at the back of the yard. The doors were closed and there was no sign of the Toyota. "My mother wants to talk to her."

Maisy shut off the hose and looked at him pointedly. "I doubt it," she said dryly. "Miz Renee is not into talking to ghosts."

Cord's mouth compressed impatiently. "Look, Maisy—"

"No, you listen to me," Maisy said fiercely. "You're not going to chase her away like you did everyone else."

Cord's eyes narrowed angrily, wondering what it was about Sarah that brought out such strong protective instincts in everyone. His mother had yelled at him, for the first time since his return. Big John had told him to make certain that she stayed at the ranch. And now Maisy was telling him off. Hell, he didn't want Sarah to leave any more than they did, but that woman had a mind of her own and short of tying her up, there wasn't a thing he could do if she wanted to leave.

Besides, she didn't need nearly as much protection as everyone thought. "Then, maybe, you shouldn't have scared her off by telling her about the gossip in town," he growled.

Maisy gripped the hose tightly, waving it back and forth. "I did no such thing! I tried to persuade her into staying! But she told me right off the bat that she was moving into town this morning. She doesn't scare easy. Not like some folks I know."

Cord's eyes glinted dangerously. "Are you accusing me of being too chicken to go into town because of gossip?"

Maisy's glance softened, but she had a point to prove and wasn't about to back down. "You've got plenty of guts. But you're just like any other man when it comes to gossip. Scares all of you."

"Is that so?" He shook his head incredulously. "Now, my mother is waiting, so maybe you'll tell me where Doc Sarah is."

A small grin tugged at Maisy's mouth. "She went to look at the office and clean her car at the car wash."

All amusement fled from Cord's face. Damn, he hadn't wanted her to walk into the place on her own. "How long ago did she leave?" he asked, striding toward his truck.

"About five minutes ago," Maisy called after him, watching the pickup charge out of the yard with a small satisfied grin. Then she held out her hand to Angel. "Come on, sweetheart. Let's have a nice chat with Miz Renee. She'll be glad to hear that things are changing around here."

Chapter 6

Cord caught up with Sarah at the edge of town. She drove slowly, looking at the houses and the high school as she passed. She must have noticed his truck, but not once did she give any indication that she realized she was being followed.

Sarah *had* noticed Cord. She had been dreading this trip for months and with every mile the tension inside her grew. But with Cord following her, she didn't feel quite so alone.

The small town was just like Simon had described it. Sleepy, quiet, peaceful. Houses stood on large parcels of land, surrounded by bushes and trees. The front lawns were still waterlogged, with dead branches littering the grass and driveways, but the windows were sparkling and the roofs and the pavements looked freshly scrubbed. Sarah noticed no fences. Bikes and tricycles stood beneath carports, unchained.

The business district of Knight's Corner was three blocks long, with Josie's Café at one end and the old Methodist church where Simon had been baptized at the other. Most of the two-story frame houses had been built around the turn of the century, she'd been told. The curbs were high, built during the days of horse-drawn wagons and buggies, making it possible for ladies to climb straight into a carriage without stepping into the street, but more importantly, so that cargo could easily be transferred from store to buckboard wagon. The stores were closed on Sundays and the street was deserted, except at the upper end near the church.

Simon's office was a white two-story corner house at the end of the first block. Sarah spotted it immediately because of the wooden boards covering the tall narrow windows.

As she pulled up at the curb, Cord drove past her into the alley behind the building. With a glance at the clean shiny cars parked near the church, Sarah started to shift into Reverse to follow him. She didn't like to attract attention to herself at the best of times and today she didn't feel up to friendly chats and condolence calls, so it would be much more sensible to park her muddy car in the rear.

Then her hand stilled. Cord wasn't parking in the rear for any of those reasons. He had driven into the back so his truck wouldn't be spotted. Did he think she didn't want to be seen with him?

Sarah's lips compressed and she shoved the gear into Park. Turning the engine off, she slid from the car and slammed the door. She jammed the keys into her pocket and strode to the back.

Cord was checking the boards covering the windows when she rounded the corner. Glancing over his shoulder, he noticed the militant spark in her eyes. His mouth twisted. He'd known that she wouldn't be pleased to have him as an escort, and if she wanted him to leave, he would.

After he'd made certain that the place was safe.

Testing the doorknob, he drawled, "Toss me the keys."

Sarah watched his face, saw the way his jaw hardened, saw the anger in his smoky dark eyes, but also noticed the

vulnerability that lay beneath it, and her heart ached for
him. She stopped a few feet away from him, her fingers
curling around the keys in her pocket. "I want to go in
through the front door," she said quietly. For a moment she
hesitated, reluctant to expose her own weakness. But his
need to be needed was greater than her fears. "I don't want
to go in alone. Will you come with me?"

Cord slowly turned around and leaned against the door.
She looked small, tired and fragile not strong enough to
fight off all the feelings coming to Knight's Corner had
churned up in her. His eyes narrowed. "Haven't you med-
dled enough for one day?" he drawled softly.

"I don't meddle," Sarah denied firmly. "I never involve
myself in other people's business."

A glint came into Cord's eyes. "Could've fooled me. Just
what were you doing back at the ranch?"

Sarah's eyes narrowed angrily. "That wasn't meddling.
Did you think I'd stand by and watch some two-bit cop insult a friend? You have some opinion of me!"

"Cops are called sheriffs or deputies around here, city
slicker," Cord scoffed. His expression grew intensely serious as he looked down at her. It was time to admit it. He
wanted her, had wanted her from the first and in a way he
had never wanted another woman before—possessively. "If
I told you my opinion of you, you'd probably run," he
drawled.

Sarah was mesmerized by the sudden flames smoldering
in his eyes. Her nerves sang with awareness. Warmth pooled
inside her, tingling, tantalizing. She told herself that she
didn't want it, that it was dangerous, but the voice of caution wasn't strong enough. She shot him a wry look. "I
don't scare that easily. And you can stop that drawl, cowboy," she said softly. "It doesn't fool me for one minute.
You only use it as a smoke screen to keep people at a distance."

"The same way you use your glasses?" he countered softly. "If I stop drawling will you take them off?" He pushed himself away from the door and advanced quietly, his stride smooth and dangerous.

"I do need them," Sarah protested, common sense warning her to keep some of her defenses up. She wanted to believe that what she felt for him was no more than the sense of kinship one battered survivor felt for another, but it was much more than that and it frightened her. At the same time, temptation curled inside her like a longing for sunshine and laughter, drawing her toward him.

He stepped close to her and his hand cupped her face, a rare tenderness welling up in him. "Perhaps I don't want you to see me clearly," he warned huskily.

The warning melted to nothing beneath the gentleness of his touch. "You told me that I was blind as a bat with or without them," she said lightly. "So there is no point in taking them off."

Cord's mouth twisted. "Don't trust me too much," he warned a little roughly. "There's a good bed upstairs in the apartment," he murmured with a wry glance at the wooden staircase zigzagging up to the second floor. "At the moment I'm tempted to drag you into it."

Sarah felt her heart beat a little faster. Small flames glinted in his smoky eyes, but the look he gave her was softer, gentler, like the one he usually reserved for her daughter. And when he smiled, it was a soft smile, a smile that made her breath catch in her throat. "But you won't," she said quietly, very sure that he would keep his word and not cross the invisible line. Of course, that didn't mean that he wouldn't try to tempt *her* into making the first move....

And, dear God, she was so tempted.

She wanted badly for him to touch her, to kiss her, to hold her. They could help each other forget, find oblivion in each other's arms and, for a short while, keep the loneliness at bay. But it wasn't smart. How could she even contemplate taking such a step? She was still trying to face up to the last blow fate had dealt her, and she simply wasn't strong enough to deal with more emotional upheaval.

At the thought, she raised her arms, her hand curling around his wrist to pull down his hand. But her hand lingered on his hair-roughened skin for long seconds, feeling the strong beat of his pulse beneath her fingertips. It took all of her determination to draw his arm down.

"Sensible, wise Sarah," Cord scoffed, looking down at her hand still holding his wrist, so white and slender compared to his. But there was strength in her grip and warmth in her touch.

Sarah looked down, unable to let go. She held her breath and counted his heartbeats, her eyes locking with his, wondering why she couldn't step back, why she couldn't release his hand and send him away. Perhaps it was because of that sense of kinship, the recognition of each other's scars, one battered survivor helping another across a difficult spot. He understood how she felt, and he wouldn't misinterpret her need for warmth and take advantage of her weakness.

With a wry grimace, she slid her hand into his big, callused one. "If we go in through the front door, do you think the ghosts will escape through the back?"

Cord's hand closed over hers firmly, warmly. "Since there's two of us, maybe they'll be petrified," he said gravely, drawing her with him to the front. But as he opened the door, he couldn't help but warn her. "It looks pretty grim on the inside."

Sarah traced the letters on the wooden plaque next to the door. It read simply: Simon Durand, M.D. "Simon always wanted me to join his practice," she said, her voice hoarse.

"Why didn't you?" Cord opened the door leading directly into the waiting room, and winced at the musty odor. Only a faint smell of antiseptic lingered.

Because I was too busy trying to be worthy of it. Shaking her head, Sarah brushed past him and tried to tamp down the rising emotions by flicking the light switch. She could only deal with one ghost at a time, she thought, as she walked into the waiting room.

Looking around her, her eyes widened with horror as she took in the destruction. Chair seats were slashed and the foam was spilling out. The gray carpeting was torn and had been ripped from its tacking, curling at the edges. The white walls were bare, nail holes and chipped plaster showing where pictures should have been. Shocked, Sarah wandered past the reception desk, glancing at the broken drawers stacked neatly beside it. She walked down the narrow hall, past two examining rooms. The destruction wasn't nearly as bad here. A few jars holding tongue depressors, gauze pads and Q-Tips had been broken and the rolls of paper sheets had been torn from the holders.

She braced her shoulders before opening the door to Simon's office at the end of the hallway, then stepped inside. Grim, Cord had warned her, but this looked more than grim. This was total devastation. She could feel a wave of hate roll toward her. There wasn't a chair cushion that hadn't been slashed. The fine old Keshan carpet Simon had been so proud of was torn and littered with fine shards of glass. In one corner of the paneled room, oak filing cabinets leaned drunkenly against each other for support. Patient files were neatly stacked on the floor beside them. Of the drawers there was no sign.

Silently she looked down at the big mahogany desk, recalling how she and Lisa had combed antique stores for weeks to find it. The polished ivory inlaid surface looked as if someone had taken a crowbar to it. The glass of the mahogany bookcases behind it was shattered and the backs of many of the medical books had been torn. She walked numbly through the door at the back of the room where Simon had stored his supplies. The shelves were empty but for a few sample boxes of sterile pads, antiseptic and bandages.

"The sheriff removed the rest of the supplies," Cord said, following her like a shadow, watching the color of her face fade a little more with each step.

Sarah nodded. Her voice was flat with control when she spoke. "I told Pilar Torres, Simon's nurse, to take what was left to the nursing home where she now works." Nausea curled in the pit of her stomach. Slowly she turned around, wrapping her arms around her against the sudden chill. "This is so senseless."

Cord reached out to wrap his arms around her and draw her back out into the sunshine, but she stepped past him, as if afraid to break down and give in to the tears burning in her eyes. "Did Simon have any enemies that you knew of?" he asked quietly.

Sarah stopped at the desk, running a finger over the ivory inlay. "If he did, he didn't tell me. He was irritated at times about the town's paranoia about illegals. Once he had a group of women protesting in his office because he didn't notify the sheriff that one of his patients had no *amica*. I wouldn't have found out about it if I hadn't called that morning and heard the commotion."

She glared at Cord. "I realize that the country isn't big enough to take in all the hungry and starving people in this world and that there has to be some control. But I still don't like the INS."

Cord raised his hands palms up, in a gesture of peace. "I quit. So you can stop glaring at me. Besides, I didn't apprehend illegals. I was after bigger game. Like drug runners and slave traders." And Harper. No matter how often he told himself that he had made the right decision, the year he had lost wouldn't seem as much of a waste if he could have stopped the man.

Sarah shivered, recalling horror stories of refugees being forced into prostitution and slave labor on *fincas* in Southern Mexico and in New York's Chinatown to pay off the *coyotes'* fees. She forced herself to glance around the office once again. "I can't imagine anyone hating Simon this much. I can't imagine anyone causing this kind of damage just because Simon helped a few poor lost souls. Besides, it doesn't make any sense to destroy the office after his death." Now that the first shock was wearing off, she began to think logically again. "I think your father was right. Whoever did this was after drugs."

Cord had never felt comfortable with the explanation. "Wouldn't an addict simply take the drugs and run?"

Sarah took a deep steadying breath, trying to control the anger and nausea. "He didn't find any drugs, at least nothing like morphine, Demerol or Valium. There are strict government regulations concerning controlled substances. Simon didn't have a license to use addictive drugs. His opinion was that if a patient was sick enough to need morphine, he should be hospitalized or under specialized care." She made a sweeping gesture with her hand. "This was done in a rage because he or she couldn't find anything stronger than codeine or amphetamines. Nothing else makes sense."

Unless, by helping illegals, Simon had run afoul of the *coyotes,* Cord thought grimly. In fact, the more he looked around, the more he became convinced that this had been a professional job, a statement, a warning of some sort. Unfortunately, most of the evidence had been destroyed when his father and Chuck had cleaned up the place. But one look into Sarah's white face and he decided to keep his suspicions to himself. At least for now. She was hanging on to control by a thin thread and all he had to go on anyway was a gut feeling. "Let's get out of here."

When she didn't answer and didn't move, Cord's control snapped. He couldn't watch her fight the pain alone anymore. Leaning against the desk, he drew her between his legs and into his arms. Sarah struggled briefly, but his hold merely tightened, pushing her head against his chest.

"Let go, Sarah." he murmured hoarsely into her hair.

Sarah shook her head, but she clung to him, because he was so solid, so warm, so strong. She turned her face into his shirt, leaned against him and absorbed some of his strength. "To Simon this town was special—his roots, a safe and friendly place, a place that still maintained the values he had been raised with, a small Eden from which he drew strength." She swallowed. "It hurts to realize that his Eden doesn't exist after all."

"I wouldn't say it doesn't exist, but every Eden has its share of snakes," Cord murmured soothingly into her hair. When the tremors didn't stop, he tilted her head up and touched his lips to hers, gently moving back and forth in a soft caress. Softly, patiently, he stroked her rigid back.

Sarah hadn't known that a kiss from a man could hold so much gentleness and tenderness. There was no demand as his lips roamed over her face, only compassion and understanding. His touch soothed her frayed nerves, calmed her angry despair and made her forget her fears. Her clenched hands relaxed, muscle by muscle. Just understanding. Slowly she reached up and took her glasses off, dropping them onto the desk.

Something began to stir inside her, a hunger, a need she had denied for years. Always before she had told herself that she was content with her life as long as she had Angel and her work.

She had lied to herself, she thought, her mouth opening beneath his, tentative, testing, still a little afraid. Her arms slid around his waist and her heart moved toward him.

Hesitantly, she brought her hand to his face, letting her fingers skim along the scar; it seemed softer somehow, as if tension was sliding away, leaving him as it was leaving her. The pain burning behind her eyes lessened. "Cord." She said his name on a sigh and melted against him.

For a moment Cord was stunned by her complete surrender. Then warnings flashed inside him. Careful. He had to be careful. Instinct warned him off, like an animal sensing fire. While he needed the warmth, wanted it desperately, he didn't want to step too close to it. But an instant after the warning passed through his head, he dismissed it. It didn't matter that his senses were reeling from her. The soft give of her body and the rich taste of her mouth blew all thoughts of caution from his mind.

The air suddenly thickened and filled with the scent of her. He wanted to carry her upstairs, lay her on the bed and take what she offered. She wouldn't resist. She had taken her glasses off and her eyes were glowing with desire and need. Perhaps she would even welcome the heat and distraction, the momentary oblivion.

But she had trusted him enough to lower her defenses, and her trust was much too precious to be betrayed for a temporary release. Fighting his own needs, he pressed his lips to her forehead and then rested his cheek in her hair. "Better?"

Nodding, Sarah drew a ragged breath. She wasn't sure she could speak. Every sense was heightened, every sense was filled with him. She wanted to stay like this, her arms around him, his heart beating against hers.

She wanted him. Not only for a few heated kisses. And certainly not for comfort. She wanted him in bed, the way she couldn't remember ever wanting a man, not even George. She wanted to look at him. All of him. She wanted to unbutton his shirt and slide it off his broad shoulders and touch every inch of his lean, golden body. She wanted him to touch her in the same way, roll over with him in one tangled heap of passion.

She realized then how fast she was falling, how vulnerable she was to him. And that thought was frightening.

What if she lost again?

It was only that thought that dragged her back from danger at the last moment. One second she was pliant against him, infinitely vulnerable. The next she was pushing, her fingers splayed tensely against his chest. "Better. Much better," she said hoarsely.

For a moment Cord didn't move, still stunned by the fierceness of his longing and puzzled by her sudden rejection.

Sarah looked at him and in those few breathless seconds she realized that his need had been as fierce and as unexpected as hers. And it was driving him still.

There was a knock on the front door. Tension ran through Cord, reality returning. Raking his hair back, he pushed himself away from the desk. "Better go and answer that, Doc," he said.

The knocking came again, louder this time. Sarah glanced toward the hall, then back at Cord, challenging him. "What are you going to do? Leave through the back door?"

Cord's eyes were unreadable when he took in her flushed cheeks and her slightly swollen, well-kissed mouth. "Maybe it's too late for that."

The knock came again, then the door opened and a woman's voice called, "Hello? Is anyone here?"

Cord's face hardened. He looked like a man ready for a fight, maybe even *looking* for a fight. Swearing silently, he strode to the front, just as a slender, dark-haired, stylish woman in her mid-forties stepped inside.

With a silent groan he recognized Alicia Hunter, the administrator of the local nursing home. Gossip had it that his father had dated her a few times a year ago. Personally, Cord didn't like the woman. She was too intense and she had a malicious streak. "Hello, Alicia, what can I do for you?" he drawled.

Momentarily taken aback by his presence, Alicia looked at him warily. "I heard that Doc Simon's daughter was in town and I thought I'd convey my condolences. What are you doing here?" Suspiciously, she glanced past him at Sarah coming down the hall. Her brown eyes glittered coldly and her carmine-painted mouth curled as she spat out,

"Haven't you caused your father enough grief? I didn't want to believe the gossip in church, but..."

Hell, the woman sounded as if she were his stepmother. Thank God there was no likelihood of it ever happening. "Then don't," Cord advised with deceptive softness. "I think you've already said more than enough." Propping one shoulder against the wall, he hooked his thumbs into his belt. "Since you're here, I may as well let you know that I plan to attend the board meeting on Thursday."

Alicia's eyes widened with shock and she stammered, "Y-you can't!"

Cord raised one brow arrogantly and drawled, "My father is not going to be here and someone has to vote on the new contract."

Flustered, trying not to show her disappointment, Alicia gnawed her bottom lip. "Well...in that case..."

Satisfied, Cord looked at Sarah, who was standing next to him. "I'd like you to meet Alicia Hunter."

Alicia was all smiles as she held out her hand, Cord noticed with satisfaction.

"Your father was the attending physician at the nursing home. He often talked about you. He couldn't wait for your training to be over, so you could join him down here."

Sarah glanced down at the long red fingernails and shuddered inwardly. "I'm afraid you must have misunderstood him. I didn't have any intentions of joining his practice." Sarah glanced at Cord. "Would you mind carrying the cleaning supplies Maisy loaned me to the apartment?"

Cord tensed. He should have brought up the question of her return to the ranch earlier. Now it was too late. Then again, maybe her move was for the best, at least for now. It would make Sarah's reception in town easier.

Alicia's eyes narrowed as Cord brushed past her. "I didn't know Maisy is at the ranch."

"Well, yes. And so is my daughter, Angel. I didn't bring Angel with me today because she's still recovering from the accident," Sarah said blandly, hiding the anger burning inside her. "I guess you heard that a bull attacked my car. If it hadn't been for Cord, I would have been stranded for the rest of the night with a five-year-old and a cat. I'm very grateful to him for giving us shelter."

Alicia shifted uncomfortably. "I'm sorry. I didn't mean to imply—" She stopped abruptly. "Are you planning to live in the apartment here?" When Sarah nodded she asked, "Does that mean that you're thinking about taking over your daddy's practice after all?"

Sarah shook her head, her voice edged with bitterness when she said, "What practice? Have you taken a look around? There is nothing left."

It was past nine when Cord carried a sleeping Angel up the stairs to the apartment.

All afternoon and evening he had told himself that the move was for the best. The place was safe. The locks were solid and the apartment itself was neat, clean and fairly comfortable. And while he hadn't been able to talk to Holt, who had taken the rest of the day off, Deputy Ryder had promised to keep a close eye on the place during the night.

But now, with Angel snuggled into his arms, he finally admitted to himself that he didn't want mother or daughter to disappear from his life again. At the thought, he stopped halfway up the stairs, shaken to realize just how perfectly Sarah and Angel would fit into his life.

And his dreams.

He shook his head as if to clear it. Dreams? He hadn't dared to dream in a long time. Until now he had only existed, living from one day to the next, marking time, wondering what he was going to do with the rest of his life but reluctant to make plans.

He had been afraid that he would wake up in the middle of the night and find himself back in the jungle, in total darkness, beneath a canopy of leaves so thick, he couldn't see the sky, couldn't see the stars.

Now, watching Sarah open the apartment door, he suddenly realized what he wanted.

A family of his own.

A wife.

And kids. Several of them, just like little Angel, to make the old ranch house ring with laughter again. And he didn't want just any woman. He wanted a woman who was as scarred by life as he himself was. He wanted Sarah. The kiss in Simon's office had left him aching and had shown him that she was as attracted to him as he was to her.

But she was a city slicker, like his mother.

It scared the hell out of him.

Entering the apartment, Sarah flicked on the light, then walked down the short narrow hall into the smaller of the bedrooms, where she turned on the bedside lamp.

Even after he had bought the house, Simon had occasionally spent the night here when he'd been too tired to make the trip out and so they had two comfortable beds, sheets and blankets, a sparsely furnished living room and even a few dishes. There was also a microwave and staples in the kitchen—everything they needed for their short stay.

Flipping back the blanket, Sarah smoothed out the sheets and fluffed up the pillow. She watched Cord lower Angel onto the bed, catching her breath softly at the tenderness on his face. He straightened slowly, as if reluctant to release her. Swiftly she tore her eyes away from his face and busied herself with sliding Angel's sneakers off.

Cord straightened and turned away, walking to the small narrow window, testing the lock. "The gossip's never bothered me before," he said, keeping his voice low. "But children are so easily influenced. I'd hate to see Angel hesitate the next time she sees me, before running to me."

Taking Angel's overalls off, Sarah glanced over her shoulder at his straight back, her heart wrenching. "I doubt that will happen. She's more likely to scratch someone's eyes out in your defense," she said, tucking in the comforter.

Cord grimaced. "I don't want that, either."

Sarah smiled slightly. "You can't have it both ways. Children usually see the world in black and white. You're Angel's white knight who chased the monster away. It would take more than gossip to change her opinion of you." Straightening, she turned off the light, watching him walk past her into the small narrow hall, a troubled look on her face. The growing attachment between Cord and Angel worried her.

Leaving the door open, she was following him outside when Sheba dashed out of the kitchen to her right. Sarah barely managed to close the door in her face. Angry and frustrated, Sheba scratched at the door.

"I don't like leaving you here," Cord growled when she joined him.

A shiver feathered over Sarah's skin and it wasn't caused by the cool night air. Temptation curled around her and drew her toward him. She didn't want him to leave, either. She dreaded the loneliness and the dark night ahead. But she didn't want to become dependent on him. Cord had stirred something in her, had touched feelings she thought could never be touched again, but she couldn't allow herself to let them grow. Whatever she felt for him was best ignored. Whatever closeness they had shared, it would end here. Tonight. "At dinner you told Maisy that it's perfectly safe."

"I changed my mind."

She surprised them both by laying a hand on his arm. "Don't worry. We'll be fine. Besides, we have Sheba to protect us," she said with an attempt at humor.

A grin tugged at his mouth. Before she could withdraw her hand he linked his fingers with hers. "That cat's nasty enough to scare off any intruder." But glancing up and down the alley, his grin vanished. The lights at the back of the stores were dim, barely illuminating the back doors. The rest of the lane was pitch dark. "This place needs a couple of strong floodlights," he said, his voice deep and rough. "I think I'll have a talk with Mayor Buckman."

A small smile curved Sarah's lips. He might not realize it, but he was beginning to involve himself in town affairs again. A hard resolve grew inside her. She had no idea how she was going to do it, but somehow, before she left, she would smooth things over for him here. "That sounds like a good idea," she agreed.

Cord's eyes narrowed. There was something about the set of her chin and the look in her eyes that warned him of her intent. "Don't go to bat for me," he warned her. "You have no idea what you're dealing with."

Apprehensively, Sarah glanced below at the wooden boards covering the windows and shivered. "Do you?"

Cord shook his head. "I'm not sure," he said grimly. "It's a gut feeling, nothing more. Devlin is involved in it somewhere, but I have yet to figure out how." Slowly he raised their linked hands and brushed his lips over her knuckles. "Sarah, come back to the ranch with me."

Sarah shook her head. There were other dangers that frightened her much more. Like falling in love with Cord.

Cord's mouth compressed. "Just what are you trying to prove to yourself by staying here?" he asked angrily. "That you're tough? That you don't need anyone?"

His words hit a raw nerve. Sarah tugged her hand free. "No. That's your line, cowboy."

So the barriers were coming up again, Cord thought, looking at her in frustration. Maybe the wise thing to do would be to allow things to slip back into casualness. But she wasn't wearing her glasses and her hair was slipping from its clasp, soft strands falling down her shoulders, making her look vulnerable, a slender fragile shadow in the night.

"Maybe it was my line, until a small angel smiled at me and thanked me for chasing her monster away. Maybe it was still true until you charged into my study, determined not to add to my troubles and ended up making me realize what I had become—an insensitive, self-absorbed, self-pitying bastard.''

"You're none of those things," Sarah said fiercely, her own fears momentarily cast aside. Cord needed far more protecting than she ever had. Her spirit was wounded, but his was more so. However gentle he was with her, he was ruthless when it came to judging himself. She couldn't, wouldn't, allow him to believe that of himself. "I won't let you talk like that."

Cord shook his head slowly, anger softening into tenderness. She didn't want him to get too close, his little tigress who scratched and hissed at him more often than not. "You're just a little thing, but you're not afraid to take on anyone. The sheriff. Alicia. Me."

The fierce look died on Sarah's face and she shook her head. She couldn't let him believe something that she wasn't. "I'm scared all the time," she said, her voice low and intense. "I'm scared of caring too deeply, scared of losing again. I'm scared of being alone. At night I sleep with a light on because I'm afraid of the dark. That's why I work the midnight shift, not because I have guts."

She took a shaky breath, then continued. She might as well make a clean sweep of it. Maybe then he would see her for what she was. A coward. A mouse. "I didn't charge into your study to help you, but to keep from becoming drawn into your fight. And I decided to move into the apartment for the same reason. I don't want any trouble. So you see, you were right in your assessment of me this morning, cowboy." She ran a shaky hand over her face, then said quietly, "Now, will you please leave."

Chapter 7

"Hell, no," Cord growled.

He stared at her for a long moment, trying to bring his churning emotions under control. He didn't believe her. Oh, he believed the part about her being afraid of falling in love and losing again. Who wouldn't in her place? She was only twenty-eight years old and she had buried two families and Angel's father, too. So many losses were enough to make anyone run from another involvement. He doubted that in her position he would have the guts to let anyone close again.

She was trying to push him away, not because she didn't care, but because she cared too much and she was frightened. Hell, he was uneasy himself. He had his own problems. He wasn't in much better shape, but he, too, cared too much already.

What bothered him most was why she thought so little of herself, why she thought of herself only in terms of flaws. Except for Simon, he hadn't met a physician who wasn't puffed up with self-importance. And her job was another thing that bothered him. How long could she work in a combat zone before it started to affect her? He felt certain that all of it had to do with her past. Unfortunately, those last days in Iran was one subject Simon had never talked about, at least not within his hearing. But he wanted, needed, to know about it. "Sarah, can you talk about what happened sixteen years ago?" he asked gently.

"Why do you want to know?" Sarah wrapped her arms around herself and crossed the landing to the railing, leaning against it. It wasn't something she talked about. Ever. Not even George had known the details of what had happened that terrible night.

Cord joined her, leaning against the railing with his back facing her. He had never wanted to know about a woman's past before, but Sarah wasn't just any woman. "Because I want to understand. I made a mistake this morning and I don't want to make another one."

Sarah gripped the metal tightly. "It's better this way. That kiss in the office should never have happened." It would be so easy to give in to this crazy attraction she felt for him. She wished he would leave.

Cord's mouth compressed. "But it did. And denying it won't change the fact that you're as attracted to me as I am to you."

Sarah shook her head, anger and fear in her voice. "I keep telling you that I'm a coward but you won't believe me. You don't understand." She couldn't allow herself to care. "I've lost everything I wanted before. I don't need the pain."

Cord said nothing, could say nothing. All he thought of was that he wanted to hold her and try to heal her as she was healing him. *Trust me, Sarah.*

The sky was so dark, she thought, without moon or stars. Looking down into the dark alley, she recalled another dark moonless night sixteen years ago. And suddenly she wanted him to understand, wanted him to know why she was so afraid. "Sometimes it seems like it happened in another lifetime. I can't even recall my parents' and brothers' faces anymore.

"They came at night after everyone had gone to bed," she said. "Our house, a compound really, with servants' quarters, separate guest rooms and stables, stood at the edge of town, surrounded by high walls. For weeks there had been warnings, unrest, but no one believed that it would amount to much. Iran was a close ally of the United States. In southern Iran, where we lived, there were so many Americans working in the oil fields, English had replaced Farsi as the official language.

"The oil companies were taking no chances, though, and were evacuating families. Simon had already sent Lisa to New York. He was trying to convince my parents to leave, too. My father refused. He was a Bakhtiar, a member of a family closely related to the crown." Sarah drew a shaky breath, then said, her voice harsh and bitter, "Bakhtiars don't run. They stay and fight."

Her words jolted Cord's memory. *I'm the only survivor of a family of dead heroes,* she had told him. *I prefer a live coward any day.* But she didn't. Rationally she might have tried to convince herself that she was lucky to have escaped. And no doubt she had tried to convince herself for years that there was no shame in survival. But deep down in her heart she felt guilty as hell. "What happened?" he asked quietly.

"Papa was sending us to safety. Mom was packing, sort of, because she didn't want to leave Papa. My brothers were fighting Papa every inch of the way." She drew a shaky breath. "In the end it made no difference. They came two days before we were scheduled to leave.

"I was sleeping over at my friend Soraya's house next door. We awoke to gunfire and screams. Soraya's parents fled. I should have taken one of their horses and ridden to the garrison nearby. Instead I crawled onto the roof and watched my family being dragged outside—" She turned slowly, arms still tightly wrapped around her. There were no tears on her face, but her eyes were dark and haunted.

"Would you have made it to the garrison in time?" he asked quietly.

Sarah shrugged. "I don't know. I'll never know," she said in a flat emotionless voice. "It was over so quickly, at least it seemed like it at the time. All I remember is how terrified I was that they would find me, too."

Cord stared at her, at the stark pain on her face. Very slowly he laid an arm across her shoulder and drew her within the circle of his arms. For a moment she resisted, then she yielded to her need for warmth. "Sarah, you were how old? Twelve? You couldn't have done a thing to help them," he said, gathering her close, trying to find words that would ease the weight of a guilt she had been dragging around with her for too long. A guilt that drove her to work in a trauma ward night after night, trying to help victims like her family, to prove to herself that she wasn't a coward after all.

Only he couldn't find the words. She had probably heard them all before anyway. So he tangled his fingers into her hair instead, pulling her head onto his shoulder, surrounding her with warmth.

"Please," Sarah whispered, her voice muffled against his shoulder. "I don't want your pity."

"I feel a whole lot of things for you, Sarah, but pity isn't one of them," Cord said into her hair, one hand running up and down her back, soothing the tremors shaking her. She was holding on by a thin thread and his heart clenched in his chest. Bending his head, he covered her mouth with his.

Longing welled up inside him. He reached out to touch her, tracing his fingertips over her cheekbones, reveling in the silkiness of her skin.

Sarah stiffened and tried to retreat. But the kiss was so gentle, so sweet, it touched the well-guarded places in her heart and soul. For a moment she tried to remember all the reasons for keeping him at a distance. She was none of the things he admired about her. She didn't deserve him, and everything she ever wanted was ripped away from her in the end anyway. She didn't need the pain, didn't think she could stand it. But the words to have him release her simply wouldn't come.

The woman in her was neither strong nor courageous, but he made her feel that she was. He made her ache with longing, made her forget about losses and pain. She lifted her hands and buried them in his thick silky hair, shimmering like burnished gold in the porch light. Pulling his head down, she kissed him back with a sweet hunger of her own.

Something ripped inside her and she felt the shock wave surge through her all the way to her toes. Heat flared, so hot and strong, it seemed to melt her very bones.

She didn't want this. Yet she wanted it more than anything in the world.

She should push him away, but he knew how to kiss her, how to touch her, how to make her feel wanted and safe. Nobody should be able to stir such need with his tongue, his lips, his hands. Her skin burned with awareness; she shivered at the light stroke of his fingers over her breasts, sensations swirled around her like stardust, heat in the cool of the night.

She hadn't wanted to feel like a woman ever again.

But it was already too late. She cared too much to draw back. She was falling in love and that, too, she couldn't stop. It was destiny.

So what was the point in denying the passion that drew them together with such magnetic force? In a few days she would return to New York and to her old life. Her lonely life. If she gave in to temptation, perhaps life wouldn't feel so lonely again, because she would have a sweet memory to carry with her.

Giving in to her needs, her hands slid down his strong corded neck and she drew him closer. "Make love to me, Cord."

Abruptly, Cord raised his head, drawing a deep shuddering breath. He wanted Sarah with a terrifying ache that went far beyond the physical. She filled the cold empty spaces in his heart and it scared the hell out of him. Always before he had been in control, but with every touch, every kiss, she was slipping deeper into him. All he could think of as he stared down into her earnest face was that he wanted to hold her, kiss her, make love to her and make her his.

But he had no right to make love to her, not with his life in a mess. If he stayed here tonight, the whole town would know about it by tomorrow morning and her life and Angel's would be hell. Besides, his "relationships" had always been aboveboard, with partners who hadn't wanted any more strings than he himself. He had never taken advantage of an innocent, and despite her training, despite her relationship with Angel's father, Sarah Durand was an innocent in many ways.

And making love to her once would never be enough.

"I wouldn't be fair to you, Sarah," he said gently. "In fact, the best thing would be for you to return to New York and let me settle Simon's affairs."

Shocked, Sarah stared at him, for a moment hardly believing that he was turning her down, that he was rejecting her. He had merely been kind to her, a friend helping a friend over a rough spot. God, how could she have seen it as anything else? Strong men despised weakness, as much in others as in themselves. She should have remembered the lesson of a lifetime and kept her fears to herself. Taking a step back, she started to walk around him. "I'm sorry," she said with quiet dignity. "I misunderstood your kindness."

Cord's hand shot out to stay her, scowling at her. "Kindness, my—foot." He couldn't leave her like this, feeling rejected, believing that he was turning her down because deep down he had been disgusted by her tale. And he certainly didn't want to add to her guilt—she was already doing a great job blaming herself. "To tell you the truth, I'm somewhat in awe of you," he rasped. Scooping her up, he carried her inside.

Startled, Sarah threw her arm around his neck and clung to him. "Me? Whatever for?"

"After everything you've been through, you're still reaching out to people. Loving scares the hell out of me," he continued quietly, carrying her through the kitchen into the small dark living room. Easing himself down on the serviceable brown couch, he settled her next to him, "It makes me turn tail and run." His arms tightened around her when she started to move away, denying her escape. "My parents can't seem to live together. But they can't seem to live without each other, either. I don't think my mother has gone out on a date since she divorced my father. My father tried a few times. Alicia Hunter, I've heard, was one of his dates."

"Was she?" Sarah grimaced. "I find that hard to believe."

"Yeah," Cord said, his voice flat. "I guess he was hurting too bad to care who he was with, as long as he wasn't alone. I swore to myself that I wasn't going to end up like him."

Sarah felt her own fears ease, her heart going out to his parents and aching for Cord. He was very much like his father and she could see why his parents' divorce had affected him so strongly.

"Anyway, I played the field. Besides, my job was dangerous. Sometimes undercover assignments lasted for weeks and it didn't seem fair to have a closer relationship."

He stopped for a moment, needing to explain a little about the trouble he had been in, but wondering how much to tell her. Baring his soul had never been easy for him. Then he took the plunge. "For years I'd been working with the

Mexican Immigration Service to gather evidence against one of their major crime figures, a *coyote* named Lobo Rodriguez who is responsible for a large share of all goods smuggled into this country. But every time we thought we had him, he managed to slip through the net. Eventually I found out that my boss, Tom Harper, was working for him, providing everything from passports and new identities for illegals to information about planned raids. But I had no proof.''

Briefly he explained about the computer file he'd found containing the Social Security numbers of the recently deceased, numbers that had been reissued. Then he told her how the file had crashed when he'd tried to copy it. He told her how Harper and Rodriguez had used Mariela Noquez to frame him for rape. And for the first time he didn't feel ice-cold rage curling in his stomach. ''I wasn't supposed to make bail. There were enough inmates with a grudge against me to arrange for a 'suicide' or an 'accident.''''

Sarah shivered at his words and leaned closer, sliding her arm around him to keep out the chill.

''I went to meet an informant out at sea who promised me enough evidence against Harper to get the FBI involved. I was followed and my boat was sunk. I managed to dive overboard.''

Sarah raised her finger and touched his scar. ''That's where you got this.'' She had heard stories like his before. One of her friends, Sue Miller, a psychiatrist, had once worked for the FBI.

Cord shrugged. ''From a piece of fiberglass. I was barely conscious at the time. A Mexican fishing boat picked me up. They took me back to their village. There was no doctor in town and they didn't want any trouble. By the time I regained consciousness four days later, I was presumed dead. If I'd returned to the States, my bail would have been revoked. If I'd let my parents know that I was alive, they would have been in danger, too. They were being watched the whole time. Harper didn't take any chances.''

Sarah sucked in her breath sharply. ''Maisy told me about Devlin's father being involved with *coyotes*. Do you think Harper paid Devlin to keep an eye on the ranch?''

He drew in a long deep breath, then said wearily, ''Probably. Harper had bounty hunters and hit men scouring Mexico for me and Devlin came into money about that time. My only hope was to find Mariela and get her to sign a confession. Rodriguez was hiding her at his *finca*. It took me nine months to locate her and another to abduct her. Luis placed her in protective custody.''

Sarah clutched his hand so hard, her short nails bit into his skin. For a moment she recalled the three terrifying days and nights of running and hiding before she and Simon had reached the fishing trawler in the Persian Gulf. And Cord had been hunted like an animal for ten long months!

''The day after Mariela signed the statement, she was found dead in her cell. There was no official hearing, which started the rumors that my father had bribed Luis, the Mexican official I had worked with all along.

''I was offered a desk job shortly afterward. A part of me wanted to hang in there and try to have another shot at Harper, but I'd had enough. After living in flea-infested huts and sleeping with one eye open for ten months, all I wanted was to put the past behind me.''

Sarah looked at his hard profile. It hadn't been an easy decision for him to turn his back on revenge, she thought. Even now she could feel the need for it churning inside him. Sue often remarked on the fact that the strongest warriors had the toughest time dealing with defeat. Tough, hard men like Cord lived by a code of honor and duty that made no allowances for failure. They never gave up. Cord may have quit his job and come home to recuperate, but nothing could remove that imaginary stain on his honor, and it was still haunting him.

With a start, she recognized some part of him in herself. She never gave up fighting for a life as long as there was a glimmer of hope. It was painful to lose a patient and she hoped she would never get used to it. But one of the first things a physician learned was to accept limitations. Men like Cord didn't.

Restless, she slid her feet off the couch and after a brief hesitation Cord released her. "Do you think that Devlin may still be working for Harper?" she asked, her voice carefully controlled, cold fear clutching her heart. Cord looked at her searchingly. For a moment he wanted to draw her back into his arms and lose himself in her soft heat. But the reason for his explanations had been to keep her from becoming involved in his affairs without adding to her guilt, and that mission had been accomplished.

"It's a possibility," he said, his voice flat, a chill creeping up his skin. "Devlin has some tough boys working for him these days. Smuggling illegals is big business. Immigration into the States is being sold in travel agencies all over the world. The price for a new identity complete with passport, Social Security number and driver's license, a safe house and a job, runs from thirty to fifty thousand dollars per person. A simple *amica,* costs around five. Those who have the money are the lucky ones. As for the others, sometimes it takes hopeful immigrants two years to work off the fees with slave labor and prostitution. If they try to escape, they are hunted relentlessly and killed so they can't turn witness."

Sarah closed her eyes against the sudden grip of pain. He may have walked away from revenge, but, like her father and brothers, he would stand and fight to defend his home. And what about Simon? Had he also become involved? Running a shaky hand over her face, she turned her back to Cord, staring through the small window out into the dark moonless night.

AN IMPORTANT MESSAGE FROM THE EDITORS OF SILHOUETTE®

Dear Reader,

Because you've chosen to read one of our fine romance novels, we'd like to say "thank you"! And, as a **special** way to thank you, we've selected <u>four more</u> of the <u>books</u> you love so well, **and** an Austrian Crystal Pendant to send you absolutely *FREE!*

Please enjoy them with our compliments...

Leslie Wainger

Senior Editor,
Silhouette Intimate Moments

P.S. And because we value our customers, we've attached something extra inside ...

PEEL OFF SEAL AND
PLACE INSIDE

HOW TO VALIDATE
YOUR
EDITOR'S FREE GIFT
"THANK YOU"

1. Peel off gift seal from front cover. Place it in space provided at right. This automatically entitles you to receive four free books and a lovely Austrian Crystal Pendant.

2. Send back this card and you'll get brand-new Silhouette Intimate Moments® novels. These books have a cover price of $3.50 each, but they are yours to keep absolutely free.

3. There's no catch. You're under no obligation to buy anything. We charge nothing—ZERO—for your first shipment. And you don't have to make any minimum number of purchases—not even one!

4. The fact is thousands of readers enjoy receiving books by mail from the Silhouette Reader Service™ months before they're available in stores. They like the convenience of home delivery and they love our discount prices!

5. We hope that after receiving your free books you'll want to remain a subscriber. But the choice is yours—to continue or cancel, anytime at all! So why not take us up on our invitation, with no risk of any kind. You'll be glad you did!

6. Don't forget to detach your FREE BOOKMARK. And remember…just for validating your Editor's Free Gift Offer, we'll send you FIVE MORE gifts, *ABSOLUTELY FREE!*

NOT ACTUAL SIZE

YOURS FREE!

*You'll look like a million dollars when you wear this lovely necklace! Its cobra-link chain is a generous 18" long, and the multi-faceted Austrian crystal sparkles like a diamond! It's yours **absolutely free** — when you accept our no-risk offer!*

Slowly Cord got to his feet. "It's time I left, or your reputation will be in shreds." He had a good idea where her thoughts had strayed. He wished he could tell her that Simon had not been involved, but he couldn't lie to her.

Sarah scowled at him fiercely. "Do you think I care a fig for what the Lorna Devlins in this town think of me?"

Something like relief shot through him, but it didn't last long. "There's Angel. I don't want her hurt," he said quietly. "Lock the doors. If you plan to stay here, it may be a good idea to get phones reconnected."

At dawn the following morning, Sarah slid quietly from her bed. Shrugging into her quilted robe, she walked across the narrow hall and looked into the smaller of the two bedrooms. At her entrance Sheba leapt off the bed and brushed against her legs, purring with contentment. Lifting her, Sarah scratched her behind the ears and the purring grew thunderous. Sheba was the only one who had wholeheartedly approved their move into town, she thought, tucking the blanket tighter around her daughter. Straightening, Sarah looked around. Both bedrooms were sparsely furnished, with pine headboards, dressers and nightstands. Mexican-style rugs covered the old plank floors. The small dormer windows needed no curtains and daylight was now seeping into the room.

Quietly Sarah closed the door and went into the blue-and-white kitchen. Filling a mug with water, she heated it in the microwave, then opened a can of cat food. Still purring with contentment, Sheba began to eat delicately.

Adding coffee crystals to the hot water, Sarah stirred the contents, then opened the front door and sat down on the top step. The morning air was cool and brisk and she wrapped her quilted robe around her bare legs. Leaning against the banister, she stared over Simon's little town. In the early-morning light it seemed so peaceful. Beyond the alley and the high wooden fence, houses were nestled among trees. Here and there, lights came on and dogs barked briefly. Occasionally she heard the sound of a car.

She hadn't slept well at all and it wasn't because she had been afraid for their safety. Twice during the night when she had gotten up, she had spotted a white cruiser drive down Main Street. The cops were keeping an eye on this place. No, her restlessness had come from a different source.

Cord.

Her hands tightened around the mug and she took a sip. Warmth flowed through her, but the coffee wasn't responsible for the strong heavy beat of her heart or the achy restless feeling settling low inside her. Losing her heart to the cowboy wasn't smart. It wasn't a choice she would have made with her practical physician's mind, but logic had nothing to do with feeling.

So whatever she felt for him was best ignored, and the sooner she left, the better it would be. For all of them. Cord didn't want to become involved with someone any more than she did. And she had Angel to think of, too. Simon had always been the father figure for her daughter and his death had left an empty space in Angel's life. What she feared was that she might be trying to fill that space with Cord. She didn't want Angel to become too attached to him.

She glanced down the alley, where shadows still pooled. Funny. She'd been here only two nights and already Manhattan seemed like a world away. She could feel herself changing. The silence suddenly seemed to hold no threats. Though he had never once said it out loud, she was well aware that Simon had moved back to Knight's Corner to make a home for them here. And she might have been tempted to join him if...

Abruptly she finished her coffee, shivering in the cool morning air. All that was left of Simon's dreams was a ransacked office and ashes.

And three beautiful Arabians, a voice inside her whispered.

And a town in need of a physician.
And a man who made her feel alive again.

Steeling herself against temptation, she rose to her feet. How could she even contemplate taking such a step? Especially now, with suspicion growing that the fire had been no accident. Rising, she slanted another look down the dark alley. It shouldn't take her more than a week to settle affairs at the bank, clean out the office and put the properties on the market. A real-estate agent and lawyers could handle the rest.

And then she could make plans for Angel and herself. Perhaps they would buy a house out in Nassau County, where she could stable the horses nearby.

Turning back toward the door, a movement below suddenly caught her attention. Gripping the railing, she watched as the slats of the wood fence moved and a boy crept through the gap. Peering cautiously up and down the alley, he limped toward the end of the block. Dark-haired, dressed in ragged jeans and a thin dark shirt, he blended with the shadows. At the end of the alley, behind Josie's Café, he stopped. With another furtive glance around, he opened a garbage can and began searching through it.

Sarah's heart wrenched at the sight. She never could pass a homeless person without giving them something or thinking of her own fate if Simon hadn't rescued her. Her father's family had been afraid to take her—the daughter of an American—in. If Simon hadn't been there, she would have ended up like so many other children: homeless, unwanted, unloved.

The boy looked about fourteen—two years older than she had been when she had lost her family and about the same age as her brother Akim had been.

Akim. The youngest of her brothers. The gentle one.

Tears burning her eyes, she ran into the kitchen, snatched a few bills from her purse and went back outside. As she lightly ran down the stairs, the boy was retracing his steps, a dirty tinfoil container clasped in his hands.

At her sudden appearance, he stopped, clutching the container to his chest.

"I'm not going to harm you," Sarah said gently, tears pricking her eyes as she looked into his gaunt, dirt-streaked face. Old, brown eyes stared back at her warily from beneath a shock of matted, blue-black hair. He inched closer to the gap in the fence, and Sarah noticed a small hole in his jeans in the upper third of his right thigh. There was a dark dried bloodstain surrounding it.

She sucked in her breath sharply. She had seen too many bullet holes not to recognize one when she saw it. "You're hurt," she said gently. "I'm a doctor. Won't you let me have a look at your leg?"

The boy lifted the slats, then hesitated. *"¿Una doctora?"*

Since a great many of Sarah's patients were Spanish-speaking, she had learned to speak the language adequately. *"Sí, yo soy una doctora. Por favor—* Let me help you," she pleaded.

Again the boy hesitated, his dark, suspicious, unwavering gaze searching her face. Then he glanced at the boarded-up office. *"El doctor es muerto."*

Sarah bit her lip, wondering if he had come here in search of help only to find the office closed. *"Sí.* The doctor was my father." Suddenly she recalled Cord's words of the night before: *Sometimes it takes hopeful immigrants two years to work off the fees with slave labor and prostitution. If they try to escape, they are hunted relentlessly and killed so they can't turn witness.*

Was this boy one of the hunted ones?

As if to answer her silent question, the sound of an engine suddenly rent the still morning.

The sound galvanized the boy into action. Swiftly he slipped through the gap, dragging his injured leg behind.

Before he could drop the slats, Sarah held the money out to him. "Take it, please."

For a moment the boy's body stiffened with unconscious pride. Then he snatched the money and dropped the slats back into place.

Sarah moved forward and stopped the slats from swinging, then raced up the steps. Heart pounding, she slipped inside and rushed to the mansard window in the kitchen. Standing back so she couldn't be seen, she watched a black pickup nose its way up the alley from the café, steer-horn trophies displayed on the front hood.

A hunter stalking its prey while the rest of the town was still asleep.

Shivering, Sarah crossed her arms in front of her.

Oh, Simon, what did you get yourself mixed-up in?

The boy was obviously an illegal and he was being hunted, not by the authorities, but by someone who didn't want to be seen, either. Fear suddenly welled up in her and for a moment she was tempted to load up the car and leave before the sun rose. Simon's little Eden was a viper's nest and it would be dangerous to linger here.

Then anger welled, a great wave surging through her, making her tremble. She wanted to run outside and wake up the folks of Knight's Corner, to make them see what was going in their midst.

She wanted to hit out at someone for killing her father.

For the violation of sanctuary.

For hunting children as one would hunt animals.

For treating her battle-scarred knight like a leper.

Her hands balled into fists, her pain growing with each breath along with her anger. Dear God, she hadn't felt so angry in years.

She couldn't leave.

Not until she found out what had happened to Simon. Simon who had rescued her, had taken her in, had loved her as dearly as if she had been his own flesh and blood. Without him she would have ended up like this boy, being hunted because she had been her mother's daughter. A foreigner.

So how could she turn her back on the child?

Chapter 8

By nine in the morning Main Street was awake. Stores opened, the sidewalks were swept and the parking spots in front of the grocery store and the post office filled up. Coming out of the alley, Sarah stopped for a moment, holding tightly on to Angel's hand, blinking at the bright sunshine, watching as people passed each other with friendly greetings or stopped for small chats before bustling into stores.

It was such a friendly, warm scene that Sarah wondered if the sinister manhunt at dawn had been a figment of her imagination. She had spent the past two hours wondering what she could do to help the boy. She had debated talking to the sheriff, but had decided against it, at least for now. For one, she had no proof that the driver had been searching for the boy. The two incidents could be totally unrelated and the threatening feeling could be all in her mind. Also, by now the boy might have hitched a ride with someone. Wherever he was, she prayed he was safe.

But just in case he was hiding nearby, she would buy food and leave it inside the fence tonight.

The one thing she was determined *not* to do, was tell Cord about the incident. She couldn't stop herself from caring for him, but she wasn't going to send him into danger again.

"Come on, Mommy, I'm hungry," Angel said, impatiently tugging at Sarah's hand.

At the thought of food, Sarah's stomach churned, but she allowed Angel to drag her along. Halfway down the block at the beauty parlor, she spotted a very pregnant young woman draw a chair outside and climb on top of it, reaching for a string of Christmas lights the storm had torn down. With an exclamation of concern Sarah rushed over, steadying the chair with one hand while holding out the other. "Let me do that. You shouldn't climb on chairs in your condition."

Startled, the woman paused, then took Sarah's hand and awkwardly climbed down. She was petite, no more than five feet with short auburn curls and merry blue eyes. "I've been asking my husband for the last two weeks to take the lights down, but he keeps putting it off," she explained once she was on solid ground again.

"It's no trouble," Sarah assured her, climbing onto the chair. Though she was taller by several inches, she had to stand on her toes to reach the top of the window. "Just do me a favor and hold on to my daughter. Angel, don't you dare move," she said, stretching to unhook the string.

The woman suddenly laughed. "If your little girl's name is Angel, you must be Sarah. I'm Mary Lou Coombs. I'm—" She stopped, bit her lip, then continued softly, "I was related to your father. Simon's mother was my grandmother's first cousin. I guess that makes us cousins in a way."

"Really?" Angel looked at Mary Lou with big shiny eyes. "I never had a cousin before."

Mary Lou hugged her. "Well, you've got one now." With a pat on her stomach she added, "And there's another one on the way." Straightening, she smiled up at Sarah. "Hi, cousin. I've been wanting to meet you for a long time."

Warmth stole through Sarah, and a sense of belonging suffused her. She smiled back. "Hi, Mary Lou. Simon told me about you, but he didn't say anything about Junior."

A shadow briefly dimmed Mary Lou's smile and she laid a protective hand on her stomach. "It's been touch and go. I had two miscarriages before."

"And you took a chance like that?" Frowning, Sarah looped the string of lights over her arm, then stretched to reach the other corner.

"I could ask you the same question," Cord growled through the open window as he parked his truck at the curb. Sliding from the cab, he leapt up on the sidewalk in one fluid move, his hands closing around Sarah's waist to steady her. She was so slender, he could almost span her waist despite the thick purple-and-orange sweater she wore. "What are you trying to do, Doc, break your neck?"

Slowly Sarah turned, smiling down at him. "I'm taller than Mary Lou and I'm not pregnant," she pointed out sensibly. She glanced over her shoulder at Mary Lou, who was watching them with a frown. Sarah decided to ignore it. "I'm sure you two know each other, so I don't have to introduce you."

"We went to school together," Cord explained dryly. He gave Mary Lou a cool nod, then winked at Angel, who smiled back at him. "Now, are you coming down from there or do I have to lift you?"

While Sarah slowly looped the string of lights over her arm, she glanced around. They were attracting considerable attention, she realized. If she'd planned the scene, she couldn't have done it better, she thought smugly. "I always wanted to be rescued by a knight," she said, placing her hands on his powerful, leather-clad shoulders. He even looked the part of the good guy; big and solid, the shirt beneath his open leather jacket a startling white against his deep tan and his blond hair ruffled by the breeze. Her fingers itched to brush it back. "So I may as well indulge my fantasy and have you lift me down."

For an instant Cord's eyes gleamed in response to the mischievous sparkle in her eyes. Then they narrowed on her face, taking in the smug look. "I warned you not to meddle," he said as he lowered her to the ground, releasing her the instant she'd regained her balance and stepped on the chair.

Sarah's smile was guileless as she looked up at him, still looping the string of lights over her arm as he took it off the hooks. He hadn't slept much, either, she thought. Lines bracketed his mouth and fanned around his eyes. "I told you, I never meddle," she said, her voice low. "But it would be nice if you said hello to Mary Lou, or Angel will begin to wonder what is going on. She's very excited about having found a cousin of sorts. She never had one before."

Cord said nothing as he jumped off the chair. When he carried it into the beauty parlor, Angel dashed after him, crying, "Cord, I've got a cousin...."

Mary Lou glanced after them, a thoughtful look in her eyes. Turning back to Sarah, she asked, "Are you staying at the ranch?"

Shaking her head, Sarah handed Mary Lou the lights, swiftly explaining the rescue and her move into the apartment. "Do you have time for a cup of decaf?"

Mary Lou shook her head. "I have an appointment in fifteen minutes." She lifted Sarah's braid. "You have beautiful hair. So shiny and thick. But the ends could do with a trim. If you want to drop by later, we can talk while I cut your hair."

"Don't you dare cut her hair," Cord growled as he joined them, carrying Angel.

Mary Lou placed her hands on her hips, her eyes beginning to twinkle. "Some things never change." Turning to Sarah, she explained, "Cord never dated girls with short hair." She speared her fingers through her carrot curls. "Perhaps that's why he never asked me for a date."

The left corner of Cord's mouth kicked up slowly. "That wasn't it. I was warned off, very painfully I might add, by a boy named Tom who was four grades above us."

Mary Lou chuckled delightedly. "I had no idea. I think I'll have a talk with that big husband of mine. Beating up on kids four years younger than him!" Abruptly, her grin vanished and she said, her voice suddenly serious, "I'm glad you're back, Cord. I've been wanting to call, but, well, you know Tom. He always was jealous of you."

Something softened in Cord's hard face. "Good Lord, even now?"

"Especially now." With a pat on her stomach, Mary Lou walked back into the beauty parlor, tossing over her shoulder, "But you're welcome to visit anytime. Bring Sarah and Angel along."

"Thanks." Cord stared after her, then shot Sarah a bland look. "How do you do it, Doc?"

Sarah chin came up. "Do what?"

Cord glanced at Angel, who was listening intently, and grimaced. "Never mind." There were shadows beneath Sarah's eyes as if she hadn't slept well. He hadn't, either. The house had seemed too empty, too silent after they had left, and he had worried about them. He would have slept better on Simon's old couch or in the truck parked outside her apartment. "Is everything all right?"

"Fine," Sarah said swiftly. "What are you doing in town?"

Cord's eyes narrowed, searching her face. She was hiding something from him. "I have some business at the bank. And I wanted to check up on you." Impatiently he glanced up and down the street. They were the cynosure of all eyes and if he hadn't known better, he would have sworn that she had planned it that way. He spotted a heavyset woman with short blue-gray hair glaring at them from across the road. Recognizing Lorna Devlin, he swore silently. "Where were you going?"

"To get breakfast. Want to join us?" The look she slanted him was pure challenge.

"Don't push it," Cord warned dryly. "Besides, I had mine hours ago."

"Please, Cord," Angel pleaded, wrapping her arms tightly around his neck.

"A cup of coffee, then. My treat." Sarah added her pleading to her daughter's.

Cord flashed her a mocking grin. "Around here, city slicker, a man still picks up the tab."

Sarah scowled. "Talk about male chauvinism."

"What's that?" Angel asked.

Sarah sent Cord a provocative look, then turned to her daughter. "A male chauvinist is a man who thinks that women are weaker, dumber and smaller than him."

"Well, Cord is bigger and stronger," Angel pointed out logically.

Sarah slanted her daughter a rueful look. "On whose side are you, anyway?"

Cord chuckled.

Angel grinned.

The sight of them standing together in the sunshine, smiling, tugged at Sarah's heart. She wished she'd had her camera with her to capture this moment out of time. Slowly she moved her eyes, only her eyes, until they met his. They were not so calm now. Fire, barely banked, burned in them and she caught her breath softly.

A shadow fell across them. Startled, Sarah glanced at a woman dressed in a blue pantsuit bearing down on them, taken aback by the look of pure hatred in her small beady eyes.

As the woman sailed past them, she muttered, "This is a disgrace. Don't you have any shame? Conducting your affair right in the middle of Main Street and in front of the little girl, too!"

Stunned, Sarah stared after the woman until she had disappeared into the beauty parlor. When she glanced back at Cord, his face was shuttered and hard. Angel's smile had vanished and she had pushed her head into the crook of Cord's neck. Sarah could have cheerfully strangled the stranger for causing Cord's withdrawal and the loss of Angel's smile. "Who was *that?*"

"Lorna Devlin." Cord lowered Angel to the ground and turned to leave. "You'll enjoy your breakfast a lot more without me," he said.

Hurt, aching with abandonment, Sarah watched Cord walk away from them with his long limbed stride. The sidewalk cleared in front of him. Two young women retreated back into the store they were just emerging from and an older man crossed the street. At the bank's entrance two men turned their backs and continued talking to each other, ignoring Cord. By the time he had disappeared inside, Sarah's eyes were blurred with tears.

"Mommy?" Angel gripped Sarah's hand tightly, a puzzled, almost hurt, look in her brown eyes. "Why don't people like Cord?"

Sarah blinked away the moisture in her eyes, hesitating before answering. "Not all people like each other. Isn't there a girl in your kindergarten that you don't like?"

"Kerry," Angel said promptly. "She always steals my crayons."

Josie's Café was the meeting place in town where people dropped by for coffee, a meal and the latest news. Today the hottest news was Sarah's arrival and the place was buzzing with it. When Sarah and Angel entered the small cheerful place, decorated in shades of brown and burnt orange, heads turned and the buzzing stopped. Being the target of all eyes unnerved Angel. Inching closer to Sarah she whispered, "Why are people staring at us?"

"Because we're strangers," Sarah explained as the buzzing started again. "This is a small town and the people all know each other."

Before she could choose a table, a tall sparse woman in her fifties with frizzed gray hair and a bright orange bow that matched the decor waved at them from behind the counter and pointed at two empty stools in front of it. "Why don't you sit right here. Everyone is curious about you and wants to meet you. So you may as well get it over with all at once."

For the next few minutes Sarah was busy shaking hands and accepting condolences, meeting people her father had mentioned occasionally. One of the women, blond, shy Rosa Lyn Jenkins, showed off her fifteen-month-old son, Pauly, whom Simon had delivered. Josie poured coffee and made Angel blueberry pancakes—from scratch.

At first Sarah felt a little overwhelmed by the welcome, but soon she relaxed. This, she thought, was the small hometown Simon had described to her, complete with the warmth and the open friendliness.

But the warmth was shattered a little while later, when Lorna Devlin sailed into the room, her hair freshly styled. Her face was red and her breath came out in short gasps as if she had run the whole way down the street. As she advanced toward Sarah, the rest of the women in the café fell silent and made room for her.

Sarah stiffened and slipped off her swivel chair to step in front of Angel. "Hello," she said calmly. "You must be Lorna Devlin. I'm Dr. Durand."

Lorna stopped in front of her, her ample bosom heaving. "I know who you are, miss. A troublemaker, just like your father."

Sarah crossed her arms in front of her, a dangerous glint in her eyes. "I think we'll leave my father out of this discussion," she said firmly. "He is not around any longer to defend himself."

Before she could stop Angel, her daughter slid off her chair and pushed past Sarah, tears filling her eyes. Her blueberry-stained lips trembled when she cried, "My grandpa was no troublemaker. You're a nasty lady."

"Hush, Angel." Sarah placed her arms around her daughter and drew her against her legs. Out of the corner of her eyes, she watched Rosa Lyn pick up Pauly and leave.

Lorna drew back, her face livid, her jowls trembling with fury. "And you're a nasty brat. But then, that's to be expected, with a mother like yours." Her small beady eyes fixed on Sarah. "Why don't you go back where you came from. We want no foreigners in this town."

Restless murmurs rose up from the other women. From a nearby table one of the men said, "That's going too far. Ought to do something."

Sarah wasn't going to wait around for anyone to interfere on her behalf. She picked up Angel, hugging her tightly. "That's enough," she said sharply, angry color staining her cheeks as she raked Lorna with a contemptuous glance. "I don't care what you call me. But have the decency to leave my daughter out of it. Now, would you let me pass."

She was standing between two swivel chairs and Lorna was standing right in front of her, two hundred and twenty pounds blocking Sarah's way. Sarah took a step toward her, but the woman stood her ground, baring her small sharp teeth like a snarling pit bull.

"If you were concerned about your daughter, you wouldn't carry on with that rapist. And if you're planning to take over your daddy's office, we'll run you out of town."

Sarah began to feel sick, nausea and apprehension curling in her stomach at the menace in the woman's voice. Her arms tightened around her daughter protectively. The other diners with whom she had joked only minutes ago were muttering protests, but no one made an attempt to stop Lorna. Anger welled up. She had never struck a person in her life, but she was so angry, she wanted to slap the woman's face. "Nothing could induce me to stay in this town," she said scornfully, shoving the woman out of her way.

Lorna stumbled backward. Before she could regain her balance, Sarah had brushed past her, then stopped and glared at the rest of the crowd. "Cord Knight is a decent, kind and honorable man who, I'd like to point out, has rid the town of some dangerous criminals in the past."

With an outraged gasp, Lorna charged after her.

It took Cord less than forty minutes to conclude his business at the bank. Leaving the building, he stopped on the sidewalk, watching the bustle around him. The encounter with Lorna was still eating at him. No one insulted a woman and a child under his protection in the middle of Main Street and got away with it.

Perhaps it was time to make the good folks of Knight's Corner realize that he had no intention of leaving again, that they couldn't chase him out of town by cutting him dead. His family owned a fair amount of the real estate on this street, including Josie's Café. People would have to deal with him if he forced them to acknowledge him. His lips compressed into a hard bitter line. It wasn't what he had wanted. Somewhere, deep down, he had hoped that they eventually would come around on their own. It would have soothed his battered pride if they had.

To hell with pride, he thought grimly. Crossing the sidewalk, he slid into his truck. As he pulled into the parking lot on the side of the café, he noticed a small crowd of people outside the entrance. Fear shot through him and he leapt from the cab. The crowd parted as he strode toward the door. Behind him he heard a siren, then the spewing of gravel as the sheriff's cruiser came to a sliding stop a few feet away. By that time, Cord was charging through the door, almost knocking Sarah down.

Right behind her was Lorna Devlin, her face bright red, screeching like a banshee, one of her pudgy ring-studded hands reaching for Sarah.

Cord caught the hand in midair, his fingers snapping around the soft wrist like a steel manacle. Lorna cried out, and clawed at Cord's face, scratching him. "Don't you dare touch me, you—"

"That's enough!" Cord said, his cold voice cutting off Lorna's insult.

Then Lorna spotted the sheriff and screamed, "I want you to arrest this man. He's assaulting me."

Sarah ducked and retreated to the corner of the room. Leaning against a booth, she buried her hand in Angel's dusky curls, pressing her small face into the crook of her neck. "It's all right, sweetheart," she said softly, soothing her daughter with the sound of her voice and soft strokes down her trembling back.

Dan Holt glanced at Lorna, a look of distaste crossing his face. "Let her go," he said to Cord with weary resignation. Then he turned to Lorna. "You're disturbing the peace, Lorna, so I'm here to stop you."

Lorna spun around and picked up a bottle of ketchup from a nearby table, holding it up threateningly. "Don't you dare come any closer," she cried. Then with a speed unexpected for someone her size, she darted behind the counter, hurling abuses, steak sauce, ketchup bottles and salt shakers at the sheriff and Cord. The last few remaining patrons dashed out the door.

At the sound of the commotion, Angel raised her head and watched. Tears fading, her eyes widened and her mouth dropped open at the sight. "Mommy, look at the nasty lady. She's making a mess."

"Now, Lorna, you stop that, or I'll have to haul you off to jail," Dan Holt shouted above the din.

"You wouldn't dare," Lorna yelled, picking up a bottle of mustard. "Hugh won't stand by and watch his mother being hauled off to jail. You'll be out of a job before the day's over."

The plastic bottle, launched from somewhere behind the counter, landed on the floor a foot away from the sheriff's boots, breaking and splattering mustard over his sharply creased pants.

Angel started giggling.

Dan Holt stared down at the mess in disgust. "That woman's getting to be a real menace. I wish someone would press charges against her, but everyone is too scared of Devlin."

Cord had jumped out of the way just in time. Retreating behind a potted plant, he cocked one brow in challenge. "Well, Sheriff, what are you going to do about it?"

Dan Holt shot Cord a wintry smile. "What would you do in my place?"

"Leap across the counter and snag her," Cord suggested tongue-in-cheek.

Dan Holt eyed the leftover pancakes Lorna had snatched from a plate. "You've got to be kidding," he growled as the pancakes came sailing through the air and joined the mustard with a splash. "There's got to be a way to get to her without hurting her and without looking like a walking advertisement for Josie's kitchen afterward."

Angel giggled again, then clapped her hand in front of her mouth.

Cord winked at her, then turned back to the sheriff. "Sure. You can call for reinforcements."

Dan Holt groaned. "To calm down one elderly woman? I'd never live that down. You know what small towns are like. They'd still be talking about it when I'm eighty."

"Yeah, I know," Cord said flatly. Then a grin kicked up. "Or you could ask, very nicely, of course, for my help.

We're both quick. If we round the counter at the same time, she'll be so frazzled—"

"What's in it for you?" Dan Holt growled, dodging a syrup bottle.

Cord shrugged, slanting a look at Sarah and Angel. "Let's just say, I have a bone to pick with Lorna for making a little girl cry. I want her locked up for a few hours."

Dan Holt looked down at his boots and pants. "Only hours? Are you kidding?" A beatific grin spread over his face. "Assaulting an officer with mustard will cost her at least one night."

They waited until Lorna threw her next missile. Before she could grab another one they ducked low and weaved between the tables in a twin assault.

It was over within seconds, each man grabbing one wrist of the screaming, struggling woman.

Lorna was still yelling threats when Cord and the sheriff led her, handcuffed, to his cruiser.

After the sheriff had left, the silence in the café was deafening. Josie came from the back of the kitchen, stared down at the bottles and the stained floor and swore beneath her breath. Sarah sank into the booth, shaking her head in disbelief.

Angel glanced around and said, "What a mess."

Josie turned around and looked at her. "You can say that again." With a sigh she walked to the door and hung the Closed sign on the window. "I don't know what the world's coming to." She turned to Sarah, an embarrassed look on her face. "I know, I should've done something besides calling the sheriff to stop Lorna," she apologized, wiping at a ketchup stain on her brown blouse.

Before Sarah could respond, Cord came back inside. He wasn't nearly so forgiving. Anger burned in his eyes and his voice was harsh when he said, "I always thought you had guts, Josie."

Josie's mouth compressed, her lined face flushing a bright angry red. "I thought you had more guts, too, so that makes us even." Despite the fact that she had closed the café for business, she sent a furtive glance around the room, as if to make certain that no one was listening before she continued, "When you disappeared, Big John lost all interest in the ranch and the town. Things have changed around here since, Cord."

Frowning, Cord asked slowly, "In what way? The town seems pretty normal to me."

"On the surface, yes." Josie sighed. "But folks who tangle with Devlin suddenly find their tires slashed and their windshields broken—or worse."

"What do you mean by 'worse'?" Sharp gray eyes locked with hazel ones, demanding information the other was afraid to give.

Josie lowered her eyes after a few seconds, wiping her damp hands on her stained apron. "Devlin went to San Antonio this morning. When he gets back there'll be hell to pay over this business with Lorna, you mark my words."

Cord's jaw hardened. "If he threatens you, let me know." Turning to Sarah, he held out his hand. "Come on, Doc. Maisy will have lunch ready soon."

Taking his hand, Sarah slipped out of the booth. "Those scratches need cleaning first."

Josie headed toward the back saying, "I'll get the first-aid kit."

Gently Sarah touched his jaw and turned it to the light, grimacing at the sight of his broken skin. "That looks nasty," she said, pushing him back down onto the seat just as Josie returned with the kit.

"I have some fresh baked chocolate-chip cookies in the back," she said. "Perhaps Angel would like to take a few with her, as how she didn't finish her breakfast."

"Mommy?" Angel looked at Sarah pleadingly, sliding out of the booth. "I'm hungry."

Sarah nodded. "One cookie only. Maisy will be disappointed if you don't eat any lunch."

"I'm very hungry."

"They're small," Josie said. Holding on to Angel's hand, she guided her around the puddles on the floor, stopping here and there to pick up bottles.

"All right. Two," Sarah called after them. Opening the kit, she said, "Why don't you take Angel with you? I'll follow you as soon as I've helped Josie clean up this mess."

"No way," Cord growled, eyeing the contents with a grimace. "I'm not letting you out of my sight again, Doc. Every time I do, you get into trouble."

Protest welled up, then vanished at the concern in his eyes. "You okay?" he asked.

Nodding, Sarah opened a bottle of disinfectant and soaked a pad. "How good are you at swinging mops?" she asked, turning his head.

"Oh, no, I did my part."

"I know," Sarah scoffed, her lips beginning to twitch. "You two were real heroes. Dodging mustard and ketchup bottles."

Cord grinned and started to turn his head, but Sarah stayed his movement. "This is going to sting," she warned, swabbing his skin with the disinfectant. Carefully she held the pad pressed against the wound to stop the trickle of blood.

Looking down at him just then, she was struck by how truly handsome he was, with his thick blond unruly hair and broad forehead, his widely spaced gray eyes, his thick dark gold-tipped lashes, straight nose and high cheekbones. Even the beard shadow that he sported heightened the intensely male line of his jaw. It was more than his features that appealed to her so vividly; it was his masculine strength, tempered by the gentleness, she knew he harbored within even when trying to control a madwoman like Lorna.

"You've got to stop fighting, cowboy, or you'll start scaring the ladies away with your scars," she teased. His wasn't the face of a safe, kind lover. He would break her heart if she gave him the chance, and, fool that she was, she was tempted to give it to him.

Just a few days of happiness, temptation whispered into her ear. What can it hurt? Just a few nights of passion and the longer you hesitate, the fewer nights there will be.

Cord stared up into her face and the air fisted in his lungs. She looked at him with midnight dark eyes that mirrored the need aching in his own soul. "I only care about one lady and she doesn't mind the scars."

Sarah's hand shook slightly. "It wouldn't be nice of the lady to mind the scars, especially since she has quite a few of her own," she said, withdrawing her hand. The bleeding had stopped, she noticed with satisfaction.

Cord stood up. "Am I going to make it, Doc?"

Sarah chuckled. "Well enough for KP, cowboy. Come on, let's get to work. Mop or broom?"

"Just a minute." Cord cupped her chin, pulling her to him with that subtle pressure alone. When his mouth met hers, her lips were still curved. This time she didn't stiffen, didn't hesitate, didn't protest. With a sigh of acceptance she opened up to him.

They left Angel with Maisy that afternoon, baking cookies. Upon Sarah's return to the office after lunch, Cord stayed to help her move the desk and other heavy pieces of furniture. In the alley the pile of broken chairs and filing cabinets grew. On their last trip outside, Sarah stopped and glanced at the fence. "Who lives behind here?"

"The Taggerts. Why?"

Sarah shrugged and said casually, "I was wondering if they heard something. Wrecking the furniture must have made a lot of noise."

"The Taggerts are in their sixties. He used to work on drilling sites, so his hearing is probably shot." Still, it was something to look in to. Walking back into the waiting room, Cord put his hand on her shoulder and slowly turned her to face him. "Will you be all right on your own for a while?" he asked. She was more composed than she had been yesterday. Still, there were shadows in her eyes and lines of tension around her mouth. He hated to leave her with this mess, but the sheriff was expecting him.

Sarah glanced around the room, stripped down to bare walls and wooden floors. No, she didn't want him to leave, but it was dangerous to become too dependent on him. Besides, she still had to make it to the grocery store, and she had a feeling that Cord would not approve of what she was about to do. "I'll be fine," she assured him.

Cord pointed at the boards covering the windows. "I'll take those off when I come back."

Sarah shook her head. "I don't think that's necessary. It won't take me but a few days to pack up this stuff."

Cord shot her a sharp look. He was beginning to dislike the thought of her leaving. But all he said was, "It would be safer. People walk past here all day long. If there's trouble, someone would notice it."

Sarah dug in her heels, a mulish set to her chin. "I feel safer with the boards up. I can always leave the door open."

Cord glared at her in exasperation. "So that anyone can walk inside."

"Oh, for heaven's sake," Sarah said. "There's little enough left to steal."

"It isn't burglars I'm worried about," Cord drawled. "You stirred up a whole lot of trouble today." He saw the light of battle leap into her eyes and raised his hand palm up in a gesture of peace, smiling crookedly. "I'm not blaming you." He slid his hands into his pockets, his smile fading abruptly, his face turning hard. "Anyone should have the freedom of standing out in the sunshine and laughing.

Anyone should be able to walk into a restaurant without being abused. This used to be a pretty nice place. Maybe not the little Eden Simon described to you, but safer than most. But things have changed around here. Just how much I didn't realize until today.''

Sarah crossed to his side, unable to stand the hard bitter look on his face. Gently she laid a hand on his arm. ''There's a Lorna Devlin in every town,'' she said quietly.

Frowning, Cord stared down at her slender hand, wondering how it had happened, but he didn't feel nearly as alone anymore. ''It isn't Lorna I'm worried about. For as long as I can remember, she's been a witch. What worries me is that no one, not Josie, or old Pete, dared to interfere,'' he said quietly.

''Josie never pulled her punches before. Old Pete, hell, he once chased a bunch of thieves from his garage with a wrench. Today he was standing outside the café. People only change that much when they're scared.''

Chapter 9

It had been more than a year since Cord had visited the sheriff's office, but the place hadn't changed. Walking into the small crowded squad room, he grimaced. Law-enforcement offices all smelled the same. The place reeked of stale smoke, burned coffee and disinfectant cleaner. He was suddenly glad that he'd quit.

The news of this morning's fight was still the main topic of conversation. Tall, lanky Larry Watson, the youngest deputy on the small, twelve-man force, was pouring himself a cup of coffee at the back of the room. At Cord's entrance he looked up and grinned. "What'd you catch? Mustard, ketchup or pancakes?"

"Scratches," Cord said with disgust.

Sharon Hart, the thirty-year-old dispatcher cum secretary, looked up from her corner desk. "You always were too good-lookin' for your own good," she joked, but winced when she saw the angry red lines on his cheeks. "Sure hope that young lady doctor of yours took care of them. Want some coffee?"

Cord glanced at the thick black brew in the pot. From past experience he knew that Sharon had a heavy hand with the coffee grinds. "Did you make that poison?" When Sharon nodded, he said dryly, "I'll pass."

"What's wrong with my coffee? It's guaranteed to make hair grow on your chest."

"Maybe his lady doctor likes his chest smooth."

Cord's eyes narrowed with warning. "I wouldn't know."

Larry caught the warning with a good-natured shrug. "Must be losing your touch, then. Because she sure is sweet on you. Defended you something fierce, I heard. Like you was the Lone Ranger. If a woman ever went to bat for me like that, I'd make for the border and marry her before she got away."

It wasn't a bad idea, Cord thought. He'd never met another woman who would suit him as well as Sarah did. And the thought of becoming Angel's father greatly appealed to him. Sarah wanted him. She even cared about him. But he had a feeling that the only reason she was allowing him close was because she planned to leave in a few days.

Dan Holt came into the room and eyed his deputy with a frown. "You gab too much, Watson, and your boots need polishing."

With a glance at Cord he said, "Let's go to my office."

Cord followed Holt down the narrow hall to his utilitarian cramped office, a watchful look in his eyes. This place may not have changed, but people's attitudes definitely had. A week ago Watson and Sharon had driven past him with no more than a polite nod. The sudden change made him uneasy. Helping Holt may have broken down a few barriers, but the real reason for their warm welcome was, Cord suspected grimly, that he had openly joined the fight against Devlin.

His suspicion proved correct. The moment the door closed behind them, Dan Holt said bluntly, "This thing with Devlin is getting out of hand. I could use your help."

Frowning, Cord leaned against the door. "Depends on what kind of help. Why don't you tell me what's going on first," he suggested slowly. He'd never taken on a job before without some knowledge of what was involved, and he wasn't going to start now.

Dan Holt leaned against the windowsill, gently touching the small feathery needles of a bonsai. Shaping young bushes into exquisite trees was his hobby. "You can't turn a blind eye any longer. As of this morning you are involved."

Cord silently acknowledged the truth. He was in even deeper than Holt knew. Not only because he suspected Harper's involvement, but because, somehow, over the past few days his feelings had changed. Revenge seemed less important now than ensuring that Sarah and Angel could walk anywhere in his town without fear. "Maybe so, but I would still like to know what I'm getting into. Why don't we start with the fire? In your opinion, was it an accident? Or arson?"

"Arson. But I can't prove it," Dan Holt warned. "Walter Bratt did some rewiring at the old house. He insists that there was nothing wrong with the fuse box and that it had a lid."

Since Bratt didn't do shoddy work, someone else must have removed the lid and tampered with the wires. Though he'd suspected it, pain and anger flashed through him and his jaw hardened. *"Damn!"*

For a moment Holt's eyes softened with compassion. He had only known Simon briefly, but he, too, had liked the man. But he had a murderer to catch and a frightened town on his hands and he couldn't afford to waste more time. "Pilar Torres, his nurse, said he received at least two threatening phone calls about that time. And then there was the uproar with Lorna when the doc treated some illegals who are working on the Turner spread."

Cord's eyes narrowed, but he didn't comment. "What else?"

"We've had an influx of illegals during the last six months and a few petty thefts, like clothing, food, cash—things a person would grab if he was on the run. I notified the INS and the FBI, but Devlin checked out clean. He only employs immigrants with *amicas*. Some of the other farmers and ranchers aren't that particular, but not in a big way. Some people were angry with the doc when he treated those two farm workers, especially after Lorna made a big fuss about it. But, hell, you don't kill a doctor for helping a human being."

Cord wasn't so sure. "Old Devlin put nine small ranchers and farmers in the area out of business. They lost everything, and in some cases the land had been in their families for generations. Folks were pretty bitter. Rusty's parents were among them."

Dan Holt's eyes widened. "You think Rusty might have—"

Cord shook his head firmly. "Rusty's a crook, but he's no murderer. And he has a thing about drugs. He wouldn't get involved with *coyotes*." Cord thought back to the conversation he'd had with the bartender two days ago. Had Rusty tried to warn him about Simon?

The sheriff pushed away from the window and walked around his neat desk. Hiking up his pants, he sat down. "Maybe. The fire was a professional job anyway—no trace of anything. What made you think of drugs? None of the DEA boys have come around and asked questions."

"That only means no one is *selling* around here. But illegals often act as couriers to pay off the *coyotes'* fees."

Holt tipped his chair back, for a moment staring into space. "Let's say Devlin is involved in it somewhere. Now, you don't need much space to hide drugs. People are a different matter, though. I keep pretty close tabs on him, but I haven't spotted anything unusual. The only vehicles larger than a pickup to enter the Devlin ranch in the last few weeks were cattle trucks.''

He pointed at the chair in front of the desk. "Do you have any suggestions on how they move their goods? I'm still new at this job. It'll take me less than thirty seconds to tell you all I know about *coyotes* and their operations.''

Cord hesitated. "Transporting illegals is only one of the steps,'' he said. "You need safe houses to hide them for a while.''

A glimmer of excitement sparked in the sheriff's eyes. "There are a few abandoned homesteads and barns in the neighborhood. D'you have time to check them out?''

Cord shook his head. "Dr. Durand is cleaning up the office and I hate to leave her alone. Not with Lorna sitting in jail.''

"I'll send Watson to keep an eye on her,'' Dan Holt said, picking up the phone. "Right now the ground is soft from the rains and we may find something. In a few days, all traces may be gone.''

The sheriff had a point. Reluctant though he was to delegate Sarah's safety to someone else, Cord pushed himself away from the door and sat down.

After Cord left, Sarah locked the doors and cleaned.

There were leftover cleaning supplies beneath the sink in the bathroom. She washed down walls, mopped floors, emptied cabinets and wiped down equipment that had escaped destruction. The only room she didn't touch was Simon's office. She couldn't handle that just yet. Also, if she wanted to salvage the old Keshan carpet, she needed help to move the heavy desk. By the time she'd finished, she had her fear and anger back under control. The place reeked of ammonia, but at least the musky odor was gone.

After locking both front and back doors securely, Sarah played with Sheba at the apartment and drank a cup of coffee. Then she walked to Bill Cowley's Supermarket on the next block. The place was small, compact and almost deserted, making Sarah feel suddenly conspicuous.

She doubted that either the elderly man behind the cash register or the two women who started a discussion on the merits of one hot sauce over another at her entrance would approve of her actions. They greeted her with friendly "howdy's," but kept their distance, as if afraid to talk to her after this morning's incident, but their eyes followed her as she pushed the cart down the aisles.

Sarah bought several cans of Sheba's favorite cat food, a quart of milk, fresh fruit, cleaning materials and rubber gloves. Then she added granola bars, trail mixes and juice in small, lunch-size containers. She hesitated over the cans of beef stew, but the selection was limited and there was no chicken soup that didn't need to be diluted with water. She had found plastic spoons in the office, so she only added a cheap can opener to the list. She waited until both women had left before paying for her purchases.

"Looks like you're planning on staying a while," Bill Cowley said as he started to ring up the items.

Sarah tensed, but his ruddy face showed no suspicion. And why should he find her purchases odd? Stew was nutritious, and he couldn't know that she didn't eat red meat. He also couldn't know about this morning's encounter. It was her own nervousness that made her jumpy and it would have to stop. "The office is quite a mess. It'll take a few days to straighten out. I have to clean it first before I can begin to pack."

"It's a shame what happened." Bill's soft drawl was tinged with regret. "I had a heart attack last year and your father saved my life. I wouldn't have made it to Kingsley County. We sure need a doctor here. But I guess after what happened this morning—" He picked up one of the cans of stew. "If you get tired of this stuff and don't want to eat at Josie's, there's a fast-food place close to the motel and a Mexican restaurant two miles past the church."

Sarah shook her head. "This morning has nothing to do with my decision." She smiled tautly, doubting that he would be quite as friendly if he knew for whom she was buying the food.

The door opened and another customer entered. At the sight of the gray-haired cowboy, his ruddy color faded and an anxious look came into his eyes. "Howdy, Rod. What brings you into town?" he asked nervously, his fingers suddenly flying over the old-fashioned register keys.

"Lorna wants some magazines while she waits for Hugh to get her out of jail." His pale blue eyes narrowed on Sarah and he advanced slowly, like a predator stalking his prey. "You'll have some fast explaining to do when the boss gets back."

Apprehension shot through Sarah as she recognized the brawler from the Coyote Lounge. His eyes were the pale, glittering blue of a desert sky at noon, cruel and merciless.

She took a paper bag from the counter and shook it out. "I'm looking forward to having a word with Mr. Devlin myself."

Rod Snyder stopped so close to her, she could feel the cold menace radiating from him. Sarah didn't dare retreat or show her nervousness, but continued bagging her purchases with a show of unconcern.

As she reached for a second can of stew, he snatched it from her hand. "What's the matter? Don't you like the food at Josie's?" he asked, tossing the can like a ball from hand to hand.

Sarah's mouth compressed. She was getting tired of being intimidated by everyone from the Devlin ranch. "I wouldn't know. I never had a chance to taste it," she said calmly. She watched him widening the distance between his hands, waiting for the opportune moment to snatch at the can. It came when the door to the store opened and a deputy walked in. As Rod glanced over his shoulder, she caught the can and dropped it into her bag. "Get your own food."

For a moment his light blue eyes narrowed menacingly. Then he shrugged and walked past her to the magazine rack.

The deputy strolled up to the cash register. "Everything all right, Bill?" he asked.

There was a moment's hesitation, then the store owner nodded. "Fine and dandy," he said, totaling up Sarah's bill.

After paying, Sarah forced herself to walk out of the store slowly. Outside, she stopped for a moment and took a deep breath of fresh air. As she started back toward the office, the deputy joined her. "Hi, I'm Deputy Watson. Cord asked me to tell you that he won't be back for a while. He thought you might need some help moving furniture." He held out his hand. "Let me carry the bag."

"It isn't heavy." Sarah's arms closed around the bag protectively. "Isn't moving furniture a little above and beyond?" she asked, battling down a surge of fear. The only explanation for the deputy's presence was that Cord had decided to work together with the sheriff. After this morning's events she should have expected it. But she didn't want him to charge into danger and possibly run into his old enemy, Harper, again. It wasn't what she'd intended when she'd decided to smooth things over for him, Sarah thought, irritation and frustration mingling with her fears. The least he could have done, was let her know what he was up to.

Watson shrugged good naturedly. "Moving furniture for a pretty woman beats trying to catch speeders." Then his easy grin vanished, a serious look replacing it. "There's going to be trouble. I wish we could keep you out of it, Doc, but unfortunately you're already involved."

"I know and I'm grateful for your presence," Sarah said, clutching the bag tighter. It seemed that from the moment she had rented her car in San Antonio, things had begun to slip out of her control. She felt as if she were sitting on a roller coaster that was picking up speed, drawing her from one danger into the next. But despite the fear curling in her stomach, she also felt a certain satisfaction. At twelve she had lost everything—her family and her home. The revolution in Iran had been beyond her control, beyond everyone's control. But this was a different fight and she was determined to help Cord win it. For Simon's sake, as well. Perhaps then she would find some peace.

It was then that she noticed a small crowd in front of Simon's office. Abruptly she slowed down. "Who are all those people, Deputy?" she asked warily.

Deputy Watson studied the group. "Looks like your welcoming committee," he said, satisfaction in his voice. "The wiry *hombre* with the salt-and-pepper hair and the big pitcher of iced tea is Pete. The woman with the pink-striped overalls and the cake pan in her hand is Mary Lou's mother, Luella. The woman with the plate of brownies is Sandy Briggs, and, of course, you know Josie. Sure hope that box in her hand is filled with chocolate-chip cookies. They're the best."

Sarah suddenly felt like grinning and a feeling of warmth stole over her.

They were no longer alone. People were coming around and joining the fight.

It was past one in the morning when Cord drove into the alley and parked beside Sarah's Toyota. He was bone weary, and his body ached, begging for sleep. They must have checked every abandoned house and barn in a fifteen-mile radius, hoping to find signs of smuggling activities. Quietly he opened the door and slid from the cab. All they had come across had been sights of cattle rustling near the abandoned chapel, ten miles out of town. But tired though he was, his mind refused to shut down.

Looking up, he saw a faint glimmer of light coming from Sarah's bedroom. He wondered if she was awake or if she was sleeping with the light on to keep the nightmares at bay. Emotions curled tightly inside him, among them a strange yearning to protect and shield her from further pain and to make this place a bright and happy haven for her and Angel. Perhaps then she would decide to stay. Walking to the office, he checked the rear door and tested the boards, then turned toward the stairs.

With his hand on the railing, he hesitated. All afternoon and evening he had wondered how to tell her about Simon's murder, but there was no gentle way, he thought grimly. No matter how he said it, she would be devastated. He didn't have to talk about it tonight, but he couldn't keep the knowledge from her indefinitely.

A cool breeze whispered in the branches of the trees on the other side of the fence. Above him, a thin cloud moved across the bright sliver of the moon. A smuggler's moon. A chill prickled down his back. His eyes narrowed watchfully as he glanced up and down the dark alley, seeing nothing but sensing a presence. The sensation remained, that of a dark intent gaze, and the hair at the back of his neck rose.

Suddenly headlights flared to life a little farther down the lane and an engine started up. Cord tensed; then, recognizing the flashers on top of the car, he relaxed. He waited until the county cruiser pulled up next to him. As the window slid down he recognized Deputy Ryder. "You scared the hell out of me," he growled.

White teeth flashed beneath a black mustache. "Just doing my job," the Deputy drawled. "Are you staying here the rest of the night?"

Cord hesitated briefly, then nodded. After today everyone in town believed they were having an affair anyway. Besides, he'd lain awake last night worrying about them. He doubted that tonight would be any different, even with the deputy stationed in the alley. "Did you notice anything unusual?"

Ryder shook his head. "Real quiet tonight. But Watson said that Rod Snyder was trying to intimidate the doc at the grocery store. And Devlin was fit to be tied when he stormed into the station about eight to pick up Lorna. The sheriff shouldn't have gone soft, if you ask me. He should have kept Lorna overnight. Devlin made all kinds of threats later at Josie's."

Cord's hands balled into fists. "What kind of threats?" he asked with dangerous softness.

"How he was going to pay the doc back for having his mother arrested. From what I heard the doc was the victim, but I guess Devlin needs to blame someone." Ryder slanted a concerned look at the apartment, then turned back to Cord. "Can't you convince her and her daughter to stay at the Circle K? Everyone would sleep a whole lot easier if they moved."

Cord nodded, a grim slant to his mouth. "I'll see what I can do." He straightened abruptly as the light outside the apartment door came on. The door opened and Sarah walked out on the landing, dressed in a yellow robe, her hair flowing loosely around her. At the sight of Cord and the police car she walked to the railing and asked anxiously, "Cord? Is something wrong?"

"No." Cord turned back to Deputy Ryder and found him staring at Sarah with an appreciative grin. Cord's control suddenly snapped, a fierce possessiveness surging through him. His voice was clipped when he said, "Thanks, Ryder. I'll take it from here."

Then he ran up the steps, taking them two at a time. On the landing he took Sarah's arm, propelled her back into the apartment and closed the door. Leaning back against it, he said, "Damn it, Sarah, I thought you had more sense than to walk outside in the middle of the night."

Sarah's eyes narrowed at his words, but one look at his tired drawn face and she swallowed her temper. "I recognized your truck from the kitchen window," she explained quietly. She had been waiting for him for hours, fearing that he had met with some kind of accident. "I realize that you don't owe me an explanation about your movements, but when you didn't drop by, I got worried about you."

With a groan Cord reached for her and drew her against him, cursing himself for his thoughtlessness. He had checked in with Chuck about six to make certain that everything was fine at the ranch. Holt had been in constant contact with the dispatcher, so he'd known that Sarah was all right. "I'm not used to someone waiting for me," he apologized, gathering her close.

For a moment Sarah leaned against him; then she pushed against his shoulders. This was what he had warned her about last night. He wanted no strings and no ties. Neither did she, but Cord made her come alive, made her want. And the more she wanted, the more she feared that it would all be taken away from her again. "I don't mean to sound possessive," she said softly.

Cord thought about the way he'd just been tempted to knock Deputy Ryder's smile off his face. Cupping her chin, he murmured, "I like it." Then he gave in to what he'd been wanting to do for hours. He lowered his head and his arms tightened around her, folding her against his length, opening his legs to pull her closer until she was pressed securely against him. His mouth closed over hers hungrily. Lord, how he wanted her. He hadn't known that he could ache for a woman so much.

He had turned her down last night, but the reasons for it no longer existed. He had wanted to keep her from involving herself in his affairs. She had done so anyway. He had wanted to spare her the gossip, but everyone already thought they were having an affair. Gently he touched her cheek, reveling in the silky softness of her skin. He ran his fingers through the shimmering waterfall of her hair, marveling at the silky weight of it.

It was as if the hours apart had left them starving for each other. Their lips fused, their tongues met, their breaths mingled and their bodies melded. Heat sprang up between them, burning away caution and fear.

It felt so right, Sarah thought, savoring the strong feel of his arms around her. Her skin tingled with awareness as his fingertips gently brushed over her face. She should push him away. She shouldn't let him—

But why not? Why not this once? When was the last time she had reached out and taken something for herself? Not for work, not for her daughter, not for someone else's cause, but for herself?

She couldn't remember. She had forgotten what it was to want a man. No, her mind corrected, she had *never* known what it was to want a man. Not the way she wanted Cord. Her relationship with George had been more a meeting of two minds, a warm friendship, but not very passionate.

She had always been afraid to love because for her the price of loving was too high. But this time she wouldn't be greedy. She wasn't asking for love, only tenderness. This time she would not dream of a lifetime but would be content with one night. This time there would be no losers, because in a few days she would leave and their paths would never cross again.

This time she was determined to cheat fate.

When he lifted her up and carried her to the bedroom, she sighed with the rightness of it. And ached with the poignancy of it.

Cord's hands weren't quite steady as he pulled down the zipper of her robe and brushed it off her shoulders. Her white cotton nightgown followed, pooling around her feet, and his breath caught when he saw her cloaked only in the veil of her hair.

With her cloud of dark hair and alabaster skin, she was Eve. Beautiful, strong and soft, and made for love. He touched her like a blind man, luring her with tenderness and gentleness, kiss by kiss drawing her away from the abyss of uncertainty. With his hands and lips he ignited a small flame of desire, then carefully nourished it, spreading the heat with ever-widening caresses.

Sarah cried out softly when he stepped away from her, leaving her suddenly shivering and cold. She didn't want any distance between them. Her hands went to the buttons of his shirt, helping him shrug out of it. For a moment he hesitated, because there were scars she hadn't seen. No one had seen them except Luis, and Luis could match him scar for scar.

Sarah thought she would cry out when she saw the still-angry patch of burned skin on his shoulder blade. There was another scar made by a bullet in his side. She touched them gently. If ever a man needed loving, it was Cord. Deep inside him was a wall of pain and distrust, an isolation from emotion he counted on to protect himself. She didn't want to break that wall. She was afraid of hurting him, knowing that she was the wrong woman for him. But she could soothe his pain with kisses and caresses. She could give him her trust. When he held out his hand she walked into his arms without reservation.

He lowered her onto the single bed. Then he reached for his billfold and the protection he still carried with him out of habit. Not for his sake, but for hers. He couldn't imagine anything more beautiful than creating another child—or two, or three—like Angel with her.

But for now he put the future from his mind. They were both realists. Their nights were filled with nightmares, not dreams.

Yet as he joined her, he felt himself change. Maybe dreams were possible, even for a man as battered by life as he was. And then all thought ceased.

She was tight, so tight, drawing him inside her warmth. And she was opening up to him, drawing him deeper, her legs wrapped around him, her arms clinging to him, urging him on.

Pleasure swirled around as they tried to reach for the stars, soaring higher and higher, becoming weightless as fears were left behind. For just this night, Sarah forgot that she never took emotional risks. All that was important was to reach out to Cord and make him whole again. Their joining was a wild ride on a dark night. Sarah heard his hoarse groan, calling to her and she was there for him, as he'd been there for her.

Afterward, they lay side by side, shudders still racking them. They remained entwined, still touching, still stroking. Their eyes never left each other, and when they finally fell asleep, there were no nightmares for either of them.

Sarah awoke before dawn, her heart pounding. Cord was curved all around her like a thick warm blanket, his calm quiet breath fanning her neck. It wasn't quite six. The smoke gray light of predawn filtered through the dormer window. Around them was silence and she was wondering what had awoken her, when she heard the slight scratch on the door. Sheba wasn't used to being shut out and was letting her know it.

Then she heard a different noise. A small thud. Exasperated, Sarah wondered what Sheba was getting into now.

Slowly, carefully, she lifted Cord's arm, which was wrapped around her waist, and started to slip from the bed. His hold tightened instantly. "Don't leave," he growled into her hair, eyes still closed. "The cat will have to get used to the fact that some places are off-limits."

Sarah turned around and kissed his bristly jaw, running her fingers through his thick blond hair. She memorized the way he looked at that moment, the first morning after she had fallen in love with him. Because that was exactly what had happened. Somehow, somewhere in the midst of yesterday's chaos, she had fallen head over heels for Cord Knight.

His bronze chest was a sculpture of lean rippling muscles, sprinkled lightly with brown hair. One arm was folded beneath his head, the other was wrapped around her, holding her as if he never wanted to let her go.

She felt her heart contract with painful fear, but she pushed the fear away. She couldn't fight how she felt for him anymore. Gently she touched his lips with her fingertips, wondering how she had gotten in so deep and so fast with a dangerous man like Cord Knight. "You're grumpy in the morning," she said.

"It's not even dawn." He captured the tips of her fingers with his teeth, nibbling on them.

Sarah snatched her hand away, and rolled out of bed. "Go back to sleep. I'll check on Angel and smooth Sheba's ruffled fur," she said, reaching for the robe and her nightgown, which were still lying in a heap on the floor.

Cord watched her dress. He didn't want to let her go. Not yet. Not before they made love again. Once hadn't been nearly enough... But then, he had known from the beginning that she would be his nemesis, hadn't he? She was his downfall, the one woman who could crack the wall around his heart and steal it like a thief in the night.

Sarah didn't know it yet, but he wasn't about to let her sneak off with it and leave an empty hole in his chest.

But she would have to come to him freely. His parents had married too young, fresh out of high school because his mother had been pregnant with him. His mother had been independent and unconventional even then and would have raised him alone. It had been his father who had pushed for marriage; he hadn't wanted to lose Renee or his child. Cord was determined not to repeat his father's mistake.

If Sarah came to him freely she would stick to him for a lifetime.

As Sarah opened the door, she glanced back at him. Sheba managed to slip through the crack and leapt onto the pine dresser, hissing at Cord.

With a cluck of annoyance Sarah went after her.

"Leave her," Cord said. Rolling onto his back, he took the sheets with him. "It's time we get to know each other."

There were many ways to conquer Sarah's heart. One of them was through those she loved.

"Good luck. Remember that she still has all her claws," Sarah reminded him with a grin.

Cord cocked one eyebrow. "She's female, isn't she?"

Sarah bristled. "What does that mean?"

"Nothing," Cord said, eyes glinting. "Just that I used to have a way with females."

"You still do, cowboy," Sarah tossed at him, then swiftly closed the door.

Angel was sound asleep when Sarah looked in on her. Quietly she closed her door, then tiptoed through the apartment. Suddenly she heard the small thud again. This time she knew it wasn't Sheba. It seemed to come from outside. She went into the kitchen and looked out the window, just in time to watch the boy replace one of the slats that apparently had fallen to the ground.

He was limping worse than the day before, Sarah noticed. Her heart wrenching for him, she went to the coat closet and took out her medical bag and the keys to the office. With her hand on the front door, she hesitated. She should warn Cord where she was going, but then again, she couldn't afford to waste time on explanations, if she wanted to catch the boy. Swiftly she went outside.

Though she had been very quiet, the boy spun around, gripping the piece of wood like a weapon. When he spotted Sarah, he relaxed and turned back, securing the slat by pounding it into the rail with his fist. Sarah ran down the steps, not realizing that she was barefoot until gravel bit into her feet. Wincing, she crossed the alley.

She was halfway across it when she heard the sound of a car. The boy froze, then cautiously lifted the wood and crawled through the hole. But as he lowered it, one of the pieces dropped off again. Sarah rushed over, trying to mend the gap before the car turned into the alley. But she wasn't wearing her glasses and in the darkness she couldn't fit the nail into the hole, even with the boy holding the piece of wood.

Twin headlights appeared at the end of the alley. Fear leapt into Sarah's throat. "Run," she told the boy.

For a moment he hesitated, as if reluctant to leave her to face his pursuers; then he parted the bushes lining the fence. Picking up the bag she left for him last night he said, *"Gracias,"* then disappeared from sight.

Chapter 10

Damn the woman for taking such risks!

Opening the front door, Cord's blood froze as he took in the scene below, of Sarah trying to fix a gap in the fence and a small shadow hobbling across the Taggerts' lawn.

And a truck stealthily moving up the alley.

Damn, if she wasn't Simon all over again. "Get back inside," he shouted, his voice low but intense, like distant thunder in the night. It was still too dark to make out much more than shapes. The driver of the pickup was as yet too far away to have spotted Sarah, who was shielded by the pile of debris. But he didn't dare wait for her response. He had no gun, nothing to protect her with. Wearing nothing but jeans, he raced down the steps. At the bottom they almost collided. "Lock the doors and stay put until I come back," Cord ordered as he brushed past her, pulling the keys to his truck out of his pocket.

Leaping inside, he slammed the cab door with one hand, while sliding the key into the ignition with the other. Seconds later the engine roared to life. Backing up, he watched as she started up the steps, her lemon yellow robe clearly visible in the early dawn light.

He turned on his brights to blind the driver, giving her a chance to get inside before she could be seen. Then he charged at the oncoming truck, reaching for one of the shotguns mounted up behind him. It wasn't much of a weapon, but it was all he had.

The approaching black pickup with bulls' horns decorating the hood came to a skidding stop, then backed out of the alley at high speed, engine whining. Cord raced after him.

At the top of the stairs, Sarah stared after his receding lights, her medical bag clutched to her chest. She stood shivering in the brisk morning air, feeling alone and frightened and as helpless as she had on that terrible night sixteen years ago.

She had no phone to call the sheriff and she didn't dare leave the apartment, not with Angel sleeping inside.

Not again, she thought, fear settling deep inside her like ice. Cord could be in serious danger. She couldn't face another loss.

If only she had sent him home last night. If she hadn't been so weak, if she hadn't wanted him so much, if she hadn't encouraged him, Cord would have been safely asleep at the ranch.

Wearily she raked back her hair. Had she really believed that she could thumb her nose at fate? That she could outwit it and snatch a few hours of happiness for herself without paying a price?

Now Cord was out there, charging into danger because of her foolish actions, barefoot and without a shirt. Rationally, she knew that clothes offered little protection against bullets. But without them men seemed so very vulnerable. Naked.

Defenseless.

Wearily, she glanced at the fence. She had managed to close the gap, but the slats were so loose, a mild breeze would blow them down. She wondered where the boy was hiding and why he hadn't been seen by anyone. Walking inside, she left her bag right next to the front door, then went into her bedroom to get dressed. Sheba was lying next to the bed, on the shirt Cord had dropped last night, and she was contentedly licking her fur. Sarah chased her off and brushed it down. Once she had dressed in jeans and sweatshirt, she shrugged into it, hugging it around her as if it were armor. Or a talisman.

Fifteen minutes later Cord charged into the apartment on a cloud of cool air, all frustration and silent rage. "I lost him," he said tautly, closing the door and locking it, his movements slow and precise with tightly leashed control. All he had was the make of the pickup, a late-model black Ford. Other than that, he had nothing. No license-plate number, no description of the driver. Angry, he slid his hands into the pockets of his jeans and followed Sarah into the kitchen. "A mile out of town I got stuck behind a slow-moving cattle truck. If the ditches weren't so muddy, I might have caught up with him."

Thank God for cattle trucks, Sarah thought, as she filled a pan with water and heated it on the stove. Then she gripped the kitchen counter tightly, her knuckles white with strain. He was back. And without a scratch on him. She drew a slow steadying breath, willing her nightmare vision to fade. The past would *not* repeat itself. No one, nothing, would take Cord away from her. Opening the cabinet, she took out two mugs and measured coffee crystals into them. "Was the cattle truck heading for Devlin's ranch? Maybe he's finally selling off some of his bulls."

"Maybe." Cord couldn't care less about the bulls right now. He wanted some answers. Barefoot, bare chested, he prowled the kitchen, muscles rippling with barely leashed anger. Then the fact that she was wearing his shirt registered and for a moment the look in his eyes softened. She had been frightened. But his own heart had stopped cold when he had seen the truck bearing down on her. "What possessed you to take a risk like that?"

Stung, Sarah raised her chin. Sliding out of his shirt, she tossed it at him. "What was I supposed to do? Climb back into bed and forget that there was a young injured boy being hunted like an animal?"

Shrugging into his shirt, Cord froze. She hadn't been out there more than three minutes before he'd gone in search of her. "This isn't the first time you've seen him." It wasn't a question, but a statement of fact. "When did you first talk to him?" he asked, his voice clipped and low.

"Yesterday morning." Sarah poured boiling water into the cups, then turned off the stove. Stirring the coffee, she quietly described yesterday morning's sinister scene, while Cord snapped the buttons of his shirt. She also told him about the food she had placed behind the fence. Handing him the mug, she added, "I don't think he speaks any English. He has a bullet wound in his leg. Today he limped worse than yesterday, which makes me think that the bullet is either still lodged inside or the wound is infected."

Cord took a careful sip, then put the mug on the counter with studied care, folding his arms across his chest to keep from shaking her or kissing her senseless. The risk she had taken made his blood freeze! "Damn it, Sarah, do you have any idea what you're dealing with?"

Sarah closed her eyes briefly against the sudden stab of pain. "Not completely, but I have a fair idea," she said, her hands curling around the warm mug. She felt cold, so cold. "Simon's death was no accident, was it?" she asked quietly, fighting tears so hard, her head felt as if it were ready to explode. "He was killed because he helped refugees like this boy."

Cord said nothing for a moment, wishing he could spare her, but knowing there wasn't anything he could do to soften the blow. Lying to her now was asking for more trouble. It amazed him how a woman who insisted that she didn't meddle and who was afraid of involvement, managed to stumble into trouble the way she did. And this particular bit of trouble just might get her killed as it had killed her father, he thought grimly, watching her face turn a pasty white, her dark eyes burning with unshed tears.

With a growl of concern he drew her into his arms, pushing her face into the crook of his neck. He didn't say anything; words were so useless at a time like this. Sliding his hands beneath her shirt, he stroked her cold skin, soothing the small tremors shaking her, surrounding her with his warmth.

For a moment Sarah took and absorbed his comfort and strength, listening to the steady beat of his heart, wondering how he always knew just what she needed. Then she pushed away from him and walked to the window. "I've suspected it from the moment I walked into the Coyote Lounge," she said. "Did Rusty tell you about Simon?"

"Not outright. His comments made me suspicious, though." Frowning, he wondered where Rusty was. When he and Dan Holt had stopped by the Coyote Lounge yesterday afternoon, they had been told that Rusty had gone to Mexico for the week. He glanced at her across the space. "And despite your suspicions you went outside to help the boy."

Alone.

Without asking for his help.

She had given herself to him, only a few hours before.

She had slept in his arms, with the light turned off, as if she trusted him to keep her nightmares at bay. Then she had left him, promising to return. Instead she had charged into danger.

While he had been lying in her bed a few steps away.

The knowledge that she hadn't trusted him enough to call him burned like acid in his throat.

"Damn it, Sarah, we're talking about organized crime. These goons don't play around. They deal in drugs, slave trade, prostitution. Don't you know better than to get mixed up in that?"

Anger flared, drowning out her fear. "What we're talking about is a human being," Sarah said, spinning around. "A young boy. No older than my brother Akim was when he died!"

So that was the key, Cord thought grimly, too furious, too shaken to speak. She was still trying to atone for the mistakes she thought she had made. She was always trying to prove to herself that she wasn't a coward, trying to pay off old debts.

And new ones, too, it seemed.

She hadn't come to him because she'd wanted him as much as he wanted her. She'd given herself to him because she felt she owed him and because the physician in her couldn't resist trying to heal his wounds.

"You have a young daughter," he finally ground out. "*She* should be your first responsibility. Did you even pause to think of her? What would happen to Angel if you got killed?"

Sarah stared at him for a moment, hugging her arms around herself. "Nothing ever happens to me," she said bitterly. "I'm like a cat with nine lives. Fate chose a much more cruel role for me. I'm cursed with burying those I love."

Cord stared at her in disbelief. The gambler in him conceded that there was a certain amount of luck involved in the turn of a card, but he didn't believe in fate. If he had, maybe he could have accepted his own failures more easily. "Who do you think you are? Superwoman?" he asked harshly, fear for her curling in the pit of his stomach. "I have news for you, Doc. If that driver *had* seen you, had realized what you were up to, you'd have found out soon enough just how mortal you are."

Stung, Sarah jammed her hands into her jeans and walked up to him. "That boy is hurt. He's starving. He's being hunted like an animal. You, of all people, should know what it feels like. I expected you to understand!"

Cord hooked his thumbs into his pockets, a chill creeping over him. "Oh, I understand why you went outside to help the boy," he drawled. "What I don't understand, what I'd like to know, is why the hell you didn't call me. I was right here."

Sarah stopped right in front of him. "There was no time for explanations." *And I wanted to keep you safe. I couldn't bear it if something happened to you. You're too important to me.* But she couldn't tell him that because Cord didn't want emotional ties any more than she did.

"But you had time to get your medical bag," Cord drawled, his hard eyes steadily fixed on her face. She had softened his scars, had made him feel again, and then she had walked from his arms, rejecting his help, rejecting *him.* "What were you really afraid of, Doc? That I would let you down? That I would turn out to be the coward everyone calls me?"

"No!" Denial instantly rose to her lips.

But before she could explain, could say a word, he continued, his voice hard and cold. "You're a great one for taking on causes. Everyone's causes, including mine. Well, I've got news for you, Doc. I don't want to be one of your strays. *I am not one of your patients.*"

Staring down at his bare feet, he shut up, striving for control.

From now on, until the danger was over, he couldn't afford to soften toward her—not if he wanted to keep her and her daughter safe. Cold rage had helped him survive ten months of being hunted by bounty hunters and hit men. Cold, hard determination had helped him snatch Mariela from Rodriguez's stronghold in the Mayan Highlands. Those were the only emotions he could allow himself to feel.

"Now, let's get your things packed and move you back to the ranch. You're not staying here by yourself anymore."

Stunned, Sarah stood there and watched him stalk into the bedroom, filled with impotent anger and pain. Tears pricked her eyes. She balled her hands into fists, trying to get a hold of her emotions, but one tear slipped down anyway. "Damn."

She hadn't thought about how he would feel if she kept her actions a secret from him. He already thought of himself as a failure and she had hurt him where he was most vulnerable—in his honor, his pride and his virility. That had been the last thing she had wanted to do, she thought as she walked to the window, watching the sun come up over the roofs of the town.

It was her own fear of losing another person she cared for that had prompted her actions—nothing more. But he didn't, couldn't, know that. Yes, the one thing she had been afraid of had happened. She had fallen in love with him.

Love. The one thing she feared above everything else.

Love. The one emotion that held the most potential for pain.

Love. The one thing she wanted desperately, but didn't deserve. Dear God, how could she have been so foolish?

"Mommy?" Angel padded into the kitchen, dressed in purple Ninja Turtle pajamas, rubbing sleep from her eyes. "What's going on? Did Cord sleep here last night?"

Sarah took a deep steadying breath and blinked away her tears before turning around. Deciding that Angel's second question was better ignored, she answered the first. "Cord and I were talking about moving back to the ranch. Would you like that?"

Angel nodded, an eager smile brightening her eyes. Then the glow vanished, replaced by concern as she noticed the trail of tears on Sarah's face. "Why are you crying?"

Sarah wiped her damp cheeks with the back of her hand. "I'm not crying. I have something in my eyes."

Angel tilted her head to one side. "Sometimes Terry cries. She always says it's because she peeled onions."

Sarah kneeled and hugged her daughter. "I guess grown-ups are often afraid to admit that they're hurting."

"Why?" Angel wiped Sarah's cheeks with her sleeve. "If you don't tell me about it, how can I make it feel better?" she asked, kissing Sarah's cheek.

Out of the mouth of babes, Sarah thought, hugging her daughter with aching tenderness. "Because when you're a grown-up you're supposed to be able to deal with your pain on your own."

But the truth was that even the strongest person needed to know that there was someone to hold on to in the darkest hour. And on one level she understood that. The physician in her had reached out and touched, given comfort and hope many times.

But the woman in her was afraid to admit that she, too, needed someone to hold on to. She was afraid of placing her hopes, her trust and her heart into someone else's hands, because she demanded guarantees the physician in her would never give.

The forever kind.

On weekdays the five single cowhands took their meals at the big house at the Circle K. As Sarah and Cord drove into the yard, the men were just leaving the kitchen. Spotting Jimmy T., Angel pounced on him with a cry of delight, demanding to see the kittens.

Cord said nothing. He merely looked at Sarah in cold, hard challenge, expecting her to spoil her daughter's and Jimmy T.'s fun because of her own fears. After a brief hesitation Sarah nodded, biting back the words of caution hovering on her lips. "She hasn't had any breakfast," she said quietly. "Would you bring her back in thirty minutes?"

Jimmy T. touched the rim of his straw hat with the tip of one finger. "No problem," he said, his gnarled fingers closing around the small pudgy hand. "Don't you worry none, Doc. All of us will keep an eye on her."

Something inside Cord softened. "Come on, Doc, lets get you settled. If you carry the cat, I'll get the rest."

Within minutes the suitcases and the cat carrier had been transferred into the guest bedroom again. Maisy smiled as she checked the towels in the bathroom. "I'm glad you're back."

"So am I." Kneeling in front of the carrier, Sarah glanced over her shoulder at Maisy, realizing that it wasn't politeness that had prompted the words. She meant it. Somehow, over the span of a few days, Maisy, Chuck and Jimmy T. had become friends, almost family.

"Is breakfast in half an hour all right?"

"I don't want to put you through a whole lot of trouble. Cereal will be fine," Sarah said as she opened Sheba's carrier. The cat shot out of it like a cannonball.

"Nonsense. Cord doesn't care for it. He likes a real breakfast, not puffed air. And you look like you could do with a decent meal." Maisy shook her head as Sheba disappeared under the bed. "That poor animal must be all mixed-up being shifted from place to place."

"I should have left her with my neighbor." Sheba wasn't the only one who was confused, Sarah thought as she filled up the litter box. What had happened to her well-ordered life? St. Anne's, the people she worked with, her apartment, even her neighbor Terry seemed as distant as if they belonged to someone else's life.

"Oh, I don't know. That cat would have missed you something fierce. You don't have to shut her in this room, you know. I like cats. And I don't think she'll run away if she happens to get out."

Sarah opened one suitcase. Hanging a pair of jeans on a hanger, she glanced at Maisy with a doubtful look. "She isn't spayed."

A mischievous twinkle came into Maisy's eyes. Spotting it, Sarah bit back a grin. "Oh, no. I agreed to take in one kitten. I don't want to be saddled with a whole litter."

"If you stayed here, it wouldn't be a problem," Maisy said tongue-in-cheek.

Pain welled up in Sarah at Maisy's words. She doubted that Cord would ever forgive her for what she had done to him. "I can't," she said, hanging up a blouse.

Maisy searched Sarah's closed face with gentle eyes. "I don't know what you two argued about, but it'll blow over. Cord isn't one to carry a grudge," she said gently.

Walking to the closet, Sarah said quietly, "It was more than an argument. But I'd rather not talk about it."

"That's all right. If you need an ear, I'll be here. Miz Renee and Big John are planning to come down on Thursday. That should ease the tension some, if it hasn't blown over by then. Vicky can't make it until Friday. It'll be nice to have the family all down here for the weekend. You'll still be here, won't you?"

Sarah nodded. She couldn't leave. Not now, knowing that Simon had been murdered. Not now, when a young boy might need her help. But the most important reason was Cord. He was in trouble, trouble she had drawn him into, so how could she turn her back on him? Forcing a smile onto her face, she said, "I'm looking forward to seeing them all again."

With a satisfied nod Maisy walked to the door and opened it, almost running into Cord who had been about to knock. Maisy stepped past him, then said, "I'll start breakfast," before walking down the hall.

At the sight of Cord, Sarah tensed defensively but continued to unpack until all that was left was the small frame of George that Angel kept on her nightstand. Placing it on the bedspread, she stored the case in the bottom of the closet, feeling Cord's gaze following her.

Closing the door, Cord walked deeper into the room and picked up the small frame. The color photo showed a young man in his mid-twenties with a round, good-humored face, curly brown hair and gentle light brown eyes. Angel's eyes, he thought. "This is Angel's father, isn't it?" he asked, staring at the man whom Sarah had loved so deeply, she had been willing to risk getting hurt again.

"Yes." Sarah closed the closet and leaned against it. His hair was still dark and damp from a recent shower. He had changed into another pair of worn jeans that rode low on his hips, molding themselves to his powerful thighs. The black sweatshirt he wore revealed the corded muscles of his neck and clung to his broad shoulders. She wished she could turn back the clock a few hours when he hadn't looked so distant, so stern, so hard. The tautness made the scar stand out sharply. Sarah's heart wrenched. She had done this to him. "Cord—will you let me explain?" she asked, determined to bring this morning's scene out into the open.

Cord glanced up from the photo in his hand. At the pleading look in her eyes, his resolve to keep her at arm's length softened. "I think I understand." His fingers tightened around the frame. "The trouble with you is that you have too many ghosts in your life." And ghosts were tough to fight, especially where Sarah was concerned, because she felt she owed every one of them for loving her. He didn't know who had planted the idea in her head that she didn't deserve love, but if he ever came up against that person, he'd cheerfully commit murder.

Sarah glanced first at his strong callused hand holding the frame, and then at his face, and a thoughtful look came into her eyes. "That's Angel's photo. She carries it with her everywhere. She never knew her father. George was killed by a psychiatric patient two weeks before our wedding. I...didn't even know I was pregnant at the time." She pushed herself away from the closet and gently took the photo out of his hands, then placed it on the nightstand on Angel's side of the big bed. "George was a good man. When he died, I was devastated. He was so solid, a big, patient, easygoing teddy bear. I thought he was a forever-kind-of-man."

Slowly Sarah turned back and met Cord's watchful gaze. She didn't want him to believe that she was still pining for George. She was many things, but morbid wasn't one of them. "It's been over for six years. I'm not mourning him anymore, if that's what you're thinking. I'm keeping his memory alive for Angel's sake."

Cord felt the rest of his anger fade, but her words made him uneasy. What she wanted, what she was searching for, was the "forever" type, a man who would never leave her, who would outlive her. "No one can make a forever-kind-of-promise," he said quietly.

"Don't you think I know that? But fears are irrational." Sarah pushed her glasses up on her nose and slowly walked around the foot of the bed. Her voice became low and intense, willing him to understand. "Every day I see men cut down in their prime by violence, and some are well-trained, experienced veterans like you." She drew a shaky breath. "The reason I didn't tell you about the boy yesterday had nothing to do with me not trusting you. It had everything to do with *my* fears."

Sarah stopped right in front of him and tilted her head back. Some of the hardness had left his eyes, she noticed. Relief flooded through her, making her voice hoarse, when she continued, "I had no intention of dealing with the situation by myself, either. The moment I was certain that the boy was still around, I'd planned to go to the sheriff."

"Sarah—" Cord groaned, framing her face with his hands and tilting it up to him. "There's no need to go on with this. I understand. Once I had calmed down—" His hands tightened with remembered fear. *He* could have lost *her*.

Sarah placed her fingers against his lips, stopping him. "I've been brooding over it for two hours, cowboy. The least you can do is listen to my apology. I had no right to make the decision for you whether you wanted to become involved—"

"Did anyone ever tell you you talk too much, city slicker?" With a moan Cord's mouth covered hers, cutting off her words. For a moment Sarah resisted, she wasn't finished yet. But then sensation took over. He tasted of toothpaste and smelled of shaving cream. She tasted his warm mouth and felt a hunger so great, it shook her, draining her resistance. She could have sworn, *had* sworn until now, that Cord didn't want this depth of emotion he drew from her. But he didn't kiss her as if he wanted no strings. He kissed her as if she were his next breath, as if she were a part of his heartbeat or a link to his soul. He kissed her until she couldn't think anymore of all the reasons why she should keep her distance. Nothing mattered anymore—not the angry pain over Simon's murder, not the clouds gathering at the horizon, not the danger or her fears. She didn't feel cautious; she felt gloriously alive. All that mattered was the here and now. Cord.

Her mouth molded to the shape of his. Her arms closed around his waist, pressing closer. She felt the thunder of his heartbeat. She felt the hardness of his belt buckle and the ache of his arousal. His kisses were rough and gentle, tender and yearning. He kissed her as if he had been empty and needed her touch to make him whole.

A forever-kind-of-kiss.

"Mommy. Maisy said breakfast is—"

At the sound of Angel's voice coming from down the hall Cord tore his mouth free.

Sarah closed her eyes. Breathing hard, Cord rested his damp forehead against Sarah's. "*Damn it,* I never meant it to go that far."

Sarah drew a shaky breath, then raised her head. "I know you didn't," she said.

Cord's eyes narrowed. "What's that supposed to mean?"

Sarah shrugged. "Just that you are not a forever-kind-of-guy." At his frown, she smiled slightly. She raised her hand and brushed back his hair with aching tenderness. "Don't worry, cowboy. I'm not angry. Strings scare me to death, remember?" But frightened as she was, she sadly admitted to herself the truth. She wanted to move back into his arms and stay there and hold on to him. She was afraid that the moment she *did* let go of him, he would disappear.

Cord scowled down at her, his mouth twisting wryly at the irony of the situation. For years he had shied away from permanent relationships. For years he had wanted to avoid the emotional strings his parents shared. But that terrifying moment on top of the steps had changed all that. In that instant, he had realized just how much Sarah meant to him. Even knowing that she planned to leave the moment Simon's affairs were settled could not change his need for her. Was this burning desire, this clawing hunger he felt for this woman what his father felt for his mother?

But before he could say anything, Angel charged into the room, a small black kitten held tightly in her arms. "Jimmy T. says it's all right to show him to Sheba," she said, her eyes bright and her cheeks flushed.

She placed it on the carpet and the black kitten sat there, motionless, staring at the three people with its bright green eyes. Then it disappeared beneath the bed. Seconds later there was a warning hiss and an indignant howl. Then Sheba shot from beneath the comforter and made for the door.

With great presence of mind, Cord caught her before she could escape into the hallway. Angry, claws unsheathed, Sheba started to swat him. Cord caught her front paws and held them firmly with one hand while stroking her fuzzy ruffled fur with the other, talking soothingly. Another brief struggle and a hiss. Slowly Sheba succumbed to the lure of his voice and the gentle stroke of his hand. She began to purr.

With a cocky grin Cord met Sarah's eyes. "She's coming around. Another day or so and I'll have her eating out of my hand."

Sarah bit her lip. For some reason she had the impression that he wasn't talking about the cat. "I didn't know you were such a dreamer, cowboy," she scoffed, her voice a little hoarse.

But watching his long fingers gently run over the fur, she desperately wanted to trade places with her cat.

Sarah had it all wrong. He wasn't a dreamer, but a hard realist. He didn't want to be in love. It wasn't a comfortable emotion, this churning need that made him ache every time he looked at her. But denying it wouldn't make it go away. He was in love. And when it came right down to it, he was a one-woman-man, like his father. A forever-kind-of-man. Sarah had stolen his heart. That was an unalterable fact.

And he didn't plan to live without his heart for the rest of his life.

Not without a fight, anyway.

Over breakfast, Cord plotted out a battle plan on how to scale the high walls Sarah was hiding behind. Or maybe scale wasn't the right expression. A show of force, after all, would bring out Sarah's fighting spirit. On the other hand, telling her about his feelings would only increase her wariness and fears. The deeper her feelings for him went, the more frightened she became of losing again.

But there were other ways to get to Sarah than a frontal attack. He would lure her out from behind her walls, using the same bait Simon had intended to use to tempt her to move to Knight's Corner.

Three Arabian horses.

The moment she'd finished eating, he rose from the table. "How good are you with currycombs and mucking out stalls, Doc? I could use some help with your horses."

Maisy glared at him over the brim of her mug. "The men aren't that busy right now."

Cord silenced her with a sharp warning look. It was true that the men weren't overworked at the moment. Wintertime was always slow. It was a time to check equipment, train cow ponies and do repairs around the ranch. In another few weeks, at calving time, everyone would work around-the-clock to make up for it. "They are today. I sent a crew out to the river pasture to check on the Brangus herd and repair the fences."

Sarah pushed back her chair and rose to her feet. "It doesn't matter if the men are busy or not. The horses are my responsibility and it's time I took *care* of them." She glanced at Cord. For days she had wondered how to bring up the matter of payment, but she had the suspicion that Cord would be as offended as Big John had been when she'd offered to pay for the locks and the replacement windows at the office. She simply would have to think of something else. Bending down, she wiped hot chocolate from Angel's mouth. "Come on, sweetheart, you can help, too."

Maisy's eyes met Cord's in silent communication. "I thought I would visit with Chuck's cousin Tina right after I've cleaned up. Brad, her husband, works here, too. They have a daughter about Angel's age. She might enjoy playing with another child."

Angel's eyes lit up with eagerness as she slid from the chair. Sarah met the twinkle in Maisy's eyes with exasperation. The more friends they made here, the harder it would be for them to leave. And it would be tough to keep Cord at some distance if the housekeeper decided to try her hand at matchmaking. But there were a few things she needed to discuss with Cord, things she didn't want Angel to hear. "Thanks. I think Angel would enjoy it more than watching us muck out stalls."

Jimmy T. had already taken care of Princess, so there were only the dapple gray and the bay left to take care of. As Sarah opened the mare's stall, she turned to Cord. "I don't even know their names."

"We don't, either." Cord walked into the stall and took the comb from a shelf at the back of the stall. "From what my father said, Simon only had the horses for a few weeks and their papers burned up with the house. My father knows the breeder, so you can get the address from him. Jimmy T. calls the black mare Princess. I just call these two Gray and Bay. The bay's name is engraved on the tack, but it's in Arabic and I can't read it." His eyes locked with hers, challenging her. "They *are* your horses, Doc. You can name them anything you want."

Sarah watched the mare walk up to Cord and nuzzle his hand, breathing in his familiar scent. She could only name them if she decided to keep them, she thought. While she wanted to, badly, she hadn't made a decision. And she definitely couldn't keep all three. Slowly she brushed past Cord and took the silver-studded halter off the hook and read the inscription. Her fingers trembled as she traced the Arabic scroll. "Zaira," she said, her voice not quite steady. "Her name is Zaira." Cord glanced at her, his eyes narrowing as he noticed her agitation. "What does it mean?"

Sarah swallowed the painful lump in her throat and blinked against the sudden sheen of tears, her fingers gripping the bridle tightly. "It's Farsi for Sarah." A hoarse, choked gasp escaped her. "Simon gave the mare my name!" She closed her eyes, trying to keep the tears from falling, but they squeezed between her lids and kept falling, silently sliding down her face.

Blindly, she reached for Cord, needing his strength, his warmth, needing his rock-steady presence while painful memories tore through her.

Cord took off her glasses and slid them into his pocket, then pushed her face into his chest, holding her while hard sobs racked her slender form, cracking the walls that contained her feelings, opening the floodgates. It wasn't what he had intended, Cord thought. He had wanted to give her a few hours of joy. He had hoped that she would be tempted enough to saddle up and take the bay for a ride. He had wanted to draw her away from the past, as well as distract her from the dangers surrounding them.

With a deep sigh, he fitted her face deeper into his shoulder and rested his chin in her hair. But she had turned to him out of her own free will. For the first time she had admitted that she needed him. She trusted him enough to cry into his shoulder instead of facing her pain alone.

He had no illusion that the battle was won. Her tears were just a relief from pain. It didn't mean that she was no longer afraid. Her kind of fear wouldn't leave overnight. He doubted that she would ever be completely free of it. Maybe fifty years down the road it would cease to matter.

And she might never be able to live and work in a place where everything reminded her of her father's murder.

Still, there was a small chance that, if he caught the men responsible for it, she might change her mind.

The trouble was, Cord suspected grimly, that the man behind this scene was the same one who had almost destroyed him once before.

What if he failed again?

Chapter 11

"Looks like the Taggerts are on vacation," Cord said two hours later as he walked down the driveway of the white one-story frame house. "The place is shut tight. No sign of a forced entry anywhere and the storm cellar is secured with a big padlock. I don't think the boy's hiding inside."

Leaning against the truck, Sarah watched him toss the hammer into the toolbox. While Cord had fixed the fence, she had walked up and down the street, looking around. This was the old part of town, where the houses were small. The yards had been allowed to grow wild. There were few streetlights, Sarah noticed. At night it would be easy for a person to move around undetected. "He can't walk any long distances with that leg," she said, a troubled look in her eyes. "What worries me is that the truck turned up both times when the boy was in the alley, as if the driver was waiting for him."

Cord closed the lid of the toolbox, recalling the uneasy sensation of being watched last night. "*You* were their target, Sarah," he said flatly, joining her. He should never have allowed her to move into town. "Someone was keeping an eye on the office on the off chance that the kid would come to you for help. I don't think they know where the boy is. If the kid was smart, he hitched a ride to San Antonio this morning."

Despite the warmth of the midmorning sun, Sarah shivered, wondering what had happened to Simon. Had they surprised him at the office? Or had they followed him home? Had they knocked him unconscious before setting the fire? She'd always wondered why he hadn't managed to escape from the flames.

Cord laid a hand on her arm. "Don't think about it," he said roughly, guessing, from the bleak look in her eyes, where her thoughts had strayed.

Sarah mutely shook her head. Simon's murder still seemed unreal. She couldn't imagine anyone wanting to kill her bluff big Texan. "I'm not going to let them get away with it," she said with quiet determination. Pushing herself away from the truck, she opened the cab door. "Whoever killed him is going to pay."

Cord looked into Sarah's pale set face, tension carving brackets on either side of his mouth. "We'll get him," he promised intensely, closing the door. Determination settled like ice as he walked around the front of the truck. He wasn't going to rest until the men responsible were caught. But he did not want Sarah involved. Her disregard for her own safety scared the hell out of him. What he needed was to find some distraction for her while he searched for the boy.

Maybe he should ask his mother or Vicky to come to the ranch today, he thought, sliding into his seat. Closing the door, he dismissed the idea almost instantly. Renee would probably join the search for Simon's murderer. And Vicky— Hell, Vicky was even worse. His sister hadn't built a small business empire by being timid. He had enough on his hands trying to keep Sarah safe. He didn't need two more headaches, he decided, starting the car.

Also the news of Simon's murder would bring Big John back sooner. Cord didn't want to have to deal with his father right now. That wound was still too raw.

"The fact that Simon's death was no accident sheds a different light on the vandalism at the office," Sarah said as they turned onto Main Street, her voice composed. "Maybe the drugs they took were just a blind. I've been making a mental inventory of the broken furniture. Every filing cabinet is destroyed. Maybe they were searching for the medical records of the illegals Simon treated."

Cord pounced on the idea. If Simon had kept records, they had probably been found and destroyed, but going through the files would keep Sarah busy for a while. "That's possible," he agreed as he pulled up next to Sarah's car and parked at the curb. "Let's pick up the files. You can look through them at the ranch."

Sarah's eyes narrowed suspiciously. She was well aware that Cord was determined to keep her out of trouble, and his protectiveness warmed her. But she couldn't remain safely hidden behind castle walls while he dealt with the trouble she had drawn him into. Getting out of the pickup, she said, "I can't take patient records to the ranch. They're confidential."

Scowling, Cord followed her to the front door. "You can lock them up in my office."

Inserting the key into the lock, Sarah shook her head. Apart from the fact that there were strict laws protecting a patient's confidentiality, she wasn't going to take potentially dangerous material to the ranch and risk the safety of everyone she had come to care for.

Frustrated, Cord glared at the boards. "I don't think you're going to find anything. The place was too thoroughly searched. Besides, why would Simon keep records of patients he'd never see again? That was asking for trouble."

Sarah opened the door, grimacing at the ammonia fumes coming at her. "Simon was meticulous. No matter whom he treated, he would have kept records. He once said that the years in Iran taught him good habits, because the hospital there had no filing system to speak of. From what I recall, they stacked charts very much like the files are stacked in Simon's office right now." She glanced up at Cord pleadingly. "I wish you'd tell the sheriff what's going on."

Cord's expression became hard and withdrawn. They had nothing, no proof of any kind. "Not without solid evidence."

Sarah compressed her lips in exasperation and apprehension. She knew his reluctance stemmed from the fact that no one had believed him about Harper. He was determined not to "cry wolf" again. But this was different. The sheriff already believed in Simon's murder; he already suspected that Devlin was involved. Only Cord was too stubborn—and too raw still—to trust anyone. "You do realize that if we find the boy, I will have to notify the sheriff about the gunshot wound."

Cord's jaw tightened. "The boy *is* evidence," he pointed out quietly. "Better than that, he's a witness. He must know the location of the safe house in this neighborhood. He can identify the men he escaped from. He also has to know about the modes of transportation. The FBI puts up roadblocks throughout this part of Texas, changing the locations constantly, but somehow Devlin has managed to get past them. I want to know how." Cord raked his hair back in frustration. "But like I said before, if the kid was smart, after this morning's incident, he left for San Antonio or crossed the border into Mexico, where he can get treatment without anyone asking questions."

Sarah started to close the door again, her chin angled determinedly. "Then I'm coming with you."

Cord put out his hand to keep it open, a mask dropping over his features. For a moment their eyes locked, antagonists caught in a battle of wills. "We seem to have had this argument before," he finally drawled.

"Yes, we have." Sarah's hands clenched, trying to control a surge of fear when she thought of the ruthless men they were up against. She wasn't going to let Cord deal with the danger by himself. He had fought alone for far too long. And somewhere deep down she hoped that if she stuck close to him, she could hold on to him.

Besides, this wasn't only his fight. *It was hers, too.*

She touched the plaque next to the door, tracing the name with a trembling fingertip. Glancing around she realized that they were attracting attention and walked into the office. It wouldn't do for people to see her arguing with Cord, she thought. That would undo all the progress they had made. People were still wary of him.

In the middle of the room she turned around, facing him. "Simon was my father. He rescued me. He took me in when no one else wanted me. My deepest regret is that I didn't join him down here earlier. I might have prevented his death."

Flicking on the light, Cord closed the door and leaned against it, frustration and exasperation in every one of his moves. Damn it, did she have to take responsibility for everything? Somehow he was going to have to cure her of that. "You are no more responsible for Simon's death than you were for your family's murder. Your father should have sent all of you to safety weeks earlier," he growled. "And Simon knew what he was up against. *He* chose to take the risks, damn it."

"Maybe." Raising her glasses, Sarah rubbed her eyes wearily, pacing to the far wall and back again. "But I can't help thinking that if I had joined his office, like he wanted me to, that he would still be alive."

"Why didn't you?" Cord asked slowly, recalling that she had evaded answering the question once before.

Sarah stopped her pacing and looked at him. "Ghosts," she prevaricated. Since coming to Knight's Corner she had confronted so many of them. Without Cord she would never have found the courage to bring them out into the open, but this particular ghost was more painful than the rest and she hesitated. Then she saw his mouth compress and his eyes becoming distant, and she plunged ahead. She had to make him believe, once and for all, that she trusted him.

"My youngest brother, Akim, didn't die immediately. He lived through the night. He was badly wounded, but his injuries wouldn't have been fatal, if a surgeon had been available. Simon tried to save him, but he lacked the skills." Briefly she closed her eyes. "Watching my brother die, so needlessly, has haunted me ever since. I swore that night that I would become a surgeon to help victims like Akim. Simon understood what drove me and encouraged me.

"I knew that both Simon and Lisa loved me. But deep down I was never certain of it. A part of me always believed that they took me in out of guilt and because after my mother's family refused to raise me, they were stuck with me. Naming that beautiful bay Zaire was Simon's way of letting me know that he would have taken me in no matter what."

She slid her hands into her pockets and tightly curled them into fists, staring at the bare walls, the chipped plaster, anywhere but at Cord. "All these years, I've been trying to atone for past mistakes. But it seems so futile suddenly. Nothing can bring my family back, nothing can change the course of past events."

Turning back to Cord, she placed her hands on his chest and looked at him with dark haunted, pleading eyes. "This is my fight, too, Cord. I need to be involved." *Most of all I need to be near you so I can keep you safe.* "So don't push me away."

Cord drew her into his strong embrace and held her tightly. Maybe, just maybe, she might change her mind and consider staying here. "I've always worked alone before," he said, brushing tendrils of hair back from her face.

"Two heads think better than one," Sarah replied persuasively against his lips.

With a groan Cord bent his head and kissed her with aching tenderness. "Under one condition. We're going to do it my way." She could think and plot all she wanted to, but in safety, at the ranch.

Sarah bristled. "Do you think I'm stupid enough to agree to that, cowboy?"

A smile softened Cord's eyes. "Your ways don't work around here, city slicker. Look at your car. It still has a dent in it. By the way, did you hear from your insurance company or Devlin yet?"

Sarah shook her head. "But I will."

"Well until you do, we'll do it my way," Cord said, kissing the protest from her lips.

He loved her, had done so since the moment she'd thrown mud at him and had welcomed him back to life. He was going to keep her safe. And if the price of her safety was another dent to his pride, he wasn't going to quibble about it. "I'm going to talk to Holt," he said, releasing her. "Meanwhile you can look through those files and see if you can find anything. And keep the doors locked."

Two hours later, Sarah leaned against the wall in the waiting room, arching her aching back. Slowly she stretched out her cramped legs and stared with frustration at the stacks of charts piled up on the floor around her. From notes scribbled on the folders, Pilar had apparently straightened out the files after the break-in. Though some reports had been destroyed, overall they were in fairly decent shape.

But there were no notes hidden among them. No clues of any kind.

Dispirited, she reached for another file but didn't open it immediately, glancing at her watch anxiously. Cord should have been back by now, she thought, fervently hoping that her faith in Dan Holt hadn't been misplaced. Perhaps the two men were searching the town. Cord tended to become as involved in his job as she did with her patients. Especially now, when he saw a second chance of clearing his name, of removing that stain from his honor.

Would he return to his job, once it was over? she wondered anxiously.

And what about her own plans? What was she going to do?

Sarah glanced at the file in her hand. A part of her wanted to continue Simon's work. It would allow her to spend more time with Angel. They were beginning to make friends here. Also, skimming through the charts, she had caught a glimpse of what was missing from her specialty. Rarely was she involved in follow-up care. Until a few days ago she had wanted it that way. She hadn't wanted the personal relationship a general practitioner developed with his patients. But now she wasn't so sure.

Or was Cord the real reason she was considering making a life for Angel and herself in this town?

With a shake of her head, Sarah closed the chart and reached for another one. She could feel herself changing; she was beginning to dream, and it wouldn't do. It was time to reestablish control over her life, because her fear of permanent relationships was as great as ever. And Cord didn't want ties, either, she told herself sternly. He was a man to rescue waifs, not marry them.

Besides, she had spent years specializing and she couldn't, wouldn't, throw it all away. Now, if she could find a place nearby where her skills were needed, she might consider a move....

"Sarah, are you in there?"

At the sound of Mary Lou's voice, Sarah scrambled to her feet and opened the door, welcoming the interruption. "Hi. I'd ask you inside, but I have no chairs," she said.

Leaning against the frame, Mary Lou smiled. "That's all right. I don't care for doctors' offices anyway. I came over to invite you for a cup of coffee and a trim for your split ends. I have an hour before my next appointment."

Sarah hesitated briefly, then nodded. "I could do with a break." Then she noticed Mary Lou's puffy face and her eyes sharpened. A glance at her swollen legs had her frowning. "Forget about the trim. You need to lie down for a while and elevate your legs."

Mary tried to see past her big stomach, hiking up her blue maternity dress. Her blue eyes showed a hint of panic as she caught a glimpse of one swollen leg. "You think there's something wrong? I still have five weeks to go."

Sarah took Mary Lou's wrist, counting her pulse while drawing her inside. "I don't think so," she said soothingly. "Water retention is common in the later stages of pregnancy, especially if you're standing on your feet all day. I'll check your blood pressure to make sure. If the swelling isn't down by tomorrow morning, though, I want you to call your gynecologist."

Mary Lou's blood pressure was up, but within normal limits. With a sigh of relief, she made for the door. Glancing at the files, she scowled. "Still packing, I see. Lord, I wish you'd stay. What are you going to do with those files?"

Sarah shrugged. "I haven't really thought that far ahead. Keep them somewhere safe until a new physician can be found, I guess. He might want them." But the thought of handing them over to a stranger bothered her. She had so little of Simon left. "I'll just put these away and then I'll join you."

Mary Lou hesitated. "Why not leave them here?" When Sarah continued to gather them, she said, "Lord, you're as fussy about them as Simon was."

Tensing, Sarah glanced at her. "What do you mean?"

"Well, he left a chart at the beauty shop accidentally one night. His car was at Pete's Garage and on his way to pick it up he dropped by. My husband was there and gave Simon a lift. Simon forgot all about the chart. He called the moment they got to Pete's. Made me swear not to read it." Mary Lou shrugged. "I never did understand why he was so upset. I mean everyone knows everything about everybody in this town."

Not everything, Sarah thought grimly. *You don't know that Simon was murdered. You also wouldn't know that it was odd for Simon to remove files from the office.* "When was this?" she asked sharply.

"Two days before the fire." Frowning, Mary Lou opened the front door. Glancing over her shoulder she added quietly, "The reason I remember it, is because it was the last time we really talked."

Sarah swallowed. She had been on the right track. Unfortunately the fire had destroyed whatever evidence the files had contained.

Suddenly Mary Lou muttered beneath her breath, "Oh, hell, that's just what we need. Devlin's parking his truck right next to your car. Want me to close the door?"

"No," Sarah said grimly. Carefully, she placed the files back down on the floor. "There's the small matter of the dent in my car." The bigger issues would have to wait, she thought as she joined Mary Lou at the door.

Hugh Devlin drove a black pickup, but no horns decorated the hood of the gleaming truck, Sarah noticed, disappointed. He was a stocky, dark-haired man in his midthirties, dressed in black jeans and a white Western-style shirt. Lines of dissipation marked his florid complexion. Gold glinted at his short thick neck and his cuffs were carefully peeled back to show off a golden Rolex on one wrist and a thick, diamond-studded bracelet on the other. On his hairy ring finger Sarah spotted an enormous signet ring with a big diamond solitaire. A black Stetson with a snakeskin band and gray snakeskin boots completed his flashy outfit.

Then Sarah noticed a tan-and-white pickup with bull horns decorating the hood pull into a parking spot a few feet down the street. Fear curled in her stomach when she recognized Rod Snyder. Devlin had arrived with reinforcements, it seemed. Nudging a suddenly apprehensive Mary Lou out onto the sidewalk she ordered sharply, "Go back to the beauty parlor."

Mary Lou laid a protective hand on her stomach, but dug in her heels. "I'm not leaving you."

"He's trying to intimidate me, that's all," Sarah whispered as Hugh Devlin stepped onto the sidewalk. "But I want you to call the sheriff, just in case."

Though reluctant, Mary Lou started down the street.

Not wanting Devlin to see the files scattered on the floor behind her, Sarah closed the door. Preferring attack to defense, she said, "I assume you've come to look over the damage your bull caused to my car."

"Among other things." Hugh Devlin stopped a foot away from her, looking her over with small dark eyes. "You're just a little thing, but you sure like to stir up trouble."

A cloud of strong, cloying cologne made Sarah want to retreat but she refused to budge. "Well, actually it's you who's causing the trouble," she said coolly. "First your bull took a swipe at my car. Then your mother attacked me. Rod Snyder tried to intimidate me at the grocery store. I'm getting tired of being harassed by your family."

Devlin's eyes narrowed with dislike. "Then why don't you go back where you came from? You can tell your insurance company that I ain't paying for your car nohow. You had my mother arrested, so I reckon we're quits," he drawled, rocking on his heels.

The overpowering scent of the cologne was stinging her nostrils. To her dismay, her eyes began to water and her nose began to itch. "I had nothing to do with your mother's arrest. She attacked the sheriff with mustard," Sarah pointed out firmly, rubbing her nose to relieve the itch. Out of the corner of her eye, she watched Rod Snyder move closer and she stiffened. Her chin went up a notch. She doubted that either man would lay a hand on her out here in the middle of town. "I don't think my insurance company or my lawyer will consider your mother's arrest adequate compensation for the dent in my fender."

"Damn New Yorkers. Always threatening to sue." One of his hairy hands shot out and clamped on Sarah's arm. "It won't work with me."

Suddenly somewhere nearby tires squealed. Then Pete's tow truck pulled up behind Devlin's pickup. Mary Lou came rushing up the sidewalk with her mother Luella in tow.

Devlin glared at the gathering crowd, dropped his arm and snarled, "All right, get the damn dent fixed."

Sarah was so stunned, not by Devlin's capitulation, but by the open support, that her fingers stilled and a big sneeze erupted. With a curse Devlin leapt back, wiping at his shirt. A second sneeze followed and Devlin retreated another step right to the high edge of the sidewalk. The high heels of his boots slipped off and he began to sway. His arms flailed as he tried to regain his balance; then he teetered over the edge. At the last moment he caught himself and landed on his feet in the street, bracing himself on his truck.

A hysterical giggle welled up in Sarah. She bit down hard on her lip. Ridiculing a vain man like Devlin would be more dangerous than baiting one of his Brahman bulls. Mary Lou clapped a hand in front of her mouth and her mother Luella said faintly, "Oh my Lord."

Coming out of the alley, Cord felt no such restraint. He chuckled out loud. But his grin vanished abruptly when he heard Devlin snarl, "You'll pay for that, you bitch."

In three long strides, Cord brushed past Sarah and leapt down the sidewalk, landing right next to Devlin like a cat. Before he hit the ground, a beet red, furious Devlin started to swing a fist at him. Cord caught his wrist in midair, twisting it behind his back. "No one insults the women on the Circle K and gets away with it. Apologize to Dr. Durand."

Sarah anxiously stared from Cord's hard taut face to Devlin's furious visage, then up and down the street.

"I called the sheriff," May Lou whispered.

Nodding, Sarah wondered how Cord always managed to appear when there was trouble afoot. Then she spotted Rod Snyder leap down the curb on the other side of her car, trying to approach Cord from the back. Pete also saw him and simply opened his door to block Rod's way, slowly sliding out of the cab. Glancing around, Sarah noticed that other shoppers had stopped and were drawing closer. Halfway up the block Bill Cowley peeked out of his store and made a thumbs-up sign before going back inside.

Devlin snarled something. When Cord released him, he rubbed his wrist and took a brief glance around. "You'll be sorry. All of you—" he threatened, shaking his fist. He broke off abruptly as a siren started to blare nearby. Climbing into his truck, he glared at Pete. "Move your truck." When Pete didn't respond, he snarled, "Fix the doc's car and send me the bill."

"Will do." Pete climbed back into his truck and drove off before Devlin could change his mind. Devlin shot out of the parking spot and raced down the street, swiftly followed by his foreman.

Cord leapt up on the sidewalk, raking Sarah's face with a swift searching look. "You okay?"

Sarah nodded. She wanted to shout at him that she didn't want to be defended. Oddly, she wanted to hug him, too. But since she didn't want to do either in plain view of everyone, she raised her chin. "Did you say city-slicker ways don't work around here?"

Behind her, Mary Lou and her mother started giggling. For a moment Sarah tried to fight the laughter bubbling up in her. Then Cord started to chuckle and her restraint vanished.

Pulling into the parking spot recently vacated by Devlin, Dan Holt climbed out of his car. Hands on hips, he surveyed the grinning group with disgust. "I guess no one wants to press charges against Devlin again."

Still giggling, Mary Lou stepped forward. "Whatever for? It was Devlin who got hurt. Maybe Devlin wants to press charges against Doc Durand. She pushed him off the sidewalk."

"She did?" Dan Holt raked Sarah's slender form. "How?"

"With a sneeze."

As laughter erupted again, Sarah's face sobered. She had made a bitter enemy. Devlin would never forgive or forget the humiliating scene. Suddenly shivering in the bright noon sun, she spun around and walked back into the office. Frowning, Cord followed her. "He didn't touch you, did he?" he asked sharply, closing the door.

Sarah shook her head. "What happened at the sheriff's office?"

Cord shrugged, but couldn't quite hide his satisfaction that Dan Holt hadn't questioned any of the information. "We were both looking for the boy when Mary Lou called." With a glance at the files he asked, "Did you find anything?"

Sarah sighed with relief. Swiftly, she told him what she'd learned from Mary Lou. Cord frowned and rubbed the back of his neck. "If Simon was concerned about the safety of those files, wouldn't he have put them in a safe place? Maybe we should make a trip out to the house and look for them." He gave her a searching glance. "Can you handle that?"

Sarah nodded. She was beginning to think that with Cord at her side she could face just about anything. "What I can't understand is why Simon didn't go to the FBI or the INS."

"Maybe he did," Cord said harshly, looking at her with hard bitter eyes. "It's entirely possible that Simon did contact the INS and talked to the one man whose name he knew. Harper." Abruptly he paced across the room, the old boards creaking beneath his weight. He opened the door and stared out into the sunshine. "Simon knew I worked with Harper. He had no reason not to trust him," he continued, his voice flat. "The bastard even publicly expressed his doubts on my guilt after my arraignment. When I disappeared, he ordered an extensive search. Hell, even my father thinks he's a good guy."

Stunned, Sarah stared at Cord's broad back. She could feel the stalking tension in him, the bitterness and the pain. It pulsed silently across the room, reaching her, sinking into her, wrapping itself around her heart. She understood suddenly why he had kept even his family at a distance. It nearly broke her heart that he thought that the members of his own family, the family he had struggled so hard to protect, also doubted him.

"Oh, Cord." Sarah went across the room to where he stood. Wrapping her arms around him from behind, she hugged him with fierce tenderness. "I don't believe it," she said into his black sweatshirt, guessing what had happened. He felt guilty about the devastation and pain he had caused the family and had isolated himself emotionally, too proud to explain himself. And he had no clue how to break through the self-imposed barriers and communicate with them properly. It didn't help that his father was cut from the same cloth. Both men were strong control types who didn't wear their hearts on their sleeves. "Did you ever try to explain to your father what happened?"

Cord turned around abruptly, taking her by surprise, and framed her face with his strong, callused hands. Words failed him when he thought of what her unquestioning belief meant to him. "I shouldn't have to explain things to him."

Sarah's heart wrenched at his words. It couldn't have been easy growing up in Big John's shadow, she thought. "He's not clairvoyant," she pointed out sensibly. "And neither are you. Maybe there are other reasons why your father spends so much time in San Antonio. Your mother for one."

"Yeah. He's the forever-kind-of-guy. Except that my mother doesn't want any part of him." Cord's mouth twisted at the irony. He had only met Sarah a few short days ago and already she had become essential to him.

Sarah shivered beneath the heat and intensity in his eyes. She could have told him that Renee was as desperately in love with her ex-husband as she was with Cord, but Cord didn't want to hear that. She wrapped her arms around his neck and kissed him instead. "Don't repeat my mistakes," she warned gently. "Talk to your father while you have the chance."

Sarah decided to get her car fixed before Devlin could change his mind and dropped it off at Pete's Garage, returning with Cord to the ranch for lunch. When Pete had warned her that it would take three days, she had almost changed her mind. Without a car she would be dependent on Cord for transportation, and she feared that he would leave her behind at the ranch.

Maisy had solved that problem by offering her car. "What with the family coming down for the weekend, I'll be much too busy for the next few days," she'd said. "And if I need something from town, you can get it for me."

During lunch, Angel entertained everyone with stories about her new friend Amy. "She let me ride her pink bicycle. It has training wheels and doesn't tip over. Can I go back and play with her after lunch? Her mother says it's all right."

"Don't you want another riding lesson?" Jimmy T. asked. "Princess is going to miss you."

"And here I thought you wanted a ride on one of them big tractors," Chuck said. "But I see you're much too busy."

Angel looked around the table with shining brown eyes. "I like it here. There's so much to do. I want to stay here forever and ever."

Tommy Lee, a young blond-haired giant with merry hazel eyes, looked at Sarah. "How about it, Doc? We'll fix up that office of yours real nice." He glanced at Cord, who was sitting at the head of the long table. "No offense, boss, but meals sure are more fun with the doc and her daughter around."

José Peña held a brown work-worn hand across the table. "Got me a big splinter in my hand."

Sarah grimaced at the sight of the sliver of wood lodged in the ball of his thumb and started to rise.

Cord put a hand on her shoulder, sending José a bland look, well aware that his men were trying their hands at matchmaking. "He's not going to die in the next five minutes." Glancing from one man to the other, he said, "Let's get one thing straight. The doc is not going to be disturbed during meals unless it's an emergency. Scratches and bruises can wait until after meals."

He paused for a moment, then continued. "There's something else. We have trouble with Devlin again. From now on everyone—and I mean *everyone,* and no exceptions—checks in with Chuck at thirty-minute intervals. And you double up if you work anywhere near Devlin's spread."

Chuck looked at Cord. "Does that go for you, too, boss?"

Before Cord could shake his head, Sarah said smugly, "'Everyone, and no exceptions' sounds pretty clear to me."

Chapter 12

During the ten-minute drive to Simon's property, Sarah sat on the edge of the seat. Not even Cord's riling comments, that it would be her responsibility to keep track of time and call in every thirty minutes, could dispel the tension.

She was dreading the visit to the site of the fire more than anything else. For weeks she'd had nightmare visions of Simon being trapped in the fire, fighting for his life. She knew a fire's merciless greed only too well. Once before she had watched everything be consumed in flames.

Bushes and small evergreens shielded the site from the road. As Cord turned onto the blacktop driveway, silence greeted them. To their left, weeds grew knee-high along a split-rail fence enclosing a big pasture and a freshly painted white barn. It looked so peaceful, Sarah thought.

Then the house, or what was left of it, came into view. Directly in front of it stood the burned-out shell of Simon's truck. After Cord parked the car, Sarah numbly walked to the edge of the front lawn, where the brown winter grass had been scorched. The heavy rains had cleansed the three low, crumbling corners of the house that were still standing like charred sentinels. On the inside, ashes had also been washed away by the storm. Here and there, patches of pale concrete slab were visible beneath the piles of charred debris.

But painful as the sight was, Sarah didn't really feel the turmoil she had steeled herself against.

Perhaps it was because the area had been somewhat cleansed. Much like her soul.

Wrapping her arms around herself, she realized that she was beginning to forgive herself.

Behind her she heard the breaking of a twig as Cord joined her. He didn't touch her, but he stood so close behind her, she could feel his breath in her hair and the warmth radiating from him. She smiled faintly. He always seemed to understand just what she needed. But then, he, too, had been through hell. She doubted that she would ever have had the courage to reach out to anyone else the way she had to Cord. Perhaps she had done so because in her imagination he had always been a golden knight. To see him being rejected, treated like an outcast, had been more than she could bear. And now, thanks to him, by forcing her to bring all the old festering wounds to the surface, they were beginning to heal.

Cord, too, was healing. Instinctively she knew this to be the truth.

But he still had to forgive himself.

She leaned against him and his arms came around her, surrounding her, warming her like a cloak. He said nothing, but she could hear the steady beat of his heart, the whisper of his breath. Suddenly the silence was no longer threatening, but pulsing with life.

She raised her face into the warm afternoon sun. Perhaps it was time to bring the last of the old ghosts to light.

"This sight reminds me strongly of my parents' home, or what was left of it after it burned down," she said. "I've often wondered if somehow I'm cursed. After my family's funeral, in the women's quarters, one of my great-aunts, an old nomad woman who was supposed to have the 'sight,' told me that I would be punished for my cowardice. That none of the persons I loved would...die of natural causes." She stirred, burrowing deeper into his embrace. "I know now that she was frightened. They all were. They were bound by their faith and family honor to take me in and to protect me. And the curse gave them a convenient—and valid—reason to rid themselves of 'the American' without looking like cowards."

She drew a weary breath. "I keep telling myself that there is no such thing as a curse. I keep telling myself that. But the indisputable fact is that none of the people I've loved, who have died since, have died of natural causes."

Frowning, Cord stared down at the haunted look in her dark exotically tilted eyes and understood at last why she had charged into danger to keep him safe. The realist in her might not believe in superstitions and karma, but there was a child hidden in every adult. And the vulnerable, shocked, grieving twelve-year-old had believed in kismet. To her it must have seemed like the ultimate punishment to be cast out of her close-knit family. The child in her still thought of herself as a coward, as worthless. Cursed. The losses she had experienced over the years had fed that belief. Somehow, Cord thought grimly, he would have to change her mind about that, or she might never have the courage to love again.

To love him.

"That woman probably saved your life," he said quietly.

Startled, Sarah tilted her head back and looked at him. "What do you mean?"

One of Cord's brows rode up questioningly. "Didn't Simon explain the situation to you when he adopted you?"

Sarah shook her head. "I know that he had problems. But I was a very frightened girl at the time. He and Lisa tried to shield me as much as possible." It seemed to her that she had been scared and frightened most of her life. And she was tired of it. "The lawyers said that Mother's older sister, Lucy, changed her mind about taking me in when she found out that I wasn't penniless. My parents had set up educational trust funds for my brothers and me in the States and my father had already transferred most of the family's assets. Simon had been my godfather and had also been one of the trustees. When Lucy found out that Simon would keep control of the funds she withdrew her offer."

Nice people, Cord thought sarcastically, but that hadn't been what he'd meant. "Simon once mentioned that he had some problems with the INS and that without permission from your Iranian family he would never have been able to get you out of the country or adopt you so easily."

Startled, Sarah turned and looked at him. "What permission? Simon smuggled me out. Right after my parents' funeral, the following day, he said that he was taking me to the States. It was what my parents had wanted, but because of what had happened, I was to tell no one about it." Frowning, she tried to recall those hazy, terror-filled days, the painful memories she had tried to erase from her mind. "Later that night, after everyone was asleep, I sneaked out of the house. In the courtyard I ran into Mehmet, my father's younger brother, who had become the head of the family. He didn't ask me where I was going. I guess he knew. He stood there with his hands balled into fists, as if trying to control his anger. Simon was there, too. I remember running to him and holding on to his hand, afraid that if I let go, he, too, would suddenly leave. Mehmet looked at me for a long time. Tears were running down his face. He didn't say anything and I thought he despised me so much he couldn't even bear to say goodbye."

Cord's arms tightened around her. He might not approve of the way her family had sent her off, but it had been effective. "If he *had* said anything, if he had hugged you, if the rest of them had welcomed you, would you have left?''

Slowly Sarah shook her head. ''They were my family,'' she said simply. Understanding dawned. She felt as if a great weight were suddenly sliding off her shoulders. Pushing her glasses on top of her head, she ran a shaky hand over her face. ''How could I have misunderstood?'' she whispered, feeling light-headed with relief. ''I loved them. They were such a warm, close-knit family. That was why their rejection hurt so much.'' She drew another shaky breath. ''All these years I thought they blamed me when all they tried to do was what was best for me and to protect themselves at the same time.''

A great surge of warmth spilled through her. It was, she thought, as if she had been given back her family. She might never see them again, might never be able to talk to them again, but she was no longer alone in the world.

She had been given back a part of herself she had denied for so long.

Slowly she turned and met Cord's warm smoky gray gaze. ''How can I ever thank you for putting up with me? You've given me back some very precious memories.'' Her voice was a little unsteady when she added, ''I hate to agree with you, cowboy, but maybe I truly am blind as a bat.''

Tenderness and humor glinted in Cord's eyes and his mouth twisted wryly. Everyone else seemed to have realized by now that he was in love with her. Everyone but Sarah. *She* still believed that all he wanted was a no-strings affair. ''I'm not going to argue with you, Doc.''

For a moment he stared down at her. There was a glow to her skin and a tenderness in her dark eyes that made him catch his breath. For what seemed like forever, but was mere seconds, he waited. Waited for her to say something. No, not just anything, he realized. He knew exactly what he wanted to hear. Odd, but he had never thought he would need to hear the words. Or need to say them himself. Yet he did. He wanted to be free to tell her that he loved her. And more than anything he wanted her to look at him and tell him that she loved him.

Then his glance strayed to the devastation beyond and reality returned.

For now he had to put aside his own wants and needs. For right now he had his hands full in keeping her safe. She didn't need the extra pressure love meant to her, and he needed a cool, clear head. For *both* their sakes he couldn't afford to become distracted anymore. Steeling himself, he took her hand and drew her toward the ruins. "Let's get to work."

An hour later, Cord tossed away the stick he'd been using to rake through the timber and debris. For a moment he watched Sarah as she shifted a small piece of charred wood near the fireplace with gloved hands. She was filthy. They both were. Her gray sweatshirt and jeans were streaked with soot, and her white sneakers were now black. Her hair, pinned loosely at the back of her head, was falling down, long strands of it clinging to her damp flushed face. There was a big smudge on her cheek, standing stark black against the paleness of her skin. She'd had enough. Looking down at himself, he grimaced. And so had he.

They had systematically searched the place, but so far, all they had found were a few china plates that somehow had been overlooked before. No fuse box lid, or fireproof box of any kind, was to be found. "It's time to check in," he reminded her.

During the past hour, clouds had moved overhead, but at ground level the air was still stifling, no breeze relieving the heat. He could almost smell the sulphur. "We're in for a thunderstorm," he stated.

Sarah straightened, wiping her brow with her sleeve, trying to mask her disappointment. She had known that the chances of finding anything had been slim. Still, the discovery of three of Lisa's precious Wedgwood plates had caused her hope to flare, if briefly. Wearily, she drew off her gloves and wiped her hands on her jeans. With a glance at the steadily darkening sky, she said, "Perhaps we should quit. I doubt that we'll find anything else."

Nodding, Cord's glance swept the surrounding land, dotted with mesquite bushes and low-growing shrubs, his eyes resting thoughtfully on the fenced-in pasture. "You check in. I'll take a swift look at the barn."

Climbing into the truck, Sarah reached for the CB, but kept a watchful eye on Cord. She felt tension running through her, like a fine electronic sensor suddenly buzzing off inside. A glance out the rear window revealed nothing. While working beside Cord, she hadn't felt threatened by the isolation and silence, but now, suddenly, her every sense was humming, perhaps, she told herself, because, with his loose-limbed stride, he was quickly moving away from her. She picked up the mike and radioed in.

"You're five minutes late," Chuck growled. "Better head on home. We're in for a thunderstorm. Messes up the signals something bad. Over."

"We plan to in a few minutes. Cord's just taking a look at the barn," Sarah said, watching him vault over the fence and stride toward the building nestled among tall oaks. "How's Angel?"

A deep chuckle came over the mike. "I don't rightly know how to tell you this, Doc, but she ain't missing you much."

Sarah bit her lip. Her daughter was becoming independent, growing away from her. A part of her, the selfish part, didn't like the idea but, deep down, she wouldn't have it any other way. She wouldn't want Angel moping around. "I'm glad," she said softly. "I don't know how to thank you. All of you. You're all so kind and patient with her."

"Don't you worry none, we'll figure out somethin'," Chuck drawled. "Watch out for them coyotes on your way home. Over and out."

Coyotes. Chuck wasn't referring to the four-legged variety, Sarah knew. Replacing the mike, her uneasiness returned. Perhaps it was being alone that bothered her, but she didn't question her need to stay close to Cord. Leaping from the truck she dashed toward the fence.

Climbing through the rails her foot hit something hidden among the knee-high weeds and her ankle twisted. Rubbing her foot, she spotted a bulky black object a few feet away. Her hand stilled. Walking closer, she parted the plants and swallowed hard.

Covered with dirt, its leather cracked from exposure, stood Simon's black medical bag.

"*Cord!*" Picking it up, she pressed it against her body and ran to the barn.

Alarmed by the sound of her voice, Cord ran outside, gun in hand.

At the sight of the gun, Sarah slowed down. She hadn't realized that he was carrying one, although she should have expected it. Her mouth suddenly dry, she held out the bag. "This is Simon's," she said, her voice hoarse. "It was over among the weeds at the fence. Simon would never have left his bag out in the open. Never in a million years." As she watched him slide the gun's safety catch on, and return it to his belt at the small of his back, Sarah felt the silence surrounding them suddenly begin to throb with danger.

"Maybe he was being followed home that last night and tossed it out." Cord took the bag from her hands and started to open it. Suddenly the hairs at the back of his neck rose like small antennae, alerting him that they were no longer alone. "We're being watched," he said sharply. Grabbing Sarah's arm he drew her inside the barn. "Check the bag's contents," he ordered. Withdrawing his gun again, he searched the land with narrowed, sharp eyes.

Lightning flashed in the distance, and thunder rolled like faraway drums.

Sitting down on the dirt floor, Sarah opened the bag.

Inside she found a folded manila envelope, wrinkled as if it had been stuffed hastily inside.

"I think I've found what we're looking for," she whispered. "Here's a letter, sealed and addressed." Taking it out, she smoothed it with a shaky hand. Holding the paper to the light, she caught her breath. "It's from Simon. You were right, Cord," she said slowly. "Simon did contact Harper. The envelope is addressed to him. Looks like he didn't have time to mail it."

Cord felt his hope flare up again, and a fresh surge of hate. Then he caught a movement among the bushes. Keeping his eyes trained on the spot, he said tersely, "Open it and look inside."

With a look at her grimy hands, Sarah took two packets of alcohol swabs from the bag and cleaned her hands. Then she carefully slid a thumbnail beneath the flap and opened it. "There are some photocopies, and a note to Harper. The photocopies are treatment records of five illegals." Swiftly she leafed through them, her excitement growing as she found signed statements by the victims. They were chilling tales of brutal beatings and rape. Names were listed and assailants described, including Devlin, Snyder and Slim.

"Snyder's specialty is floggings," Cord said, his voice hard and grim. "I once saw him beat a sixteen-year-old wetback to within an inch of his life, because he tried to escape from the Devlin ranch. Snyder would have killed him if Vicky and I hadn't come along and rescued him."

Sarah thought of the man's merciless blue eyes and shivered. "I hope he hasn't found the boy in town."

"I doubt it. I told you the kid probably left." A brief hard smile flashed across Cord's face. "But if he hasn't and we find him, I know just where to send him. To that same wetback Vicky and I rescued and hid in a line shack for over a week. Now Luis is a colonel with Mexican Immigration. He was the one who helped me find Mariela. They'd be good for each other, I think."

Sarah looked at him with aching tenderness. Beneath that tough hide of his he was such a caring, tender man. And suddenly the words she had been afraid to say, above all else, slipped naturally from her lips. "I love you, Cord."

Cord's head jerked around, and their eyes connected. He had known that she cared, and cared more deeply than she wanted to admit even to herself. But until she'd said those three little words, he hadn't realized how much he needed to hear her say them. And how much he needed to say them himself. "I love you, too, Sarah."

Suddenly a bullet slammed into the wood mere inches away from his face. Cursing, he leapt back, raking Sarah's taut white face with a brief hard glance. "You do choose your moments, Doc," he growled, inching forward to take another glance outside. He saw the bushes close to the driveway move briefly as the sniper shifted position. He would have given his eyeteeth for a high-powered rifle just then. "I won't let you take back those words," he told her with quiet determination.

Sarah felt a lump of ice-cold fear clogging her throat. She wanted to leap to her feet and run. Instead, she forced herself to remain seated on the dirt floor. "I don't want to take them back. But I do wish that my fears weren't being tested quite so soon. That sniper could have had the decency to give us at least time for one kiss," she said with the unflappable calm that had once irritated the hell out of Cord.

Now he found it reassuring. He smiled, a brief hard smile, edged with determination. "I'll make it up to you, Doc."

Sarah's fingers gripped the papers in her hands, wrinkling them. "I'll hold you to that promise, cowboy," she said, blinking against the sudden moisture in her eyes. She couldn't bear it if something happened to him, she thought. But thinking that way was madness. If they wanted to come out of this alive, she couldn't afford to fall apart. Not now. Pushing back her fears, she smoothed out the wrinkled papers and skimmed the pages. The information in them just might save their lives. "Oh my God," she said, "Three of the victims claimed they were flown across the border in a small plane, then taken to a safe house near here in a cattle truck. Apparently there was a closed-in section in the front of the trailer. The rest was filled with rodeo bulls."

Cord swore softly, viciously. "I should have guessed," he muttered, sending a worried glance at the swiftly darkening sky.

Sarah frowned. She wouldn't allow him to blame himself. "So should have the sheriff, and Chuck and the INS men keeping an eye on Devlin. Do you think you're so much smarter than they are?"

A brief, almost cocky smile flashed across Cord's face. "Yeah, and my mother has a box full of commendations and medals to prove it." Then a brooding look came into his eyes. "I spent eight years chasing guys like Devlin. But when it came to a crunch, those medals were just so much scrap metal."

"You didn't do it for the medals, Cord," Sarah pointed out quietly. "You helped. You made a difference. That knowledge no one can take away from you."

"Maybe." Cord raised one brow and taunted, "I thought you didn't like heroes."

Sarah bit her lip. It wasn't quite true and they both knew it. It was the fear of losing them that she detested. And the mere thought of him possibly returning to his old job made her blood freeze, but her love for him was strong. Above all else she wanted him whole again. "Well, I have to admit that at this moment a hero would be a bit more useful than a coward," she said dryly.

A chuckle escaped Cord. Guessing what that remark must have cost her, he said gently, "We'll make it, Doc. I've survived worse odds."

Sarah thought of the scars and bit her lip. "Do you know how many are out there?"

"One. He probably saw you find the bag. That's what he's after, I guess." Cord kept his voice low, calm, even. "He's holed up in the bushes along the road. He can't get any closer because there's very little cover. The shot was a warning. He's letting us know that he's got us trapped. He must have followed us, or listened to the CB."

Sarah drew in a sharp breath. "I'm sorry, I didn't think of that."

Cord shrugged. "If I hadn't thought it was worth the risk, I wouldn't have gone along with it. The trouble is, with this storm about to break, we can't afford to wait for Chuck. Once it starts pouring, that sniper will have all the cover he needs. And he may have radioed for reinforcements." Lightning flashed across the sky and thunder grumbled. The storm was much closer now. Cord slanted another glance at the dark sky. He figured they had about another five minutes before the storm broke. "I'm going to get the truck."

Sarah slid the sheets back into the envelope and got to her feet. Folding it, she stuck it into the front of her jeans. "I'm going with you." She wasn't going to stay behind in safety while someone she loved took all the risks. Not this time. Never again.

Cord didn't waste time arguing with her. They had about two hundred feet of open space to cross before the sky's floodgates opened. His hand closed hard over Sarah's. Crouching, they waited until lightning flashed again. Once the sky darkened they dashed outside. The smell of sulphur was stronger now and thunder clapped almost instantly, loud and strong. Bending low, they raced across the pasture, Cord dragging her along, keeping his body between her and the sniper.

No shots fell until they neared the fence.

Sarah knew she couldn't match his easy leap over the top rail and tried to twist her hand free as the fence loomed up in front of them. "Run on ahead," she gasped.

Cord's hand tightened. "Don't waste your breath."

The first drops of rain fell as they reached the fence. When the shots suddenly rang out, the bullets thumped into the ground and the posts beside them. Together they dived between the bottom and middle rails, landing facedown in the knee-high weeds. The shots abruptly stopped.

Cord allowed Sarah a few seconds to catch her breath. "You're out of shape, Doc," he growled, deliberately riling her to distract her.

During their mad dash Sarah had lost her glasses and her hair was tumbling down. Breathing hard, she wiped hair and weeds from her face, then shot him a nasty look. "You weren't forced to race at twice your normal jogging speed."

"You're that slow? Got to do better than that or you'll never keep up with me."

"Should I want to?"

The rain started to come down harder. They had another twenty feet of ground to cross before reaching the safety of the truck. Cord grasped her hand. "Come on, Doc, you can argue with me later. After you get your breath back."

"Show-off!" Sarah grumbled, her hand curling around his.

They shot from the weeds and dashed across the space just as the sky opened up. Only one bullet was fired, and that was way off the mark.

Scrambling into the passenger side of the pickup, Cord slid across the bench, wiping moisture from his face. By the time Sarah slammed her door, he had started the engine and the pickup was racing down the drive. "Keep your head down and call Chuck on the CB," he ordered. Inwardly he cursed the rain. It was so heavy, he could barely see five feet in front of him.

Flattening her body on the bench, Sarah tried to reach Chuck, but there was too much static in the air. "I can't get through," she said after several attempts, hanging up the mike. Lightning flashed and thunder clapped in quick succession. The storm was right above them. Cord turned on the wipers, but not the lights. The fact that the sniper was holding his fire was little cause for comfort. As he shot out of the drive, a black pickup appeared right behind him out of the curtain of rain. As lightning lit the sky yet again, the bull horns on the front hood gleamed wickedly.

Cord floored the gas pedal, cursing viciously. Without Sarah he would have stopped, but he wasn't going to take any chances with her life. She had put on her seat belt, he noted with approval, and was reaching for the mike again. "Keep calling," he said. "The base station has more power and might hear the signal."

The pickup behind them inched closer. At the next thunder clap, the rear window shattered. The bullet hit one of the shotgun barrels and ricocheted into the floor behind them. Sarah sat up and brushed glass from her face and hair, her eyes widening with horror as she spotted a big obstacle suddenly charging through the rain, coming at them at high speed. "Watch out," she cried, gripping the door handle tightly and bracing herself with her feet.

Cord had already seen it. "It's that damn cattle truck again." His hands tightened on the wheel. "This is a trap. Hold on tight, Sarah. I'll try passing it on the shoulder. If we get stuck, run into the pasture. And keep running. Don't look back. Promise you won't wait for me."

Protest rose hotly to her lips, but, with one look at his grim hard face, she swallowed it. His scar stood out sharply. Then she recalled this morning's scene, when she had left him behind to protect him. Dear Lord, had it only been this morning?

A sudden jolt from behind sent their pickup spinning across the narrow road, right into the truck's path. "Promise!" Cord demanded through clenched teeth, pulling the wheel in the opposite direction so sharply, the pickup tilted onto two wheels. For long seconds it hung there precariously, and then the wheels dropped back down.

Sarah shot an anguished look at Cord's set face. "I promise. As long as you stay close behind me." Grimly, she clung to the door handle as their pickup shot across the road. The big truck was no more then five feet in front of them. "If you do something stupid, cowboy, I'll haunt you forever," she threatened on a near sob.

"Deal." Cord sent the pickup hurtling through the muddy ditch, felt himself losing speed. He held his breath until he could feel the big front tires grip the grass covering the slope.

Another shot ran out.

Cord cursed as he felt one of the rear tires go flat and the pickup slow down even more. Leaning across Sarah, he flung the door open, unsnapped her safety belt, then shoved her out of the cab. *"Run."*

Sarah hit the ground and started racing up the slope. Rain lashed her face, soaking her in seconds. The grass was slippery beneath her sneakers and she pulled herself up with her hands on tufts of grass. She almost didn't see the fence in the downpour. Throwing herself on the ground, she rolled beneath the wire, her sweatshirt snagging on the barbs. Then she was up and running, trying to listen for Cord's steps behind her, but unable to hear anything above the drumming in her ears.

Then she heard a volley of shots.

Sarah spun around. She slipped on the wet grass and fell, just as the black vehicle came halfway up the slope, its headlights turned on Cord's white pickup. What she saw made her blood freeze. *Cord wasn't following her.* He was crouched behind the pickup, shooting at the cattle truck and the black pickup every time their doors opened. A sob escaped her. That stupid, valiant idiot. He was holding the men off to give her a chance to get away. If she ever got her hands on him—

Then, to her horror, the window of the cattle truck slid down and a gun appeared, spraying the pickup with a hail of bullets. Sarah knew little about guns, but even she recognized the sound of machine-gun fire. While Cord took cover behind the front tire, two men leapt down from the far side of the truck and continued shooting at Cord's pickup. From the opposite side, the driver leaped from the black truck, also opening fire.

A scream ripped from her throat. *Not again. Not again.* she repeated in her mind as her nightmare took on grim reality. Mindlessly, blindly, she started sliding down the slope, her one thought that she had to reach Cord.

Apparently her scream had been heard above the sound of the rain and gunfire. Abruptly, they both died down. Into the sudden silence a man shouted, "Get the woman."

Suddenly, bellows erupted from the cattle truck, horns butted against metal, chains rattled. There were shouts and screams coming from the trailer, too.

"Where'd she go?" a man yelled, raising his voice above the din.

Cord hadn't been able to clearly identify the first voice. But there was no doubt about the second man. It was Devlin.

"Don't know. Just get her. Can't let her get away," the first voice ordered again.

Harper! He aimed at the man making for the slope. Cord's finger tightened on the trigger and the man reeled back with a cry of pain, clutching his shoulder. A smile of grim satisfaction curled Cord's lips as he recognized Snyder. "Leave her be, Harper," he yelled. "She has nothing to do with this." His blood froze at the thought of what the man would do to Sarah if he caught up with her.

"You should've learned your lesson the last time, and stopped messing with me. But your kind never learns," the driver of the black pickup jeered. "The doc was another idealistic fool. Talking about the doc, I want the stuff he promised to send to me."

"Let the woman go, and I'll give it to you."

"No deal. Rodriguez wants you real bad. You stole Mariela right from under his nose, and he's blaming me for it. Reckon he'll be mighty pleased to get his hands on your woman."

Ice-cold fury welled up in Cord. He knew he was playing right into Harper's hands, but couldn't stop himself. He leapt to the rear end of his truck and fired at the windshield of the black pickup. A scream told him that he had hit his target, but there was no telling how badly wounded Harper was. A volley of shots ripped through the air. Cord flinched as one of them gouged his shoulder. Ignoring the burning sensation, he retreated behind the front wheel and slid a fresh clip into his gun.

Suddenly, a movement to his far right attracted his attention. His heart froze as he spotted Sarah crawling out of the ditch behind the cattle truck, her gray sweatshirt barely visible in the rain. Damned if he ever let her out of his sight again, he swore, then opened fire once more to cover her.

Harper. Devlin. Snyder. Each one of the names sent terror racing through her. Sarah dashed behind the cattle truck and leaped onto the running board, trying to push the words she'd overheard to the back of her mind. Chuck would have missed them by now. He would be here soon. If she could buy them time by creating a diversion, they might make it.

For a moment she clung to the truck doors, studying the locking mechanism. The bulls were so frightened by now, they were rocking the trailer and kicking against the doors. Standing on her toes, she reached for the heavy metal crossbar which was secured with a pin at the side of the truck. No locks, she noticed as she tugged at the slippery pin with both hands, probably because no sane person would want to free the Brahmans. With the bulls leaning on and kicking the gate, it seemed forever before she finally managed to slide it up.

Finally, the pin slipped out. Spring action made the bar swing back, releasing the locks and opening the gate completely. The first Brahman exploded from the trailer like a cannonball, brushing past Sarah with less than an inch to spare. The leap to the hard road momentarily jolted the bull. As he hit the pavement, he stumbled and went down. Then the second bull charged from the other side of the center partition, just as the first one recovered and leapt to his feet. He veered to avoid a collision and raced toward the front in a blind, panicked rage.

Sarah flattened herself against the side of the truck and held her breath, hoping that the bull wouldn't notice her. He didn't. The second one also passed with inches to spare.

Cord was running along the ditch, had been running since he had watched the first bull explode from the trailer. Bullets whizzed past him. Then curses erupted. "The damn bulls are loose!"

As the men fired shots into the air, Cord dashed across the road. Reaching Sarah, who stood as if glued to the side of the trailer, he grabbed her hand and drew her behind it. Around them bulls bellowed, men shouted and a car horn blared.

For a brief moment, Sarah clung to Cord. "It worked," she cried, raising her voice above the din.

Cord kissed her, hard. Gripping her hand tightly, he drew her down the road. The rain was slowing down now and the storm was passing. He wanted to put as much distance between them and Harper as possible. Suddenly, far ahead, he noticed a pair of headlights, then a second, and a third set. Was it Chuck coming to the rescue? Or were they Devlin's men?

The gunmen also noticed the approaching lights. Cursing, they raced to their trucks, Devlin yelling, "Let's get the hell—" The shout ended in a high-pitched scream as one of the Brahmans caught him as he started to climb into the cab, pinning his leg to the truck with its horns.

The scream made Sarah spin around. Then they heard an engine racing and tires spinning and raced up the slope, both realizing that if the cattle truck moved, Harper would have a clear shot at them. Because the barbed wire wasn't high enough off the ground for Sarah to roll beneath it, Cord had to lift her across it. Then, glancing over his shoulder, he saw the black pickup nose its way past the cattle truck.

"Get down," he shouted at Sarah. Gripping the post, he vaulted over the fence. But the gouge in his shoulder had made him unexpectedly clumsy, and he didn't clear the wires completely. His jeans snagged. He felt them rip, and he hit the ground a split second too late. The black pickup was charging up the slope behind him and Harper fired. Cord felt a bullet slam into his back.

"Damn," he snarled as his knees buckled and a wave of pain washed over him. For a moment the world went dark and he crashed to the ground. Blinking, he fought the dizziness that immediately assailed him, his one thought to keep Sarah safe. He crawled over to her, covering her with his body while bullets flew past them. Suddenly they stopped. Raising his head, Cord watched the pickup make a U-turn before squeezing past the cattle truck and race down the road, swimming in and out of focus.

Damn it to hell, the son of a bitch had won after all.

Sarah heard Cord curse, then felt his weight settle on top of her. For a moment she was too shaken, too stunned to move, unable to believe that they were safe. But she could feel Cord's warm breath blowing into her ear and the rapid thud of his heart against her back. Squirming, she pushed against his weight. "Get off me, Cord," she muttered, needing to see if he had been hurt. She didn't dare believe that anyone could dash through a hail of bullets and not get hit.

Cord kept her down, keeping the encroaching darkness away by sheer force of will. His glance narrowed on the pickups coming closer at high speed. Recognizing Chuck's tan one, he shifted his weight to his side, allowing Sarah to turn. Then he threw one leg over hers, brushing wet strands of hair from her face. "You just used up all of those nine lives in one big swoop, Doc," he growled, framing her face with unsteady hands. "I told you to run. Damn it, you promised you wouldn't wait for me."

Sarah frowned at the breathless sound of his voice. Her eyes narrowed on his grimy wet face. "Are you hurt?" she asked sharply. Even as she asked, she noticed the rip at his right shoulder. Again she tried to squirm from beneath him, but he wouldn't move. Gripping the fabric with both hands, she ripped it, raising her head to look at the damage. It was no more than a cut, perhaps three inches long and only bleeding sluggishly.

Shock, she thought. He was going into shock. She had nothing to keep him warm. Until Chuck arrived, the warmest place was right where he was, on top of her. "God, you scared the hell out of me, cowboy," she said hoarsely, framing his face, raining kisses all over it. She could have lost him, she thought. But she hadn't. She might lose him tomorrow, or the next day, or years from now. But he would be in her heart, with her forever, whether he lived to be a hundred, or died tomorrow.

Still, she very much wanted those next seventy years. "You were supposed to follow me," she said fiercely, her hands running up and down his sopping black sweatshirt in search of injuries. He didn't flinch, and when she looked at her hands they had no blood on them. "I told you, I hate heroes."

"Don't hate this one too much," Cord whispered. "I'm in no condition to follow you if you decide to leave." He felt cold suddenly, so damn cold. Darkness was closing in on him—a canopy of green leaves. He couldn't feel his legs anymore, either. His speech was beginning to slur, too, he realized. Funny how shock crystallized some senses, though. His need for Sarah was just as sharp as ever. He kissed her fiercely—the forever-kind-of-kiss. Then his head began to swim, and he rested his forehead against hers. At that moment, the cattle truck started to move. He had failed again, Cord thought. "About Harper and Devlin—"

"Don't worry about them," Sarah said. "The sheriff'll take care of them."

Sarah could hear the pickups nearby now. Something was wrong, badly wrong, she thought, reaching for his wrist. His pulse was weak, his respiration rapid and shallow. He was slipping away from her. She raised his head. His eyes were still focusing intently on her, as if she were the center of his universe. "Cord, where are you hurt?" she asked sharply. Even as she asked, she tried to squirm from beneath him, but he was a deadweight on top of her, and his hands held her firmly.

"Somewhere in the back." He managed a crooked grin. "What are you going to do, Doc? Run or stick around?"

His back! Sarah froze at his words. "I'll stick around, cowboy," she promised hoarsely. Tears were pricking her eyes, but her voice was steady and firm. "And not because you're hurt—you'll be up in no time, bossing everyone around—but because I just realized something. You know what forever means?"

He could hear the first pickup skid to a stop. She wouldn't be alone now. He could let go. "I don't think I can make forever, Doc."

She hugged him tightly, tears running down her face. "You can do it, cowboy," she said fiercely. "Forever is the time between two heartbeats. I can handle that. How about you? Can you hang in there? Just reach for the next beat? One at a time?"

He might, just might, be able to handle that. "I'll try."

Chapter 13

As long as she lived, Sarah would never forget the drive to Kingsley County General. She didn't dare wait for an ambulance. A quick examination had shown that the bullet was lodged close to the spine. A few inches above his waist there was very little blood, and his blood pressure was dropping rapidly. He was hemorrhaging internally. She prayed that the bullet had missed the aorta.

They lifted him into the back of Jimmy T.'s truck, the only pickup with a camper top. With only one blanket to help keep him warm, Sarah lay down next to him, holding him, talking to him, one hand on his wrist, monitoring his pulse, willing him to hang on.

From one heartbeat to the next.

He slipped in and out of consciousness, and she felt as helpless as she had during that dark night so long ago. The contents of Simon's medical bag, which Chuck had retrieved, were woefully inadequate, but she didn't stop talking, couldn't stop talking, afraid that she would lose him if

she did. "You know, cowboy, I've never belonged anywhere, not since I left Iran. I always felt like a refugee in this
country, an outsider, unwanted. Then I came down here and
I felt I was home again. Despite everything that's happened, I want to belong here."

"I never truly belonged to another person, except Angel.
I could have, but I was too afraid. Maybe you can't belong
anywhere or to anyone until you stop being afraid and are
willing to fight for it. I'm willing to, cowboy. I'm going to
fight for you and I have the skills now to do it. You're the
best thing that's ever happened to me and Angel and *I'm not
going to let you go, but I need your help, so don't you dare
leave me.*"

Cord hung in there, like he'd promised.

From one heartbeat to the next.

Sarah started to believe that they might make it when she
heard the ambulance in the distance. Halfway to Kingsley,
Cord was transferred gently, swiftly and with great effi-
ciency. Cord refused to let go of her hand during the trans-
fer but lost consciousness soon afterward. The moment the
doors closed, one of the paramedics, Jim, started an IV
while Sarah washed her hands and face.

"We'll have to take him to San Antonio, Doc," he said,
placing the oxygen mask over Cord's face. "Kingsley
County General doesn't have the facilities to take care of
him. It's a small eighty-bed hospital. We only have two surgeons. Dr. Adams is at a seminar in Houston and Dr.
Breining is in his sixties. Would have retired by now if they
could find another surgeon to take his place. He can't handle a case like this."

"He doesn't have to," Sarah said sharply, ripping Cord's
sweatshirt and peeling it off him. "I'm a trauma surgeon.
I'll need someone to assist me, that's all. This patient is not
going to make it to San Antonio and you know it."

Jim placed the blood pressure cuff on Cord's arm. "It's not my decision. Depends on what Dr. Breining says. He's the chief of service."

Dr. Breining was about to leave the hospital when Sarah reached him on the phone. He listened to Sarah's crisp clear diagnosis, then said quietly, "I'll take a look at him. But if your evaluation is correct, the best I can do is try to stabilize him, then send him on to San Antonio by helicopter. I can't let you operate here. You don't have a Texas license and you're not on staff. If something goes wrong, the hospital may lose its license."

Frustrated, Sarah checked Cord's blood pressure again. It was still dropping and his respiration was shallow and rapid. Damn it, she wasn't going to lose him to bureaucracy. Despite the blankets covering him, he was cold and, beneath his tan, his skin looked gray. She checked his pupils; they were dilating. "Then hire me," she said fiercely. "Jim says that you're looking for a surgeon. I have a valid New York State license in traumatology. I'm eligible for licensure in Texas and the law allows me to practice here while I apply for it. If you need references, call St. Anne's in New York. Also, I'm Doc Simon's daughter. My father was on your staff. Surely, for his sake—"

"You're Simon's daughter? Why didn't you say so?" Dr. Breining interrupted. "Hell, I'll hire you on the spot. Sure hope you're as good as Simon said you were."

So do I, Sarah thought. Gripping Cord's wrist, she felt his increasingly weakening pulse. With her fingers pressed on it she whispered, "I just burned all my bridges for you. So you better hang in there, cowboy. All I want in return is forever, forever, forever. . . .

He fought. And so did she.

At St. Anne's, Sarah dealt with injuries like Cord's every day. But there she worked together with a team of specialists, with well-trained technicians and ultramodern equipment. Kingsley County General had only one operating room, two lab technicians and one X-ray technician. The radiologist lived in San Antonio and read films on Tuesdays and Fridays. The plasma supply was low and the nearest blood bank was fifty miles away. But Dr. Breining, a thin cadaverous-looking man with a shock of white hair, was an expert at reading films. Round, hazel-eyed Nurse Gray was a wizard at unearthing supplies, and the anesthesiologist was cracking jokes about hiring surgeons for a day, distracting her from the fact that this patient was the man she loved. But her hands were steady as she repaired the damage. The bullet had passed the aorta and had nicked the renal artery instead.

Carefully she extracted the bullet lodged near the spine and dropped it into the tray. The last of her doubts and guilt vanished. She had redeemed herself. She was free of guilt at last.

She could have changed her mind about working here once Cord was in recovery. In fact they were prepared for it. It was Dr. Breining who signed the necessary forms so there would be no complications of any kind. On paper Sarah had merely assisted him.

Sarah herself almost panicked when she talked to Dr. Breining for a few minutes afterward. Her decision had been made under extreme stress. What if she had misread Cord's feelings for her? All he had said was that he loved her. The phrase was overused these days and often meaningless. People loved cars, houses, clothes. Perhaps she was presuming too much.

But she had never heard Cord use the phrase before.

He was cautious about love.

Then again, her admission may have prompted his. They had been in a very dangerous situation at the time and he may have said it to reassure her. After all, how was a guy to respond when the woman he had made love to the night before told him out of the blue—and with a sniper outside somewhat forcing the issue—that she loved him?

And since when did love mean marriage in this sophisticated day and age? Cord wasn't the marrying kind, remember? He had told her so himself only a few days ago.

Then she realized the truth. Her love for Cord might have influenced her decision to move to Knight's Corner, but with or without him she would eventually have decided to make the change. She could continue Simon's work. She could keep the horses, she might even find the time to ride them. Angel already loved it here, she would be happy about the move. Slowly she turned to Dr. Breining and took the leap. "I would have to work out my notice at St. Anne's," she said. "Then there would be the move down here. I couldn't possibly start before April," she warned.

"Sounds fine with me. But we can deal with all the particulars at a later time."

Nurse Gray bustled in. "There's a crowd of people waiting for you outside in the hall, Dr. Durand. Mr. and Mrs. Knight have just arrived. And the sheriff wants to see you."

Sarah briefly stopped by the recovery room to check on Cord. His vital signs had stabilized. Reflexes in both legs were normal. "You did great, cowboy," she said softly, brushing her lips over his hair, his cheek, his mouth. "You deserve some rest. I'll be here when you wake up."

There *was* a crowd waiting outside the surgery. Most of the ranch hands were there. Mary Lou, Josie and Pete. Maisy had brought Angel along with her, a pale, teary-eyed Angel who was badly in need of reassurance. Sarah hugged her daughter fiercely. "Cord's fine, sweetheart."

"Can I see him? I helped Maisy make pecan pie for him. It's his favorite."

Sarah shook her had. "He's sleeping now, but you can see him tomorrow. Can you wait that long?" When Angel nodded, she whispered into her ear, "I'll even help you smuggle a piece of that pie into Cord's room."

A small grin lit Angel's face. Then, eyes still damp with tears, she ran back to the cowhands. Gripping Maisy's hand, she said, "I told you my mommy would make him all better."

Sarah pushed strands of hair back with a suddenly shaky hand. The urgency, the rush of adrenaline, was wearing off. How could she have faced Angel, all of them, if the news had been bad? With a grateful smile at Maisy, Sarah turned to Renee and Big John. She was so glad to see them, she could have cried. She had made the right decision, she thought. This was where she belonged.

Slowly she smiled at Renee and held out her hand. "He's going to be fine," she said. Renee must have been working in her studio when she had received the news. She was still wearing paint-stained jeans and a bright orange smock that should have clashed with her auburn curls, but didn't.

Renee hugged Sarah tightly, her slender body suddenly shaking with emotions, tears running down her sensitive, exquisitely beautiful face. "Lord, I'm glad you were there. I couldn't have borne going through it all again. Losing a child once is something no mother should go through. But a second time—"

Letting go of Sarah's hands, she scrubbed her eyes and sniffed. "Oh, Lord, I don't have a tissue."

"You never do," Big John drawled, handing her a white handkerchief. As he watched Renee dry her tears, Sarah spied a look of such aching tenderness in his steel gray eyes, she caught her breath. But the moment Renee looked up, the look vanished.

For a moment, while Big John was concentrating on Renee, Sarah studied him. There were only eighteen years separating the father from the son and the likeness between them was striking. Gray streaked Big John's tawny hair at the temples and his brows were thicker than Cord's. His deeply tanned face was even less expressive than his son's. Control had become second nature to him. When he turned to Sarah and found her studying him so intently, he cocked one brow, just like his son. "I promise I won't cry on your shoulder like Renee," he said, holding out his hand. "But—" Emotion briefly roughened his voice and he stopped to snatch at control. "But, well, I too am grateful."

The very idea of this tough, controlled man crying on anyone's shoulder brought a fleeting smile to Sarah's face. But tears pricked her eyes, and her own control suddenly slipped dangerously. Grasping his work-roughened hand, she said a little unsteadily, "Don't thank me yet. It's only fair to warn you, Big John, that I plan to strangle him once he's well."

Always sensitive to other's feelings, Renee's eyes focused with sudden perception on Sarah's face. What she saw brought on fresh tears and the first glimmer of a smile. "I could stand that kind of loss. Lord, it wouldn't be a loss at all."

Withdrawing his hand, Big John glanced at Renee. "What are you talking about?"

"I'll tell you later. First I want to see Cord," she said with a questioning look at Sarah.

Sarah nodded. The hospital had no ICU or security guards, and the safest place for Cord right now was the recovery room. She planned to keep him there for as long as possible. Suddenly anxious to get back herself, she looked for the sheriff. During their mad drive to Kingsley, Sarah had told Chuck everything and had asked him to take the envelope to the sheriff. Finding the sheriff standing nearby she asked, "Is there any news?"

"We picked up Rod and Devlin. Both were flown to San Antonio for treatment. The black pickup escaped," Dan

Holt said, regret softening his brown eyes. "But we'll find him."

"Damn right, we will," Big John said grimly.

Sarah felt a fresh rush of fear. As long as Harper was free, Cord would be in danger. He was so defenseless now, so vulnerable. "Have you checked with the hospitals? I think Harper was injured."

Big John frowned. "Harper? *Tom* Harper?"

Sarah nodded, watching him closely as she said, "It was raining hard and the black pickup had tinted glass and the driver was careful to keep out of sight, but Cord called him Harper and he didn't dispute it." Swiftly she relayed the words she had overheard. Big John's frown deepened but he didn't interrupt her until she finished.

Then he said, "It isn't much. Not enough to get the FBI involved."

At Big John's words, Sarah expelled a sigh of relief, then said slowly, "Cord had the impression that you didn't believe his allegations about Harper."

Big John gave her a startled look. "You're kidding. I trust Harper about as far as I can throw him. That's why I've been sticking close. But that wimp is so smooth, he never makes a wrong move."

"But he did." Sarah looked at Dan Holt pleadingly. "Will you explain about Simon? I can't deal with it right now. I just wanted to let you know that the black pickup was the same one I spotted in the alley. The boy is afraid of it—"

"Excuse me." Nurse Gray stood by the double doors. "Mr. Knight is awake. He wants to see you, Dr. Durand."

Renee stood outside the recovery room, wiping tears with a crumpled tissue. "He's awake. He recognized me."

Sarah gently squeezed her shoulder and turned her toward the doors. "Tell Big John the good news."

Cord's eyes were closed again, but he wasn't asleep. He was concentrating on staying awake long enough to talk to

Sarah. The memories of what had happened after the bullet had hit him were hazy. What he remembered about the trip to the hospital was the sound of Sarah's voice. It had kept the darkness away. He recalled reaching for it again and again. Fighting. Trying to prove to her that he was the forever-kind-of-guy. He had made it, he thought wearily. Barely.

He knew the moment she entered the room, even before she laid her hand on his wrist. He opened his eyes and studied her. She looked different in her blue-gray surgical togs. Competent, aloof, distant. Oh, hell, he had expected it after the ordeal he had put her through.

Sarah bent over him. The gurney was almost too short for him. He was lying on his side, a white sheet covering the bandage on his back. "Hi, cowboy. How do you feel?"

Humor briefly glinted in Cord's eyes. "Like someone used me for target practice." Then his eyes searched her face. She looked tired. There were shadows beneath her eyes and tension around her mouth. "You okay?"

Squeezing his wrist, she nodded. "Let's check you over first."

Cord endured the poking and prodding stoically and with closed eyes, waiting with growing impatience for the nurse to leave. By the time she did, he was nearly floating off again, but he didn't dare. Not yet. "Is the sheriff here?"

"Yes." Sarah bent over the guardrail and tenderly brushed back his tousled hair. "I talked to him and your father's here. Don't worry about anything but getting well."

Cord frowned. "Try to keep them from worrying. Make them go to the ranch."

Sarah sighed. He worried about them, but he still tried to keep them at a distance. Now, though, wasn't the time to argue with him. "I'll see what I can do."

Cord felt himself floating off again. "How's Angel?"

"Making plans to smuggle pecan pie into your room to-morrow."

He smiled faintly and opened his eyes again. "I want you to leave me with my parents, Sarah."

Sarah gripped the rail tightly against the sharp pain. "I'm sticking around. I've news for you, cowboy. Right now *I'm* giving the orders."

He smiled at her faintly. "Care to put that to the test? Kiss me, Sarah."

Sarah framed his face, her lips trembling. "I should make you beg, Cord. Just to prove my point. But I—" Suddenly the emotions she had tried so carefully to control broke free. She leaned her forehead against his. "Damn it, Cord, *you* owe *me* for scaring the hell out of me."

He moved his hand, by sheer effort of will, sliding from her shoulder up her neck. "Then you meant it," he said, his thumb stroking her cheek. "Forever wasn't just a trick to draw me up the hill?"

Sarah shook her head. "I thought you might not remember."

He frowned, hearing her voice again, recalling fragments, and what he remembered made him smile. "Only part of it." *Forever.* He wanted a million years to start with, but he wasn't greedy, didn't dare to be greedy. Lady Luck was beginning to smile again, but he didn't trust any woman. Except Sarah. "In Texas we seal that kind of bargain with a kiss."

"In New York, too, cowboy. I guess we have something in common after all." Slowly, with aching tenderness, she brushed her lips across his mouth. She felt him respond for long aching seconds. Then he floated off.

It was past five in the morning when Cord was wheeled into a private room on the second floor. Dr. Breining had down-scaled his condition from critical to serious an hour ago. His remarkable progress, Sarah suspected, was mainly due to the fact that Harper was still at large.

Holding the IV pouch high to keep the catheter from tangling, she watched the orderly and Big John help Cord into bed. Vicky, who had arrived by chartered plane from New Orleans around nine, had persuaded Renee to check into a nearby motel. Big John had refused to leave. After arranging protection with the local sheriff's office he had dozed in the waiting room, always, Sarah suspected, with one eye open and glued on the swinging doors.

Sarah hung the pouch onto the pole and adjusted the drip. She was so tired, her vision was beginning to blur. She had spent most of the night in a chair next to Cord, too uneasy to sleep, waiting for dawn. When the orderly rolled out the stretcher, Sarah quietly followed him to the nurses' station in search of coffee, giving father and son a few minutes alone.

Exhausted, Cord waited until the orderly had left, his eyes closed, trying to recoup the strength the move had taken out of him. He could hear his father walk to the window and open the curtains, wishing he wasn't so damn weak and could meet his father eye to eye. Wishing he would leave. Finally he couldn't take the silence anymore. Opening his eyes, he said wearily, "Why don't you check into the motel and try to snatch a few hours' sleep, Big John?"

John glanced over his shoulder at his son. He wasn't leaving, not before they'd cleared up some misunderstandings. He just didn't know where to start. He never did. "I can remember a time when you used to call me Dad. When did I stop being your father, Cord?"

Oh, Lord. A guarded look came into Cord's eyes. This was going way back and he didn't feel up to raking up the past. "Can't we leave this for another time?"

Shaking his head, John turned around. "With your track record there may not *be* another time," he said quietly.

Walking across the room, he drew a chair close to the bed. "Since Sarah so tactfully left us alone, we may as well make use of it. I'll be doing most of the talking anyway. All you need to do is stay awake long enough to listen."

Stretching out his long legs, he crossed his ankles, resting one boot on top of the other. "Did you know that I hate the name Big John?" When Cord shook his head, he shrugged. "To me, the *big* stands for responsibility and isolation. I'm good at both of them."

Slouching deeper into the chair, he leaned his head back wearily. "I know you've heard the story of how I got that dumb name a hundred times, but never from my side. Your grandfather was a very sick man for a long time. When he committed suicide, he left me with a mountain of debts, and your grandmother and your aunt and uncle to take care of. But that wasn't enough responsibility for an eighteen-year-old. The night he died, you were created and I added a wife and a son to the burden." He looked at Cord. "Don't misunderstand me. I wanted you. But, hell, you could have given me four or five years to straighten out the mess my dad left me."

Cord's mouth twisted wryly. "That's one thing I refuse to take the blame for."

With a rueful shrug John continued. "Anyway, by the time the ranch was solvent and your aunt and uncle were in college, I didn't know how to talk to your mother, or to you or your baby sister. But I tried to show you how I felt, and I thought you understood that you could come to me with anything." He stopped briefly, clearing his voice. "I can remember the day you started calling me Big John. It was the day you and Vicky hid that Mexican kid in the line shack."

Cord went very still. He wanted his father to stop talking because from here on things were going to get rough. Then he remembered Sarah's warning. He had almost left it too late once before. He smiled faintly. "I should have known we couldn't hide a thing like that from you."

"Yeah," John growled. "I knew every blade of grass on the ranch, but I didn't know how to talk to my kids. What hurt like hell was that they felt they couldn't tell me about what they had done and ask me to help. It wasn't something to be ashamed of! I guess that was the day when I started hating the name Big John."

Cord expelled a long breath. "I swore Vicky to secrecy. And it had nothing to do with not being able to come to you. You'd promised me a car for my sixteenth birthday and I was afraid you'd feel I lacked responsibility."

John looked at his son with exasperation. "You and I both know that's not the real reason. I'll tell you why you kept it a secret. You were afraid I'd call the sheriff and hand the kid over to him. Do you know how that made me feel? And it got worse over the years. You did it last year again. I felt like a damned failure when I realized that you'd stayed in Mexico because you thought I wouldn't keep my mouth shut or protect my family."

Shaken, Cord looked at his father, his throat working, but no words came out. Finally he said, "Oh, hell. That wasn't why. I just wanted to be as big as you."

A bitter smile twisted John's mouth. "Oh, hell, is right." He sighed wearily. "I wish you'd stop trying to measure up to me, Cord. You're twice the man I ever was and I sure as hell *don't want you to become like me.*"

Cord squeezed the moisture from his eyes. His voice was rough when he drawled, "Oh, I don't know. You were one hell of father, even if we did get our lines crossed somewhere along the line. You still are, for that matter. I always knew I could count on you. Big John. I've always liked that name. Suits you just fine. But you've got to do something about your communications skills, Dad. They're even worse than mine, and that's saying something." Opening his eyes, he smiled at his father, then glanced at the door.

Suddenly he noticed that dawn was creeping into the room. Sarah had been gone a long time. Frowning, he pressed the call button and said sharply, "I'd like to talk to Dr. Durand."

"I'm sorry, Mr. Knight," a disembodied voice answered. "She isn't here right now. She went to the ER a few minutes ago. Sheriff Holt brought in a young boy and was asking for her."

Cord leaned back against the pillow, wishing he wasn't so damn weak. Why hadn't she told him or had someone else relay a message? "Can you give me the number of the ER?"

"I'll make the call for you" the nurse said. Cord could hear her doing something on the other end and waited impatiently, watching his father get to this feet and walk to the window. "They're not picking up down there. Must be busy. I'll have her paged."

Thanking the nurse, Cord let go of the call button. Almost immediately he heard Sarah's name being called over the intercom. He gave her a whole minute to answer it; then he pushed back the light blanket. "Something's wrong," he said hoarsely. Sweat broke out on his forehead as he slid his legs to the edge of the bed. When his father strode over to help him Cord shook his head. "Sarah said she put my gun into my left boot," he said between clenched teeth. "Will you get it for me?"

Frowning, Big John hesitated. "There's a deputy outside. You're in no condition—"

Cord cautiously slid his legs off the bed, fighting dizziness. Drawing a shaky breath, he challenged his father. "If it was mother out there what would you do?"

Without a word, John went to the closet, returning seconds later with the gun. Silently Cord held out his hand, gray eyes meeting gray eyes and clashing in a battle of wills.

"I can't fight you for the gun," Cord finally said, his voice little more than a hoarse whisper. "I haven't the strength for it. But if something happens to her—"

With a sigh, against his better judgement, Big John put the gun on the bed, then strode to the door. "I'll send the deputy to look for her."

Cord nodded. "And see if you can find Dan Holt."

Cord listened to his father talk with the deputy, wishing he wasn't as weak as a newborn foal. Pushing the button, he raised the head of the bed, and, picking up the gun, he leaned against the pillow to conserve his strength.

A minute passed and then another one. The only warning he had was a small, swiftly muffled shriek outside. Seconds later the door burst open and Sarah slowly came into the room, her pale face devoid of expression. From the stiff way she held herself, Cord guessed that the brown-haired, stocky, soft-skinned bastard following her had a gun pressed into her back. Harper's left arm was in a sling and judging from his pale, sweating face he was in agony.

Good. That would even the odds somewhat, Cord thought with grim satisfaction. Leaning back against the pillow, he eased his legs back on the bed and drew the blanket up. "You haven't a snowball's chance in hell of getting away, Harper," he drawled. Beneath the blanket, his fingers curled around the butt of his gun, gently releasing the safety catch.

Closing the door behind him, Harper leaned against it, wiping his face with a shaky hand. The gun in his hand was trembling with weakness and hate for the man who had become his nemesis. "Get up, Knight, I'm taking both of you to Rodriguez."

Beneath the cover Cord pointed the gun at Harper's head. He didn't look at Sarah. If he did, he would lose what little control he had. There was no more room for mistakes, he thought, keeping his eyes focused on his enemy's face. One blink and he stood to lose everything. "Don't be stupid, Harper," he growled. "Even if you made it to the border, you wouldn't survive. You've become a liability and Rodriguez won't take the risk of you turning witness. He's going to kill you, like he killed his mistress. And he's going to do it slowly. There'll be blood everywhere."

At the mention of blood, Harper's already waxlike skin turned a sickly shade of green. "Get up—" he snarled, digging his gun into Sarah's back to enforce his order.

"He can't. He's going to faint if he does," Sarah said, her voice flat, emotions tightly under control. She tried not to think of the fact that this man had murdered Simon and had nearly succeeded in killing Cord, twice.

"Cord lost an awful lot of blood," she explained. "If he tries to stand up, he'll open the stitches and start bleeding again."

Harper shuddered.

"He's only going to slow you down," Sarah continued persuasively, her eyes fastened on Cord's hard, expressionless face. Harper would have to shoot her before she allowed Cord to be dragged from the bed. "I'll come with you without a struggle."

She could only pray that Harper was unaware of the fact that Dan Holt, and at least one deputy, were somewhere in the building. Trying to lure him out of the room, she added persuasively, "But we have to leave now, before the police get here."

Cord didn't waste his strength arguing with Harper or Sarah. Shifting in his bed to mask the sound, he gently cocked his gun.

Suddenly, sirens wailed in the distance, prompting Harper into action. "Let's go," he snarled. Pressing the gun to Sarah's temple, he backed into the small bathroom, immediately adjacent to the room's door, and ordered her to turn around and slowly open the door.

The hall appeared empty and silent, and the nursing desk across from the room was deserted. Suddenly, Dan Holt leaped forward and kicked the door open all the way, wedging Sarah between it and the wall. Harper leaped back further into the bathroom, hitting the doorjamb with his injured shoulder. Groaning, he doubled over and slid to the floor, dropping his gun. Kicking it out of his reach, Dan Holt hauled the man to his feet and dragged him out into the hall.

For a moment, Sarah merely leaned against the wall for support. Then she pushed the door closed and rushed over to Cord. "I'm sorry," she cried, anxiously scanning his face. He looked exhausted. There was a grayish tinge to his skin and deep grooves bracketed his mouth. But his pulse was strong, his lips were curving and his eyes smiling.

Framing his face with trembling hands, Sarah kissed him passionately. "I'm sorry I led Harper straight to your room. Dan Holt brought in the boy and I went down to take a look at his leg. The bullet went right through the fleshy part of his thigh. It's badly infected and it took me some time to clean it. When I realized just how long I'd been gone, I didn't bother to wait for the elevator and rushed up the stairs. Harper was hiding in the stairwell. He said he'd been there for hours, waiting for you to be transferred to another room."

With a groan, Cord pulled her head down. "Don't think about it anymore. It's over," he whispered against her lips. He still couldn't quite grasp that he was free of the past. That would take hours or days to really sink in. Slowly, tenderly, he brushed his mouth against hers. "Marry me. Sarah."

For a moment Sarah caught her breath, then she asked quietly, "Are you sure? You're taking on an awful lot. A child, three horses, a cat and my demanding job."

Cord frowned at her and went very still. "Whom are you trying to talk out of it? Yourself or me?" he asked quietly.

Suddenly the door burst open again and Vicky charged in, her red hair flying wildly around her head. Renee and Big John followed in her wake and the nurse bustled in after them. Cord glared at his family. "Your timing stinks. I was just asking Sarah to marry me."

Unperturbed, Vicky rounded the bed, sat down next to him and looked at Sarah. "Don't let him bully you into it."

"I agree with Vicky," Renee said, stopping at the foot of the bed. "Cord, you should give her time to recover from the shock."

Torn between amusement and frustration, Cord looked at his father for help. Big John merely shrugged. "They have a point. But you would be doing all of us a great favor, Sarah, if you'd take him on and keep him from charging into danger again."

Slowly, Sarah's glance went from one family member to the next, their welcoming smiles warming her heart. "How can I resist?" she said, laughter welling up. "Yes," she said, her eyes meeting Cord's. "Yes, yes, yes..."

Cord stayed in the hospital for ten days.

On the day before his release, Chuck and Jimmy T. took down the boards at the office, then returned to the ranch. While Angel played in the alley with her new friend, Rico Garcia, Sarah and Maisy cleaned the windows.

Rico, the boy Harper had been hunting, was still recovering from the gunshot wound, but the infection was clearing up fast. He barely limped anymore.

A year ago, he and his mother had left Ecuador in search of a new life and had fallen into Rodriguez's hands. They had been separated by the smugglers shortly after their arrival in Mexico. Rico had worked off the *coyotes'* fees on a *finca* in Southern Mexico before he had been taken to the

States, where he was supposed to have been reunited with his mother. When, upon his arrival in the States, he had found out that his mother was working in a bordello in Mexico, he had decided to search for her. During his escape from the safe house—an old abandoned church ten miles south of Knight's Corner—he had been shot by one of the guards and had hidden in the Taggerts' garage, waiting for his leg to heal.

Sarah had signed a partnership agreement with Dr. Breining. The men from the Circle K and several of the friends she had made in Knight's Corner were fixing up the office. Despite the fact that she was returning to New York in two days, she had decided to take down the boards. Knight's Corner once again had become Simon's small sleepy town.

"What are you going to do with the boy?" Maisy asked as they carried the cleaning supplies to their cars parked in the alley.

Sarah studied Rico's closed face and dark old eyes from where she stood. "Keep him here, until we've found his mother. Cord knows someone in Mexico who can help him in his search. He's also offered to use his influence with the INS to get them *amicas*."

The news of Harper's arrest had brought several of Cord's former colleagues to the hospital and he had been offered his old job back. That, Sarah recalled, had caused her some bad moments. To her relief, however, Cord had turned the offer down, without regret.

Suddenly a pickup came down the alley, stopping a few feet away. Sarah turned, frowning when she spotted Cord getting out of the truck. Arms akimbo, she demanded, "What are you doing here? You weren't supposed to be discharged until tomorrow."

"One day won't make a difference. I was lonely," he said.

Angel turned to Rico. "That's my daddy. Well, he's not my daddy yet, but he's going to be. And he says I can call him anything I want. I've never had a real daddy before. Did you?"

Rico nodded, then turned abruptly away and walked toward Main Street.

Watching Cord pick up Angel, Sarah ran after Rico and stopped him on the sidewalk outside the office. Though Rico understood some English, he could not speak it and Sarah always talked to him in Spanish to make him feel less of an outsider. "We'll find your mother," she said, laying a comforting hand on his shoulder. "Cord has contacts in Mexico."

Rico nodded. Looking down, he kicked a small pebble with his brand-new boot. Sarah's heart wrenched for him. She knew how he felt—alone, an outsider, wanting love but afraid to reach for it, the way she had been until three long weeks ago. She hoped that Knight's Corner would also heal him a little, the way it had healed her. "You'll have a place here for as long as you want. Come back with me and meet Cord."

Afterward, while Maisy bundled Angel and Rico into her car, Cord scowled at the office windows, sparkling in the sunshine. "You could have waited another day to take the boards down," he said, frustration in his voice. "There isn't another place where I can make love with you. The ranch is overrun with relatives. Did Mother and Dad have to invite everyone to stay?"

"I like them." Sarah's chin came up in challenge. "And so do you."

"Sometimes." Cord's hand curled around Sarah's neck. Tilting her face up to his, he kissed her hungrily. "But not right now. You are leaving in two days and I don't want to share you with them."

"It's only for four weeks," Sarah said, but her arms tightened around his neck at the thought of being separated from him for a month. But they both would be busy. Cord had agreed to help the FBI and INS to build a strong case against Harper, Devlin and Snyder. All three men had been indicted with Simon's murder. Cord was determined that they would be locked up for a long time even if there wasn't enough proof to make the murder charges stick.

"Only?" Cord grumbled, drawing her to the stairs. His legs were still a little wobbly and he had hoped he wouldn't have to climb them. "It's been days, and I'm aching to hold you and make love with you."

Sarah wrapped her arm around his waist. "So am I," she admitted, letting him lean on her as they climbed the stairs. Together. Once inside, she cupped his face. "I love you." The more often she said the words, the easier they became.

"I love you." He, too, needed to say them often. They were the only guarantee that there was a forever. And for them, there would be.

*   *   *   *   *   *

CAN YOU STAND THE HEAT?

SUMMER Sizzlers '94

You're in for a serious heat wave with Silhouette's latest selection of sizzling summer reading. This sensuous collection of three short stories provides the perfect vacation escape! And what better authors to relax with than

ANNETTE BROADRICK
JACKIE MERRITT
JUSTINE DAVIS

And that's not all....

With the purchase of *Silhouette Summer Sizzlers '94*, you can send in for a FREE Summer Sizzlers beach bag!

SUMMER JUST GOT HOTTER— WITH SILHOUETTE BOOKS!

Take 4 bestselling love stories FREE

Plus get a FREE surprise gift!

Special Limited-time Offer

Mail to Silhouette Reader Service™

3010 Walden Avenue
P.O. Box 1867
Buffalo, N.Y. 14269-1867

YES! Please send me 4 free Silhouette Intimate Moments® novels and my free surprise gift. Then send me 6 brand-new novels every month, which I will receive months before they appear in bookstores. Bill me at the low price of $2.89 each plus 25¢ delivery and applicable sales tax, if any.* That's the complete price and—compared to the cover prices of $3.50 each—quite a bargain! I understand that accepting the books and gift places me under no obligation ever to buy any books. I can always return a shipment and cancel at any time. Even if I never buy another book from Silhouette, the 4 free books and the surprise gift are mine to keep forever.

245 BPA ANRR

Name	(PLEASE PRINT)	
Address	Apt. No.	
City	State	Zip

This offer is limited to one order per household and not valid to present Silhouette Intimate Moments® subscribers. *Terms and prices are subject to change without notice. Sales tax applicable in N.Y.

UMOM-94R

©1990 Harlequin Enterprises Limited

Rugged and lean...and the best-looking, sweetest-talking men to be found in the entire Lone Star state!

Diana Palmer

LONG, TALL TEXANS

In July 1994, Silhouette is very proud to bring you Diana Palmer's first three LONG, TALL TEXANS. CALHOUN, JUSTIN and TYLER—the three cowboys who started the legend. Now they're back by popular demand in one classic volume—and they're ready to lasso your heart! Beautifully repackaged for this special event, this collection is sure to be a longtime keepsake!

"Diana Palmer makes a reader want to find a Texan of her own to love!"
—*Affaire de Coeur*

LONG, TALL TEXANS—the first three— reunited in this special roundup!

Available in July, wherever Silhouette books are sold.

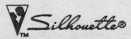

INTIMATE MOMENTS®
Silhouette®

It's those rambunctious Rawlings brothers again!
You met Gable and Cooper Rawlings in IM #523
and IM #553. Now meet their youngest brother,
Flynn Rawlings, in

THE WILD WEST

by Linda Turner

Fun-loving rodeo cowboy Flynn Rawlings
couldn't believe it. From the moment he'd
approached beautiful barrel racer Tate Baxter,
she'd been intent on freezing him out. But Tate
was the woman he'd been waiting for all his life,
and he wasn't about to take no for an answer!

Don't miss FLYNN (IM #572), available in June.
And look for his sister, Kat's, story as
Linda Turner's thrilling saga concludes in

THE WILD WEST

Coming to you throughout 1994...only from
Silhouette Intimate Moments.

SILHOUETTE®

Desire®

They're sexy, they're determined, they're trouble with a capital T!

Meet six of the steamiest, most stubborn heroes you'd ever want to know, and learn *everything* about them....

August's *Man of the Month*, Quinn Donovan, in **FUSION** by Cait London

Mr. Bad Timing, Dan Kingman, in **DREAMS AND SCHEMES** by Merline Lovelace

Mr. Marriage-phobic, Connor Devlin, in **WHAT ARE FRIENDS FOR?** by Naomi Horton

Mr. Sensible, Lucas McCall, in **HOT PROPERTY** by Rita Rainville

Mr. Know-it-all, Thomas Kane, in **NIGHTFIRE** by Barbara McCauley

Mr. Macho, Jake Powers, in **LOVE POWER** by Susan Carroll

Look for them on the covers so you can see just how handsome and irresistible they are!

Coming in August only from Silhouette Desire!   CENTER

HE'S AN

AMERICAN HERO

Men of mettle. Men of integrity. Real men who know the real meaning of love. Each month, Intimate Moments salutes these true American Heroes.

For July: THAT SAME OLD FEELING,
by Judith Duncan.
Chase McCall had come home a new man. Yet old lover Devon Manyfeathers soon stirred familiar feelings—and renewed desire.

For August: MICHAEL'S GIFT,
by Marilyn Pappano.
Michael Bennett knew his visions prophesied certain death. Yet he would move the high heavens to change beautiful Valery Navarre's fate.

For September: DEFENDER,
by Kathleen Eagle.
Gideon Defender had reformed his bad-boy ways to become a leader among his people. Yet one habit—loving Raina McKenny—had never died, especially after Gideon learned she'd returned home.

AMERICAN HEROES: Men who give all they've got for their country, their work—the women they love.

Only from

SILHOUETTE... Where Passion Lives

Don't miss these Silhouette favorites by some of our most distinguished authors! And now, you can receive a discount by ordering two or more titles!

D#05706	HOMETOWN MAN by Jo Ann Algermissen	$2.89	☐
D#05795	DEREK by Leslie Davis Guccione	$2.99	☐
D#05802	THE SEDUCER by Linda Turner	$2.99	☐
D#05804	ESCAPADES by Cathie Linz	$2.99	☐
IM#07478	DEEP IN THE HEART by Elley Crain	$3.39	☐
IM#07507	STANDOFF by Lee Magner	$3.50	☐
IM#07537	DAUGHTER OF THE DAWN by Christine Flynn	$3.50	☐
IM#07539	A GENTLEMAN AND A SCHOLAR by Alexandra Sellers	$3.50	☐
SE#09829	MORE THAN HE BARGAINED FOR by Carole Halston	$3.50	☐
SE#09833	BORN INNOCENT by Christine Rimmer	$3.50	☐
SE#09840	A LOVE LIKE ROMEO AND JULIET by Natalie Bishop	$3.50	☐
SE#09844	RETURN ENGAGEMENT by Elizabeth Bevarly	$3.50	☐
SR#08952	INSTANT FATHER by Lucy Gordon	$2.75	☐
SR#08957	THE PRODIGAL HUSBAND by Pamela Dalton	$2.75	☐
SR#08960	DARK PRINCE by Elizabeth Krueger	$2.75	☐
SR#08972	POOR LITTLE RICH GIRL by Joan Smith	$2.75	☐
SS#27003	STRANGER IN THE MIST by Lee Karr	$3.50	☐
SS#27009	BREAK THE NIGHT by Anne Stuart	$3.50	☐
SS#27016	WHAT WAITS BELOW by Jane Toombs	$3.50	☐
SS#27020	DREAM A DEADLY DREAM by Allie Harrison	$3.50	☐

(limited quantities available on certain titles)

	AMOUNT	$_____
DEDUCT:	10% DISCOUNT FOR 2+ BOOKS	$_____
	POSTAGE & HANDLING	$_____
	($1.00 for one book, 50¢ for each additional)	
	APPLICABLE TAXES*	$_____
	TOTAL PAYABLE	$_____
	(check or money order—please do not send cash)	

To order, complete this form and send it, along with a check or money order for the total above, payable to Silhouette Books, to: **In the U.S.:** 3010 Walden Avenue, P.O. Box 9077, Buffalo, NY 14269-9077; **In Canada:** P.O. Box 636, Fort Erie, Ontario, L2A 5X3.

Name: _____

Address: _____ City: _____

State/Prov.: _____ Zip/Postal Code: _____

*New York residents remit applicable sales taxes.
Canadian residents remit applicable GST and provincial taxes.

Silhouette®

SBACK-AJR